COUNT THE PETALS OF THE MOON DAISY

A love story. A mystery. So many seeds of truth.

MARTIN KIRBY

First published in Great Britain in 2007 by Pegasus
This edition published by Mother's Garden in 2025

Copyright © Martin Kirby 2025

A CIP catalogue record for this book is available from the British Library.

ISBN 978-1-969282-16-4

By the Same Author

Albion
Norfolk Century – Nature
No Going Back
Shaking The Tree

The Boy On The Stairs

For Frank Prendergast and Charlie Gauvain

Table of Contents

Moon Daisy (*chrysanthemum leucanthemum*)

Wild flower also known as the ox-eye daisy or marguerite: A very common north European perennial of grasslands and roadsides that can now be found across North America.

1

14th April, 1989

The crimson sun has slipped away, and the shadow of night rises like water, drowning the colours of day. With the darkness flows the great flood of memory: America, the dying, the crying, the pain of loss.

A storm is coming. Eyes pinch tight.

Get to sleep, Jessica. Sleep now. Remember. Remember the rhyme …

> *Rest your head, my little one, and count with me*
>
> *The perfect petals of the moon daisy.*

Close your eyes, and you will find

The lovely moon flower in your mind.

Count the petals, one by one, Round and round the heart of gold 'Til it's done.

Close your eyes, my child, my sweet. Count them all,

And then to sleep.

Her mind's eye fills with a bloom. She succumbs to sleep.

In the cool light of midnight, an armada of moon-silver clouds, aligned to the curve of the world, drags shadows across the wetland toward the sand hills and sea. They are the vanguard of the storm. Those that follow billow and merge into blackness as the anger grows, pushing waves through the hissing reeds and across the iron-grey water.

At the back of the reeds, in a tiny cottage cocooned by rippling alder leaves, the woman lies on her side on a brass bed, covered by a patchwork quilt of green, crimson, and blue. A candle burns low on the table beside her, next to matches, an unopened packet of cigarettes, and a small, oval-framed sepia photograph of a woman of years. The flickering flame, spilling wax, illuminates the corner of the bed, the sleeping woman's face, her bare arm, and the fist that clutches the quilt beneath her chin. Loose pages of a music score are scattered on the floorboards next to shoes and clothes. An old journal lies on top, open at the final page, words she has read countless times.

I feel for the seeds in my pocket. They are my comfort.

My mind and my heart are so overwhelmed that I can hardly breathe or dip this pen into the inkwell. There are the ink blotches of tears. I care not, for they tell the truth.

This life is over. The sum of it, these precious years, have been taken from me, and now I must depart. Yet I am compelled before I end these pages to sow words of gratitude. I have had the rarest, most loving of times among the whispering reeds and blue heaven, drawn daily from within to stand among my flowers, to open my arms and soul to the majesty of nature's rawness, its brilliance, its honesty.

The music of the water and the cries and melodies of the fowl; my beloved Jacob, God cherish him; and these people, a race apart who merge into this great wetland and know its secrets, wrath, wisdom, and wonder. They have my heart. I leave it here.

By the window, where the draught stirs the curtain and the first heavy drops of rain tap at the glass, sits the woman from the photograph, the keeper of the journal. She occupies a nursing chair, straight-backed and motionless in the shadows. Her thick, shoulder-length grey hair is swept back from her forehead and tucked behind her ears. Her thin face is ghostly pale, serene, and thoughtful. She wears a white blouse with an aquamarine brooch at the throat that matches the colour of her eyes. A black shawl wraps around her narrow shoulders, and her slender hands are locked on the lap of an ankle-length black dress. Her long neck turns slightly toward the bed. Her unblinking gaze is fixed on the faintest rise and fall of the quilt– the quilt she had made.

On the other side of the room, beside the latched door to the narrow wooden stairs that lead steeply down to the living room, a younger man stands with his arms folded, his shoulders and head resting against the wall. He wears a baggy, deep-green roll-necked jumper and faded jeans gaping at the knees and rolled to the ankles. His crossed feet are bare, the hue of seasoned pine. His hair and eyebrows are strong and wild, the jaw of his broad, weathered face shadowed by stubble. His mouth is slightly open, and his brown, deep-set eyes are also locked on the bed.

Thunder rumbles in the middle distance. The two watchers narrow their gaze, willing the woman not to wake.

She hears nothing. Sleep is deep. Her dreaming mind continues the thoughts that crowded her before slumber: the year that was, the incredible year that was.

2

6th April, 1988

It must be noon. The Easter sun reaches the sofa about noon. It stings the eyes. Jess is lying on her side again, curled, her forearm a shield. The feather sofa is deformed, moulded to her shape. She hauls herself upright, then flops backwards and stares vacantly at the window. There is the familiar odour of vomit. She looks down at her crumpled clothes, the encrusted stain on her jumper. She pulls it off and throws it aside. Fingers fumble to light a cigarette. She cannot block it out. Why live like this? Why live?

A short, stout woman with dyed red hair and rainbow beads had found her. She did not leave. She did not ignore. She helped. Jess had been lying on the toilet floor of a London pub, cheek pressed to the ingrained tiles, black and grey. She could see where she had thrown up by the sink. More sick welled in her mouth. She had backed into a cubicle to try and pee, sat, and then pitched forwards.

She had pushed herself half up when she heard the woman come in. The woman gave her toilet paper to wipe her mouth. "Oh, and you've gone an' cut yourself. Hold still now." Jess felt warmth running down the side of her face beside her right eye. She touched it and stared as the blood trickled down her finger. The woman dabbed at the small gash on the corner of Jess's brow.

"I'll get help."

"No." Jess started to tug at her knickers round her knees. She got unsteadily to her feet, pulled her knickers up, and let the hem of her dress fall.

"Wait." The woman began to wipe at the vomit on Jess's jumper. Jess brushed past her, pausing to look down, to gently squeeze her wrist. A touch of gratitude through defiance and hopelessness.

"Where do you live? I can walk with you."

Jess shook her head, let go, and made for the door, the street, the air. Her chin crumpled as she leant her shoulder and head against the wall. People spilled out of the pub. She pushed on, heading unsteadily for the blackness of the London common.

Her forehead thumps. She rubs at the skin of her face, and there is the different pain of a cut. She touches the small wound on the side of her eye socket, and it makes her wince. She sits for a few seconds, coughing, looking down at the empty half-bottle of vodka and the glass on the table. She slowly turns her head and stares at the empty shelf where her violin would normally rest during rehearsals and performances. But now it is gone. The foundation who owned it, who had permanently loaned the precious instrument to her, had kept it after the concert collapse and returned it to their bank vault for safekeeping. Jess could not be trusted with it any more. The empty shelf holds her gaze.

The artistic director of the Thames Concert Hall had taken a huge risk. Her televised comeback concert after three years–playing Schubert's Violin Concerto in D Major, D. 345 "Konzertstück" with the Royal

Philharmonic—came to a shattering end when, during the rondo, she suddenly stopped playing, sank to her knees, and let go of the violin. The orchestra had come to a stuttering halt. Then from Jess there came a cry, a deeply emotional torn-soul cry that seemed to suck the air from the concert hall. The audience had gasped, and for several seconds, an eternity, there was a deathly silence. The conductor and leader of the orchestra helped her to her feet and guided her from the stage. Then a wave of voices rose from the auditorium. Someone gathered up her violin and bow and followed. It was Suzy. Her accompanist, her life support. She had been with her when others would not. She was loving, honest, loyal. She had counselled strongly against the concert, saying Jess was suffering from depression, was close to a mental breakdown. She needed help, not this pressure. But Jess needed the money. There was no choice.

In the confusion, the artistic director had blundered into Jess's dressing room and pushed past the music manager and agent, who backed away into the corridor when Suzy told them to give Jess some air. Jess was slumped on a chair, staring blankly at the ground. The director froze, said nothing to begin with, then realised she had been drinking. He said he could smell it. He was incredulous and had to be physically forced out by Suzy, who banged the door shut, then squatted by Jess, stroked her hair, and said simply, "I understand."

Suzy had stayed close through the weeks that followed, forsaking her young family to sometimes sleep over, trying to counter Jess's anxiety. But they both knew it was ingrained. It had once been manageable, had fuelled intensity and focus, enhancing some of the greatest performances ever given. Now it was strangling her.

Jess stands, strips, and stumbles to the kitchen, gulping a glass of water. Then another. She turns and heads to the bathroom.

She gets a small plaster from the crowded cabinet above the sink and covers the wound. She catches sight of herself in the mirror. She sits on the toilet, leaning forward, head in hands, hair draped on thighs. Her mind continues to wake. She had drained what was left in the bottle before leaving the flat. She sat in a corner of the pub with nameless faces until numbness flooded her veins. A hollow-cheeked man with sallow skin and lazy, bloodshot eyes sat down next to her. He was grinning, talking crap. She never acknowledged him. He sniffed her glass, refilled it, put his hand on her knee, then between.

She looks up through her hair at the sleeping pills on top of the cabinet. Thoughts of ending it seep in once more. She runs the shower.

The phone rings. Jess darts to the bathroom door, slams and bolts it.

The London rush hour chokes both the street and the damp Easter air. The heavy sky threatens. Jess waits by the letterbox on the street corner for a break in the traffic. How many times has she done this? She hunches her shoulders, pushes her scarf against her neck, and looks up at the first floor of the Georgian house on the other corner. She freezes.

Why am I here? What was I thinking? Is it the music? The happiness? Maybe. Yes. And the music bonds like blood. What has happened here pervades her conscience. Indelible. Why? Francis is dead. It is not the same. She tries to think straight, about how it might be, what she should say. It was something Rudi had said. She couldn't ignore it, but now doubts and questions blur in her head, and panic begins to rise. She is about to turn away when the anxious face of the old man appears between the half-drawn curtains at one of the two tall windows. Rudi sees her and waves.

She slowly climbs the stairs, the steps she would race up. She hovers. The light is dim, the air stale. She hears a door open, and he calls her name. As she reaches the first floor, the bent old man is waiting for her at the door to his flat. She hasn't seen her teacher for eight months. The funeral. He is leaning on a stick that is shaking. He seems even smaller, more round-shouldered. His wispy white hair has thinned to almost nothing. The bags under his kind eyes seem a deeper, deathly blue. But his gaze and broad mouth are alight with a smile.

He looks at her and sees her fear, senses her brittleness. She looks pale as china, worse than when he saw her last summer, and aged far beyond her fifty-seven years. Her wide eyes have the pink soreness of tears.

"Come in, come in! Oh, it's so lovely to see you, Jessica. So lovely!"

He almost sings it. He wrinkles his nose and grins as he gently lets the stick fall and pats her cheeks with spindly fingers; the fingers she used to watch for countless hours dancing on violin strings and guiding a bow as gently as her Nana in Massachusetts would sew. His touch is cold.

"How are you? I'm so glad you've come. So glad. Come by the fire. Come. Warm yourself." She picks up the stick and gives it to him. He takes her arm, and his fingers grip her, holding her until the door is shut.

Jess quivers. The crowded room is still as it was when she first walked into it on a bitter January morning thirty-eight years before. It had always been a haven. But it doesn't feel the same now. There is a deafening stillness. No more the sense of peace and sanctuary.

With Rudi's hand on her arm, they take small, slow steps towards the fireplace. With his head down, watching his feet, he keeps repeating between shallow breaths how happy he is. His grip transmits the pain.

Her eyes dart around, looking for the ghost.

The facing side walls are weighed down by shelves of music scores, ranks of books and records. The only breaks are the chimney breast on the left and the doorway on the right that leads to other rooms Jess glances left, into the darkest corner. The dining table hasn't moved an inch. It is wedged in by chairs and is still covered with piles of paper and scores, some towering out of cardboard boxes. Lined in front of them, next to the permanent cream standard lamp, are the open-topped loose-leaf tea tins that Rudi kept his pens and pencils in. At the end is his "throne"–the Windsor chair with the sheepskin, yellowed by years; and facing it is the green portable Olivetti typewriter she once thought about carrying away to break into a thousand pieces. Francis bought it for Rudi on some distant birthday to replace the ancient black Imperial that the old man would play like an instrument. She can remember Rudi's momentary, fudged smile on opening the present, how the old typewriter was put on the floor beneath the table. She can see it's still there. The gift was a mistake, never mentioned. As they shuffle on towards the fireplace, she wants to, but can't, ask Rudi why he continues to use the Olivetti now Francis is dead.

When Jess had first gazed nervously about the room all those years before, the sight of the tall, flat-faced Imperial with its gold lettering had stunned her. It reminded her of the one she would tap in her Grandpa's study, which had its back to the picture window that looked out onto the porch, the dunes, and the sands of Cape Cod. She had tried to trace it, to have it as a part of him, of them, of that life, but years had passed by then. Everything had gone.

Her mind floods with the distant dream world of her youth: timber slat houses warmed by sunrise; spending time with Nana, adoring her; walking with her through her flowers where, year by year, her English poppies would spread their red a little more among the white and yellow of the moon daisies; playing violin with Grandpa; watching Mummy paint; running on the wooden bridge over the lagoon and along the seam of sea with her grandparents' dogs, Nell and Blue; sailing on Cockle Cove or east to Chatham, learning ropes; loving the rhythm and depth of Grandpa's voice; following his finger with fresh eyes towards South Monomoy Island to where, before the European settlers, the First Nation had come in summer for shellfish and to hunt; feeling the air season her skin; hearing from her pillow the waves lap or roar; sitting reading on the porch; listening to the typewriter as Grandpa sat hunched at his desk, his face—the steady, deep-set eyes dark beneath furrowed brow, the grey and ginger beard he would habitually twist with his fingers; one arm opening to her as she entered his study, the other clinging to a thought; his cardigan that sagged; the smell of the wool; the comfort of him, the enormous love she felt.

Her family were rocks on the shifting shore, beneath the cries of the herring gulls and cast of salt. They had watched her run, flare, discover, grow. She was an outsider, shoeless on the sands, unafraid to walk alone in nature. The whole family stood apart from much of other human life: her mother mentally frail, fighting demons, forever staring, hiding when people came, drinking; her grandfather consumed by the economy of words, in ink and spoken, the sanctuary of his violin, making time to bestow his love and need of it; him teaching her music; Nana weaving the nest, washing the table and replenishing it, tending her garden, tending them all. They understood the fire Jess carried, her raw spirit, her capacity, her needs. She would push, erupt at frustrations. So they let her go, to sense all, to begin to fathom. Then they listened as music welled in her and embroidered her soul.

As fast as crystal memories of family come, they are crushed. Waking in hospital; remembering nothing of the accident; disbelieving; shaking, screaming; wishing so hard that she, too, had died.

She tries to wrench her mind free. Her eyes blink to the wooden library ladder waiting beside the shelves. It is where she would perch, scanning books and music scores open on her legs while Rudi and Francis flirted and cackled in the kitchen, arguing about who was making the tea. All those years ago, after the long first days of doubt, of not knowing, she belonged. They let her in. It was a haven, an affinity, the closest she'd come to any sense of contentment since Mummy, Grandpa, and Nana had been snatched from her.

During the bewildering beginnings at the Royal Academy, her times with professor of violin Rudi and his partner Francis were moments to almost forget how everything she understood, loved, and wanted had disappeared in the blink of an eye. Almost. She had been twelve years old. She'd then spent the rest of every day blocking out, hitting out, running. All she had to cling to was the music. The feelings well because it was here, in this room, for a short while at least, that she found a semblance of love again.

Jess's world had ruptured on the night of 16th December 1943.

The doctors said it was a miracle she was alive, how the accident was caused by a falling branch during an Atlantic squall that tore roofs from houses and uprooted trees across the Cape. The driver of the furniture truck that hit the branch before flipping onto its side was not to blame.

The crash killed Mummy and Grandpa instantly. Nana, who was sitting next to Jess as always in the back of the family's rusty Chevrolet, was in a coma for a week before she died. Jess regained consciousness ten days later. She'd suffered severe head injuries, a punctured left lung, broken ribs, and a deep wound in her left leg just above the knee. She left hospital after six weeks. She was immediately confined, boxed in. It was a nightmare. The children's home was in a former red brick school. So many people, so alone. War consumed: fear in eyes, the bravado of boys, the stifling rules, the blacked-out windows. Claustrophobia. She would scream, punch, wreck, refuse food. They gave her pills. They forced her to eat. News was of military sacrifice, not loss, never numbers. Europe was on fire. The Pacific and Asia were on fire. She would never go home. She went down to the basement and played her violin until her fingers were raw.

Months after peace was proclaimed, a tall Englishman in a navy uniform with brass buttons came and stood over her. He had very short brown and grey hair and wore heavy, black-rimmed glasses that he kept pushing back up his nose. He clutched at his cap and at his duty. He said his name was Frederick Montgomery, her father. He flinched a smile. He offered his hand. She stared. He stepped back, spoke in half sentences. He was out of his depth. He locked onto practicalities, said she would live with him at his home in England. Everything was arranged, and everything would change. Only it wouldn't. She had fallen into water and was still being swept by currents. Her life would never be her own again. The only constants were the music and that crescent scar on her thigh, the branding when her real family, the touch of fingers interlocking, everything she adored, vanished.

Her father, of few words and no physical contact, took her to lay flowers on graves, then drove to the airport. She never went to Cape Cod again.

Jess knew her parents were never married. When she was old enough to think to ask, her mother dissolved, rushed out, and howled. It was her Nana who said, "All that matters is we have you. We love you."

On the flight, Jess sat in silence beside the stranger. She was frightened. Everything lurched. The noise was ceaseless, her legs cold. The man was by the window looking out. He uttered nothing at first. He was frowning, searching, then spilled. It was a mistake, he said. He had been in America for government work. He had met her mother at a gallery exhibition in Boston. She was working there. It was not love. They met just that once. He had given her his name and address, but they never spoke or met again. He had no idea he was a father. Then there was war. When he was contacted and told about the accident, it was the first he knew he had a daughter. He wanted to do the right thing, but he was on active service. It had been impossible to do anything. He was now bound to help, even if he was not her father. It was the worst of explanations. She wondered what he had not said. She pictured her mother's distress, her struggle. Jess remained silent and clung to the seat as the plane shook. She threw up.

In England there was a car waiting to collect them. The driver, also in uniform, saluted and called the man sir. The man said he had to go to a ministry in London to deliver something. Jess realised he had not gone to America just to fetch her. She stared out of the window at bombed buildings, twisted metal, and piles of rubble. Teams of people were working to clear shattered streets. They turned into a guarded square, and she waited in the car for nearly an hour. He came out and said they would be going to his house in Oxford. But he could not stay. A friend would look after her. The world changed again. There was no destruction in the famous university city. The house was new, set back on a tree-lined road. He put her bag and violin case in a small room with a single bed. From the window she could just make out in the fading light a long strip of cut grass. There were no trees, no flowers. He told her to change and refresh because they would be dining out. She said she had nothing except pyjamas, her coat, a work smock, and two aprons. He tried and failed to mask his irritation. As they walked, it was as if the war had passed the city by. He had long strides, did not stop to let her catch up, and she had to keep running. It was a maze of living history, of medieval marvels, of learning, just as her grandpa had described it. People swept by, black gowns billowing. There were glimpses of neat green through college gates, the aura of privilege. The man called for her to come. He turned a corner, pressing on past a line of small shops. He peered into a restaurant, acknowledged someone, and ushered Jess in.

An equally stilted woman with lacquered blonde hair precisely pinned in waves was standing in a tailored green two-piece suit with fur collar. She was introduced as Cecile. She smiled with her mouth but not her eyes. The man said she was French. She had worked with him for the government during the war. Now she worked at the university. Jess looked at white lace gloves lying on the table. Cecile was like a mannequin, someone in a magazine advertisement. They were her things Jess had seen in the bathroom. She, too, was brittle, unsure. Jess still said nothing. None of them could relate and never would. When had she first found out he had a daughter? As they ate, Jess saw them exchange a glance. Her father said he'd found a boarding school in Sussex with a renowned music department.

Jess blinks again and shivers. She looks at the armchairs and the fireplace as she and Rudi approach them. The once open hearth that Francis would constantly tend and feed with balls of Coalite from a brass scuttle is now plugged with a gas fire. The marble mantelpiece is still lined with pictures of the two men, either side of the large, round-topped wooden clock. She notices a more recent photograph of Francis in a gold frame, looking gaunt but handsome, mop-haired and laughing, sailing a boat. She remembers him standing there, by the fire, cheekily daring her to smile at him, then trying to make her and Rudi laugh with one of what he called his "nonsense poems", though she never thought of them like that. She loved them. She loved him.

Rudi helps her off with her coat.

"Sit. Please."

She stands for a second or two more.

In the far corner of the room was the open roll-top writing desk. Rudi, in a fluster of embarrassment, would stuff her fee into any one of the six small drawers. The desk was still lost beneath paper and towers of books. In front of the windows, the shining black Bösendorfer grand piano is unmoved, as ever apart from the chaos, only now the keyboard lid is down. Just beyond it, between the piano stool and the outside world, is the same metal music stand where Jess would practise for hours on end. To the side of it she can just see Rudi's violin case in its usual place, lying on the bottom shelf below the stereo and behind the open door to the small hall that leads to the kitchen, the two bedrooms, bathroom, and what was once, maybe still, Francis's colourful, ordered study, which he always called his playroom.

She watches Rudi gingerly lower himself into his chair. She tries to think of his tenderness and generous wisdom but sees only the closeness of death. He settles himself, looks up, and beams She wants to leave. She looks away and sits.

"So good to see you, Jessica, so good." His smile drops. He sees the plaster under her hair. "But you've hurt yourself."

"It's nothing."

His eyes flutter, and he wonders where to begin. "Well, you can see little has changed, mmm? Save the dust, maybe. There's probably a little less thanks to Esther. Wretched woman has boundless energy. She usually pops round in the late afternoon to see if I'm still alive. But she's away at the moment. She'll be sorry she missed you. Now, what can I offer you? I have some scones. I thought—"

"No. No, thank you."

"Something to drink, then? You must remember I like to have tea in the middle of the afternoon. It gave us a rest, didn't it? Now I've become so English that I can't live without my 'cuppa'. I usually have about four cups a day, if I'm honest. That was Francis, you know. Of course you do. All part of his fussing." Rudi freezes for a second, not breathing. "But now, clearly, I don't have tea to give me a rest from playing. Not any more. That, naturally—" he holds up his hands and looks at them for a second, "is precious little now. Age is a bugger, isn't it? My hands and my brain talk less and less. I love my violin, of course, to touch it, to feel it. Only I don't like to hear how I play now. The piano too. But—" He slaps his hands onto his thigh bones. "There are other things to take comfort in. I may look pretty feeble, but I'm still moving, just—and some brain cells are alive. I think!"

14

Jess says nothing. The silence goes on too long.

Rudi, eyes blinking in thought, suddenly offers up a question as if she asked it. "How do I pass the time? There are days, I must admit, when I'm not feeling too clever, when I stay in bed and do very little, save reading, snoozing, enduring a lecture from Esther about tidiness. Otherwise, when I'm not over there–" He nods in the direction of the papers and typewriter on the dining room table. "Or there–" Then towards his piano and violin. "I spend countless hours in this chair listening to my music. By that, of course, I mean listening to you and my other pupils. There is nothing more important now. I want you to know how important it is to me. How much I love it and how it helps me."

He looks for any warmth in her, any softening, but she is looking down at her hands.

"A-and, as I said, I'm still working, sort of, just a few hours a week, but for how much longer I don't know. I'm scribbling mostly, but I still do a little teaching–just Monday and Friday mornings for an hour–does me good, I think, although I'm always exhausted afterwards. A couple of bright young things who, like you, have something. And the girl, Rachel, from Cumbria originally, if I remember correctly, reminds me of you a little, in a way. As for the writing, I'm still digging about researching music and doing the occasional thing for magazines. It brings in a little too. Remember how I'd devote more time to that than I should have? Well, I'd give it up now, of course, for the chance to play like I did. It's just that my fingers are stiffening so much. They ache too. But you, you, Jessica my darling, are much, much younger."

Jess closes her eyes.

Rudi bites his lip, thinking what to say. He mustn't push too hard. But he goes on. "I loved it so much when we worked here together. You must remember. I tingle thinking about it, you know–thinking this is genius. Listening to you, watching you as you played."

"No–"

15

"Such depth, such unbelievable gifts for one so—"

"NO!" Jess stands. Her eyes and fists are pinched shut. The clock steps out of the shadows again. She turns to grab her coat and scarf from the arm of the chair.

Rudi reaches out his arms "Please don't."

"Why, Rudi? Why? I don't want your help. I don't need anybody's BLOODY help! SHIT!"

Rudi waits for a second. "I'm not offering it." His voice is weak again. "That's not why I rang you. Believe me. Please. As I said in my message, Jessica my darling, it's me that needs your help. I'm sorry. I'm truly sorry. Forgive me. Old fool. Don't go. Please. Please. Sit. Tea, mmm? I've got everything ready in the kitchen. Let's have some tea." He struggles to his feet and shuffles away, then stops and half turns. "You are not to worry about the Thames Concert Hall director, by the way. Let that anxiety go. I have spoken to him."

Jess sinks back onto the chair.

"Do you know Norfolk?"

Jess looks at Rudi. The words ring a tiny bell in the back of her mind. She finds herself remembering her Nana from her dream the night before, that same recurring dream, seeing her smiling mouth move with words she can't quite recall. She was from Norfolk County, Massachusetts. How can he know this? She blinks wide-eyed, paralysed, as Rudi asks again.

"On the east coast. You know where I mean, don't you—that so-called flat county on England's east coast? Not New England, Jessica. England. Here. It's that great curve jutting out into the North Sea, facing Holland. You all right?"

Jess is breathing faster. She nods slightly. Rudi goes on.

"It's where Francis's mother came from. The land of Abraham Lincoln's forefathers, actually. Did you know that? His ancestors came from there, along, no doubt, with those of a great many of your fellow Americans. One of the English kings, Charles, I think it was, wrongly dismissed Norfolk as being so flat and uninteresting that the only use he could think of for it was to be dug up and used for making roads. Not that that's why I think so many people were so keen to sail across the Atlantic to the New World. Poverty, politics, religion, a whole host of reasons, no doubt. No, Norfolk's a beguiling place, an incredibly beautiful and fertile place. The king did it a service, to my mind. It's been left alone, unspoilt for the most part. There's a vast wetland there—the Broads. You must have heard of the Broads." Jess shakes her head, shakes her thoughts from her mind, looks down, and tries to sip from her cup. She can't take this. Rudi, seeing her slipping away, tries to keep talking. "I'm sure we told you about our American trip, didn't we? I must have."

She doesn't remember. She's barely listening. It's been such a long time since they talked, properly talked, when she had sat listening to him like this. He's talking as if nothing has changed, as if they're still close like all those years before. There is that familiar tenderness in his voice, yet everything else is wrong, so horribly wrong or so far in the past. A deep anxiety begins to well in her. She bites into her lip.

Rudi goes on. "Four or five years ago it's got to be now. Francis had just been diagnosed. There was an urgency, a fire in him to defy the disease. He organised everything, and we flew to Boston and drove to all those places with Norfolk names. We went to several Norwichs, one on the coast in Connecticut, very beautiful, and another in New York State I think, then we pottered around in Norfolk County for a few days, where JFK and a couple of other US presidents were born, apparently. We even went down to Norfolk, Virginia, and drove along a highway named after a Norfolk man who married a Native American Indian called Pocahontas—Rolfe, yes, Rolfe, that's it. The Rolfe Highway or something like that. It was just a road as far as I was concerned, but Francis was so excited, you know? Big kid, as always. When he got a bee in his bonnet it was wonderful to see, and, yes, of course, the whole thing was great fun; and it was very beautiful; the autumn; golden colours; I learned a lot; so much really. New

England is gorgeous." Rudi's face clouds. His eyes glaze. "Made me wonder about that time when we left Prague in that bitter January 1938, before that bastard Hitler... well... and we came to London, and what my life would have been like if I had gone on to America, something that was discussed. My father wanted to stay here to help those left behind in Czechoslovakia, his sisters and their families, others. He so nearly went back. Mother was distraught. I said I would go. I was thirty. I had friends and contacts who might help. But he would not have it. It was too great a risk. I had a life, a chance, he said. He had worked for the government and could do far more. In the end even he could not get back. So, he worked with the British Committee for Refugees from Czechoslovakia, and about three and a half thousand were saved before the Nazis stopped the trains. It haunted him, though, that he failed to get any of the rest of the family out before the war, the Holocaust. They refused to leave until it was too late." His voice drops to a whisper. "Belsen... Auschwitz..."

Jess had no idea. They had never talked about Rudi's past, his family, like this before. "Father wanted me to go ahead to America, but I refused. Then, anyway, London, Britain, was consumed by the conflict. I did whatever I could."

A deep breath, a sad smile. "And if I had gone, I'd have not met Francis, would I?"

"The America trip. That is the memory I want. We had a few nights in Manhattan at the end, which made me very dizzy. But, you know, until Francis got hooked on the subject and then started planning, I hadn't realised—had no reason to, I suppose—that so many of the settlers came from Norfolk, Suffolk, and the east of England. We'd talked a bit about it before then because it came out of something we'd both read, that mentions someone leaving to start a new life in America just over a hundred years ago. It was in an old journal, something that became very important to Francis in the last couple of years. Come to think of it, you ought to read it, you really should. Then a friend from Boston, Hugh—Hugh Carlton Brock—an artist who'd based himself here in London for a while, told Francis he'd traced his roots back to a village in Suffolk, England. Francis started then. When he found out that the first counties named by the settlers included Norfolk and Suffolk, that was it, he was like a dog with a bone. But it is amazing, isn't it, this history, the stories of the people who went to America, where they came from? Well, for me it is, now that I know Norfolk, Norfolk here, I mean, that now I've learned a little about it, especially the wetland, and a little of its past, the people, how they lived. It's only a little piece of the story of your country, but it makes you really think, doesn't it, things like that?"

Jess is sitting like stone, staring blankly back at him. She's heard only words, not sentences. She glimpses Francis. Fragments of her younger life are flashing through her mind.

Rudi wants to tell her of their visit to the Cape but stops himself. He suddenly feels clumsy, foolish. There is no breaking through to her. This is the wrong tack. He must get to the point.

"Sorry, only given that you are from there, I thought... Oh, forgive me. Twittering on again. And why should I expect you to know about the Broads?" He drops his gaze. With mellow, thoughtful eyes on the orange glow of the gas fire, he rubs one slippered foot with the other. "To be honest, I wouldn't have known either if it wasn't for Francis. It's been a vital place for me. For us."

They drift, each in their own world, to a more comfortable calmness. Then Rudi eases his head away from the wing of the chair and looks at Jess, a hint of a smile on his thin lips. "We've a house there. You never knew, did you?"

Jess, surprised, moves her head very slowly from side to side.

"We, or rather Francis I should say, inherited it a few years after we got together. About... oh... 1963, I think. My God..." The smile falls away, and the eyes glaze and begin to water. He tries in vain to smile again. "Where has the time gone? Where has it gone? I miss him, Jessica. I miss him so much."

Jess suddenly wants to reach out, to touch him. Tears begin to run down her cheeks too. She glances up again at the picture of Francis, and memories of him flood back. She remembers the awful bleakness of the funeral, that unanswerable emptiness; then, looking again at him, happier thoughts come to her, of what an incredibly bright light he was; thoughts of the mischief and the laughter, when the flat was alive with music and banter and a magic of secrets and abandonment, somehow far removed from the outside world. Francis had been living with Rudi for about a year when she first knew them. Rudi's joy had been unbridled.

She tries. "What sort of house?"

"Oh–" Rudi wipes his face with a handkerchief. "A little cottage. Very little. Tiny, really. A place for bare feet on floorboards; roaring fires and candlelight." The old man struggles forward in his armchair and points at the teacup on the low table between them. "Pass the wretched thing, will you?"

Jess leans across with the cup and saucer. "Actually, I have been to Norfolk. Once. I vaguely remember it–Norwich, I mean, the old city– sometime around the mid-seventies, maybe. I gave a recital of Bach's second violin concerto, I think. In the huge cathedral; middle of the night; no time."

"You didn't see that beautiful city then?"

"No."

"That was typical, yes?"

Jess nods.

"Hardly a love affair."

"No."

"I don't know about you, but I think living in London all the time, there's so much we don't want to see that we don't see much at all. Maybe it's my age. I don't need reminding how I used to rave about being here. Loved it. Simply adored it. Knew nothing else, wanted nothing else after we came over from Hanover, except during the war, of course, but even then it seemed so vital, was gripped with this most incredible spirit during even the most terrible and worrying times. Later, after the war, there was such optimism and life here. How it changed, for the better mostly, becoming so liberal and open. But I'm tired of it, you know? Too old, far too old. I can't explain it very well, but I can't do it any more. I don't have the energy, I suppose. It's not a place to be decrepit. But there's something else that's changed my perspective. Away from here, for a long time now, I've learned to–and simply love to–stand and use my eyes and ears. Somewhere natural, beautiful–peaceful–yes, that's it, peaceful. To be lost, if you can understand that." Rudi's voice drops to a whisper. "Away from bloody people. Nature. It's... life-giving. That's what Francis would say. We all have our favourite haunts, don't we? Mine used to be the Royal Academy, galleries and libraries–and concert halls, of course. And they still are, in the London sense, though much less so now. But–"

He pats and rubs his thighs through the blanket and looks at the fire. "I'm so glad I found Norfolk. It was Francis's gift. Francis's ashes are there, in the garden of the cottage. I will join him. That is my wish."

They sit and think of different things. Jess cradles her tea and looks into it. Rudi leans forward a little.

"I'm sorry I upset you earlier, Jessica. Thank you for not leaving."

"No. I'm sorry."

"I don't get to see many people these days. There are not many I want to see, actually. You understand."

Jess nods.

"Esther normally comes about this time. Blasted woman. Anyone would think I was a child. Her child. Oh, I love her, of course I do. Best sister a brother ever had and all that. But I'm not a total invalid–not yet–and I don't understand, and never will, the mind of someone who relishes domestic arrangements. If only she'd married and left me to gather dust happily."

"How old is she now?"

"God only knows. Let me think... she's seventy-six. May 18th. I'm going to give her my ticket for Michael's lunchtime concert at St John's next month, in fact."

Jess stops breathing. Michael. Her son.

"Dear boy sent it to me, but I won't be going. I have an outpatient's appointment that day. I'll pay for her taxi and organise a meal, or something. Are you going?"

Jess shakes her head. She looks away. Rudi sees that her cup is shaking and, silently, he curses his clumsiness. He has to raise it, but not like this.

Two car horns duel on Marylebone High Street.

"Esther's in Ramsgate or somewhere or other. Forgotten exactly where. Wasn't listening. Gone with a friend she plays bridge with is one fact that did sink in. Still living in her little house in Amery Gardens. Still there. Very handy indeed for both the Jubilee and Bakerloo lines, both of which lead to my door, virtually. Not that I agree with her using the tube these days." Rudi sighs deeply. "I suppose I'd be dead by now if it wasn't for her. As I said, she's here almost daily. Nothing like as regular as that, of course, when Francis was alive. Ha. No. Heavens, no. You can't really begin to imagine, can you? She was always phoning and writing and did call in, yes, but never unannounced. It was only when Francis passed that she started turning up again just as she did all those years ago. Remarkable, really. She doesn't talk about it. Not that she talks about anything other than how I don't look after myself."

Jess whispers. "I saw her at the funeral."

"Yes, that's true. To be fair, that's true. In fact, if I'm honest, she has always been there. When I have needed her, or when she has thought I needed her which, I suppose, is the same thing. I've never understood why, though. I'm a cantankerous old queen and, more important than anything to her, an unorthodox Jew. I'm not, in her case, one to give much back."

Heavy rain starts to splash against the windows.

"Be a love and turn the lamps on, would you? And I'd be grateful if you'd pull the curtains while you're at it. Shut the ruddy world out."

The red velvet deadens the noise of London. Jess moves to the second window which, like the first, opens onto a tiny balcony. She turns on the standard lamp in the corner of the room. She grabs at the curtains, then stops, facing herself in the glass. Her flat, straight, shoulder-length brown hair hangs limp and lifeless around the shadows of her face. Here, in the far corner of the room by the piano, she'd stood all those years before and played and played.

"Do you–," Rudi hesitates. "Do you still see Tom occasionally?"

"No," Jess says softly. "Sometimes."

In her mind she sees him with Michael, hovering by the door of the green room at her last concert four years before. They didn't speak. She barely spoke to anyone. They'd been together twice more, with Rudi and Francis too, when Michael's quartet had won the Wigmore prize two years later. Again, nothing was said. Then there was the funeral.

Rudi repeats her thought. "We were all at the Wigmore for Michael's big night, weren't we?"

"Yes."

"That was quite a moment. Michael has your vitality. You must be very proud."

Jess looks through herself out onto the wet street shining under the yellow lamps. It's almost dark. She loves her son. She hates herself. Her words are a mumble. "Michael's much more like Tom, though." Her voice drops to a whisper Rudi cannot hear. "He's not me."

"He respects you enormously, Jessica. You know that, don't you? He walked me the few yards home after the concert. He'd so hoped you would stay afterwards to tell him what you thought."

23

Jess shouts in her head that it wasn't Michael but all the other people she was escaping. That she had no more courage. That it hurts so much to hear Michael's thoughts from someone else. Rudi talks on.

"He has been to see me quite a few times, actually. He's sensitive. And astute."

Jess swings round.

"What the hell does that mean?"

"That he sees what I see. That we agree. But–sorry. Uncalled for. Sorry."

Rudi flops back into his chair and holds up his palms He knows he must stop.

"No, I have said far too much. It's just that you're special, Jessica. And I feel I can say this–I have to say this–because I love you. Because Francis loved you." He turns and pulls at the cushion at his back.

"But enough. Enough. Anyway, I want to talk about the favour I need to ask of you."

Jess takes a very deep breath. Her anger falls away to an ache in the middle of her, the ache that lives with her. She folds her arms across it. There is no point in rage now. She cannot find the words anyway. She never can. She needs a drink. Her shoulders drop, and she bends forward and leans against the piano, resting her crossed arms on top of it.

"We–I mean I–need someone, someone I can trust, to open the windows and clear the dust for me. Our Norfolk cottage."

"Me?"

"Yes, you, Jessica. You. Francis and I have always trusted you. There is no one else I can think of who I would want to do this. He would want this too. You can put coal into a stove, can't you? What month is it now? April? The place will be chilled. Lovely Margaret, from the nearby farm, pops in and fires up the wood burner and kitchen Rayburn occasionally to stop things deteriorating, but it needs living in again. You'll love it. Now, you must be prepared for a little hardship—"

"I haven't said—"

"I know, Jessica. But promise me you'll think about it? Go for a couple of days at least? For me? If I'm truthful, I'm at a loss to know what to do with it all and would value your thoughts. I think you'll understand what I mean when you get there. When Francis died, I locked myself away there for three weeks. Kept putting off sowing his ashes until I was about to leave. September. Brought it home to me, though, that I can't cope with it on my own. Not as I am. Not at my age, in my state. Worried now, though, because it's been empty all winter. I'd truly appreciate it if you'd have a look. I trust you. And the truth is, even if I could, I'm not sure I want to go any more, now that Francis is gone. Only when I am dead too."

"I don't know."

"It can be our secret. Nobody needs to know. Francis and I loved secrets. Absolutely loved them. We'd tell people we were off to Italy or somewhere, but more often than not we were there, in Norfolk. Blissful isolation. As much as three months a year, counting weekends, and we spent many wonderful Christmases there too. Sharp frosts, snow once. Francis referred to it as his Valhalla. He inherited it from his uncle, a lawyer with no family, who was potty about ornithology. Wilfred—that was his name. His book collection is all there—I hope. Had an office and home in Norwich and used to trundle over to the Broads whenever he could. Francis said his mother called it her brother's disappearing act, but, apparently, he involved his whole family, letting his nieces and nephews come whenever they wanted, if he was there. Francis was an only child, as I think you know, but there was another uncle who had three children, although they didn't visit the cottage anything like as much. Any chance he got, Francis would be there. And I think Wilfred and Francis's mother Elsie were quite close. He was older, and she relied on him quite a bit, I think, after her husband died. Anyway, the family would all come together at the cottage occasionally, more so when the children were young. The old boy used to call his nieces and nephews his tulips—equally colourful yet

25

independent, like a vase of tulips. You know, how they are all alike in one way, but will each twist and turn differently. Beautiful. We all have flowers we have reason to love especially, don't we? And for Francis it was tulips. Certainly, he was very fond of his uncle, looked up to him." Rudi addresses the fire again. "The family were rather shocked, all the same, when he left it to Francis, along with his savings and his library. Francis had been here in London for quite a few years. His mother had died. His other uncle wasn't very happy about it at all, saying it wasn't fair on his children, although they were left the Norwich house, which was worth a pretty penny. They came here once. It was very difficult. Horrible. Francis was quite ill about it. We invited them because we thought it might help clear things up, which, on reflection, was a mistake. Never heard anything from them again after that. It hurt Francis deeply, you know, because he didn't have any other family. He would have let them use it, but I don't think it was just about the cottage."

"What happened to his father? I knew he died abroad somewhere. But Francis never spoke about it, about his family or anything like that, and I never asked."

"None of us did, did we? Talk about families, the past. Not easy."

Jess shakes her head and looks down.

"He was killed in South Africa, when Francis was about seven. A street mugging. He wouldn't give them what they wanted, apparently, so they stabbed him. Before that, Francis had spent all his life in the Bahamas. Born there. Was a wonderful life for a child. He told me he didn't wear shoes until he was seven, though, typically, that must have been an exaggeration. Makes sense, though, doesn't it, when you think how he was, always going barefoot—or naked—given half the chance? His father was a diplomat of some sort. He'd been posted. The family was just about to up sticks and move to South Africa—not sure exactly where—when his father was murdered. The mother immediately packed up the children and came home to England. Settled in north Norfolk where she'd grown up."

Jess thinks about Francis again. Senses him.

"Where is this cottage?"

"Close to the coast, on the edge of Hickling Broad. In fact—what a marvellous idea!" Rudi's face lights up. "You must, simply must travel to it by river. You sailed a lot as a child, didn't you? Well, don't worry a bit, it will all come back to you, like riding a bicycle—you never forget how. Otter, our sailing cruiser, is at Ludham. She's a beautiful little boat, you'll adore her. I'll call, and someone at the yard will get her rigged and hopefully get you on your way. She should be ready for the season by now, and they'll be glad to be rid of her. Need the space."

Jess's mind clouds over. This is ridiculous. Absurd. She can't remember how to sail. She doesn't want to even think about going anywhere. It's crazy. It's a dream. All she says is, "I don't drive."

"Yes, yes. I know. All the more reason to take the boat on the last leg. All you've got to do is get British bloody Rail to get you to Wroxham."

Rudi beams "Oh, and I should have said. The cottage is called Whispering Reeds."

3

The rail timetable is a whirl of letters and numbers clicking continuously above the ebb and flow of travelers. Jess's head thumps. Her eyelids are heavy, and she tries to stifle a yawn. Lifting her sunglasses for a few seconds, she squints up at the East Anglian destinations: Norwich, platform 6, 11:25. She has eighteen minutes. She pulls at the high collar of her coat, takes a tissue out of her pocket to blow her nose, and then looks down at the plastic bag propped between her knees. It sits on top of her holdall–the bag Rudi had given her a couple of hours earlier. The bastard. She had never been able to defy him. He always wanted more. What made her go to him?

The doorbell had kept buzzing and buzzing.

Jess angrily pulled on her dressing gown, paced up and down before shouting at the door, "Who is it? What d'you want?"

When she heard Rudi call his name back, her heart stopped for a second. She pulled at her hair and swore silently over and over for having let on that she was there. She couldn't ignore him. She couldn't.

"Jessica! Good morning, good morning."

Rudi was talking before her door was half open.

"I hope you don't mind, but I've brought some things for you to read on the train."

The heavy plastic bag was pushed into her chest as he shuffled past into the flat. He was using his walking stick, but he seemed different, stronger.

"I mentioned today, yes? Wasn't sure you'd remember, so I thought I'd get in a taxi, get over here, and give you a little help. I've woken you, haven't I?"

"Wha—what time is it?"

"Gone 9:30 now. You'll need to be ready to leave in an hour to allow yourself plenty of time to get the 11:25 out of Liverpool Street. Best train. Suggest you wear something warm, though—jumper and jeans would be sensible—and pack some rubber-soled shoes if you have them."

"I'm not feeling very good, Rudi. I'm... I'm full of cold."

"A cold? Dose yourself up and get the hell out of London. Fresh air, that's what you need."

He turned and looked her in the eye. His voice dropped an octave. There was the old light in his eyes.

"Trust me, Jessica. Trust me. I know what you need. This will do you the power of good, believe me. Believe me."

He turned away and continued to walk into her flat. He patted his pocket. "Now, I've got the rail ticket here, an open-ended return, and I've ordered you a taxi too, so you don't have to worry about anything.

29

That train gives you plenty of daylight the other end to get your bearings. I've also written a few notes for you. They're in the bag too, with the keys."

He waved his stick back towards the door without stopping or looking. "Oh, and this is Nigel, by the way. A sort of pupil..." A freckly, ginger-haired teenager in a duffle coat was hovering outside in the hallway, smiling timidly. "...in that he does the washing up and runs a few errands in exchange for a little wisdom. He's a good chap. And you owe him an apology. He's supposed to be having a lesson but agreed to prop me up on the journey over here. The deal was he would get to meet the famous you, Jessica Healey. Shall I make a pot of tea?"

The day, from the second the doorbell had pierced her sleep, is like a dreadful dream. Jess feels helpless, like being carried by a current.

She hadn't said yes to any of Rudi's pleas or suggestions, but she hadn't said no. Listening to him in his flat two weeks earlier, she couldn't remotely conceive of doing what he was asking. She was numb. But she hadn't said no. It was a case of thinking of other things and other times and only vaguely taking in what he was saying, then walking away and almost blocking it out. Almost.

After Rudi's first telephone message, Jess told herself she had to go to see him because she might never see her old teacher again, but that wasn't it. He was impossible to refuse. He was once her guide, someone—once, maybe the only person apart from her mother and her Nana and Grandpa—that she trusted; him and Francis. But after this last time, in his flat, she felt she never wanted to see him again. She never wanted to go there again.

A week later, his second telephone message and the way he'd glibly talked about travel arrangements as if everything had been agreed made her cry with despair. She cursed herself for having gone to see him. She screamed at the walls and drummed them with her fists. The shock that he was serious, that he actually expected her help, for her to do something, "to go to his damned cottage, FOR CHRIST'S SAKE!"

30

made her shake. She had gulped from a bottle, coughing. She laughed and cried, telling herself over and over again, all she had to do—yes, all she had to do—was to say nothing and do nothing, to cloud it out like everything else that was pressing down on her; to avoid it, to avoid him. He'll find someone else. It wasn't important. It wasn't important.

It never crossed her mind for a second that he'd come. That morning, before opening her door, her knees had buckled and she fell back against the wall. She could barely find the strength to breathe.

Alone in the middle of busy Liverpool Street railway station, Jess takes deep breaths. But the hollowness that grows and shrinks yet never leaves is still deep. No chance of a drink now. Her chin and eyes drop. She can see that the gaping bag between her knees contains a large bulging brown envelope, a thinner white one, and two books, a hardback and a paperback. The lime green hardback looks old and has a tatty-edged, torn dust cover. The thinner paperback looks new. Then a coldness runs down her back.

"Shit."

She picks up the bag and holdall and walks to a newsstand. She buys cigarettes and gets some change for the phone.

"Suzy, it's me. Jess."

"You OK?"

Jess waits, says nothing.

"Shall I come? I can be there in about two hours—"

"No."

"Where are you? Sounds like an airport. What's happened?"

"At a railway station. Er—look, um..."

"What?"

31

"Are you working?"

"No. Monday morning. Drinking coffee, staring at the piano and thinking about it."

"I–I need a favor. I've done a stupid thing. Michael's been in California for a couple of weeks. I've got to go away for a couple of days. When you get a chance sometime today, could you go round to my flat? Do you still have the key?"

"Of course. And I have Henry's too if you want that back. They are both hanging on the dresser."

"Please go and thoroughly check my kitchen. Today. Would you? I might have left a knob open or something. Stupid."

"Paranoid? Stupid." Suzy's Australian accent weights the word.

"Can you take care of this for me? Please?"

"Ok."

"Shall I tell Henry?"

Jess looks blankly at the three 20p coins she has stacked on top of the payphone.

"Jess? Jess–are you still there?"

"S–sorry?"

"Shall I tell him?"

"What?"

"Tell him. Henry."

"Tell him that I've asked you to go to my flat?"

"No. Tell him you're away. We're dearest friends, you and me, Jess, but he is my brother. He mentioned the other day that even after all this time you've still got some of his stuff. CDs, that sort of thing.

But–if you don't want him to know then I won't tell him."

"I'd rather he didn't–know, I mean."

"OK. I won't."

"H–he's all right?"

The phone starts to beep and Jess pushes another 20p into the slot.

"Jess, if you really want to know, he's fine. Absolutely fine."

"Could you get round there today? I'm not going to be gone for very long, only–"

"Of course, I will."

"Yes. Er... Ignore..."

"Ignore what?"

"The mess."

"Jess. Stop it. I keep telling you. I understand. When are you back?"

"Don't know. Thursday, maybe. Sorry."

"Stop worrying. I'll come see you when you get home. You just take very good care of yourself now. And for God's sake either turn your answer phone off or return my calls, eh? Better still, give me a ring tonight whenever you get to where you're going. Oh yeah–where are you going?"

The train gathers speed through the chimney pots of Stratford. The young man facing Jess across the table looks blankly out of the window, chewing gum, head lolling towards the dirt-speckled glass and propped by a fist. Other people are scattered through the smokers' carriage that is already fudged by a gray haze. Jess stubs out her cigarette and immediately lights another. She empties Rudi's bag onto the table.

33

The hardback is *The Broads* by E. A. Ellis. The dust cover has a photograph of some sort of river barge with a huge black sail. The book looks about thirty or forty years old. She opens it and some old newspaper cuttings fall out of the back. One is from *The Telegraph*, the other from the *Eastern Daily Press*. Both date from the late '70s and appear to be about early boating holidays, and the larger *Eastern Daily Press* cutting has Victorian or Edwardian pictures of an old sailing boat that looks a bit like the one on the dust cover. Young, barrel-chested men in blazers and caps are posing about the deck, some with hands on hips.

Jess puts the cuttings back, pushes the book aside, and looks at the pristine paperback with a painting of a clifftop church on the cover. *Norfolk Life*, by Lilias Rider Haggard and Henry Williamson. She snatches a few words and lines as she flicks through it. She puts it down again, draws on her cigarette, and feels the large and heavy unmarked brown envelope which bends in her hands and seems to contain an inch-and-a-half-thick wad of A4 paper. Then her hands and eyes move to the much lighter white envelope which has her Christian name on it, written so distinctly by Rudi's rhythmic hand, the letters like small waves rebounding from a wall. Inside is a battered Ordnance Survey map, a typed letter spilling over four pages, and two smaller sealed white envelopes. One is addressed to Margaret and the other to Helen and Ted.

Jessica,

There is a distinct probability that you are having a few colourful thoughts about me at this time. I know I have bullied you into this and I also know there is nothing remotely appealing to you about what I have asked you to undertake. Endure, please, for my sake. And for yours, I presume to hope.

Let's start with the keys.

Jess upends the white envelope and three keys fall onto the table, each tagged with a coloured sticker.

Treasure them. Blue is for back door, green is for shed, and red unlocks the French doors. While I remember, a spare key for the piano resides with the teaspoons in the front of the cutlery drawer in the kitchen, although you will probably find the piano unlocked.

I mentioned Margaret, didn't I? She's Irish and a lovely, lovely person. She's married to Philip Bunn, a local man of few words but very friendly all the same, and they have a son, David, who's about 15 and who you will no doubt meet. The other two children, girls, Lizzie and Jackie, have flown the nest—one's at art college in London, I think, and the other's a nurse, like her mother used to be, and living in Norwich. They may well be around at some point. If you get the chance, ask Margaret how she came to marry a Norfolk farmer—it's a great love story. But I digress. They live at the farm about 500 yards back along the lane towards Hickling Heath, and they have a large dairy herd that keeps them very busy. It also means someone is usually about. The pasture to the rear of the cottage is theirs, or they rent it from the Norfolk Wildlife Trust, I'm not sure. Either way, I'm certain they won't mind if you walk there—but watch out for the dykes, and I'd suggest you don't go exploring if it's foggy. There are paths which go through the reeds too, which Francis knew like the back of his hand, but you may prefer, as I always did, to use Otter to enjoy the wetland (tea-making facilities on hand at all times!)

Since Francis's illness became acute some 18 months ago and he couldn't travel anymore, I started paying Margaret a little to stop the cottage from rotting, an arrangement which has worked very well because the family are free to use the cottage if they need space, and we've always let them keep their sailing cruiser berthed there in the summer. It won't be there this year, though, because they are having the hull done, so it would be nice for Otter to be around should they want to use her. Margaret can tell you the form with regard to essentials—fuel, milk, bread, papers, etc.—and is a mine of information about the wildlife and local area. There is a letter for her, and one for Helen and her father, Ted, at the boatyard. I would be glad if you would play postwoman for me. Helen and Ted are wonderful people too, and I have telephoned them so they know to expect you. The boat is ready, but more of that anon.

First, though, can I urge you to study the map and use a few minutes of the time on the train to get your bearings. I've marked it to show you the best route to the yard at Womack Water.

Jess opens the map. A green line trails north of Norwich along a rail line to Wroxham and then turns east along the A1062 through Horning to Ludham. Rudi has printed "BOATYARD" in blue ink where the map shows a patch of blue called Womack Water. From there the green trail follows a river north towards the coast, then east, ending with the letters "WR" close to the edge of a lake marked as Hickling Broad. The nearest civilization appears to be Hickling Heath, a few houses clustered along a lane at the far end of the broad. Further off, but probably still walkable, there is the village of Hickling. Stalham, obviously a town, has to be about four miles away around the other side of the expanse of water. The gentle curve of the Norfolk coast looks no further than a mile or so away to the north.

For a split second, Jess sees herself alone on a beach, and she wonders if it is anything like Cape Cod.

You could dodge the sailing trip and go straight to the cottage, but you'll have to ask my friend Gordon Crang to run you there and he may not have the time. It's about three times further than it is to the boatyard, and as for getting back, it could prove difficult.

Anyway, you should remember you will need Otter to get around, plus I feel sure you will enjoy sailing her. I hope you agree to taking the boat because traveling by river is the only sensible option–honestly.

If the train is running to schedule when you get to Norwich station, there should be another one leaving in 20 minutes to Sheringham. You don't need a new ticket–the one I gave you is from London to Wroxham. Wroxham is the second stop after you change trains, about 10 to 15 minutes' journey if I remember correctly. You will know when you are there as the train has to cross the river just before it stops.

There is only one exit from the station. Turn right. About three houses along after a car park, you will find a small hotel—Honeylands. It is owned by Gordon and he will run you out to Womack. He's expecting you. If the weather looks ghastly when you get there, you can always hole up at the hotel overnight.

Jess stops reading and looks out of the window. The sky is gray and heavy above the shrinking city. The train has passed the terraces of the East End. Now the gardens are larger. There are more trees. She feels the train speed up. Looking back, she can see the NatWest tower in the distance, almost touching the cloud. She watches it until the London horizon is lost in the folds of suburban Essex.

She pushes everything including the half-read letter back into the bag, rubs the back of her neck, and decides to go in search of coffee. She fishes her purse out of the holdall, throws her coat onto her seat, and leaves everything else on the table. There is a queue at the buffet and by the time she gets back, the train is rattling through deep swathes in the countryside. As she sips the hot drink and looks blankly at the world whizzing by, the window is suddenly filled for a second by a gray mare and brown foal standing motionless in the middle of a very small field where all the grass, save a faint veil of green, has been gnawed away. The horses are just yards from the railway line. Both animals have their eyes shut, ears flat, and radiate unhappiness. Jess looks the other way.

"Please forgive me, but are you traveling to Norwich?"

The woman on the other side of carriage is smiling at her.

"I'm sorry—only I saw the map. North Norfolk's so beautiful. Is this a holiday?"

Vogue magazine lay on the table in front of the woman, and a small case and neatly folded blue Barbour jacket are on the seat beside her. Her dense jet-black hair is at odds with her lined face. She speaks quickly.

"And, if you don't mind me asking, you're Jessica Healey, the violinist, aren't you?"

Jess doesn't answer. She just looks at the woman. The young man sitting opposite Jess stops chewing and stares at her.

"Am I mistaken?"

"Yes."

"Oh. I'm so sorry. Only–"

The train starts to slow. Jess hurriedly bundles the books, letters, keys, and envelopes into the plastic bag, picks everything up, and heads back towards the buffet and the nearest door.

"The next station is Chelmsford. Chelmsford," says a voice over the carriage loudspeaker. "We will shortly be arriving at Chelmsford."

Three young women, chatting and laughing, get up and block the door as the train slows. Jess slides into the seats they have left. "I could get off here. I could," she thinks, her heart racing. If the women weren't in her way, she would. This is crazy. Crazy. She doesn't know what to do. She sits and watches as the train slides to a stop, the doors bang open and closed, and people walk past, including the woman with the dyed hair. She obviously can't get off here now, but maybe at the next stop. She thinks about her flat and wants to be there, to lock the door. She doesn't want Suzy to see the chaos. But with Michael away, there was nobody else she felt she could ask. Suzy only lives a couple of miles away. She knows Jess. She knows.

Jess takes some deep breaths. She thinks about Suzy, how they met some ten years ago and first worked together on a contemporary music festival at the Barbican. How she'd already been told about Suzy, five years younger than her, the Brisbane-raised daughter of a British lawyer and Australian doctor, who'd been based in London for most of her career and had long established herself as an outstanding accompanist. How, from their first rehearsals, Jess found her tolerant, forgiving.

How there was an optimism and an understanding, even at the bleakest time. How, through the years, Suzy had seen Jess at her worst and somehow seemed prepared to live with it, to work through it. How many times she'd done that. They toured in America and Europe, as well as Britain. There were the recordings too. That was all that was left. Their last partnership was fourteen months ago. Fauré's Violin Sonatas for the Hyperion label.

The train jolts forward.

Jess thinks about Henry too and her stomach tightens. How old she felt, how lost for words or actions she became as his knowledge of her grew. How part of her wished it would end and knew it was bound to, and how the thought hurt so much.

Henry pushed his way into her life three years ago. He later admitted that he was fascinated by her openness when playing the violin compared to her well-known reticence, her dark silences, away from music. He was nine years younger than her. They'd met once before, the previous year, when he was visiting his sister. Suzy and Henry were in the audience at the Thames Concert Hall to hear Jess play Delius's Violin Concerto with the Philharmonia. It was her last public performance. Jess collapsed in her dressing room. Henry and Suzy took her home. The following year Henry moved from Australia and was working for the BBC in London. He came to hear his sister play at a Schubertiad at the Wigmore. It was January. Jess hadn't wanted to go. Henry arranged tickets and pressed her. Jess found herself sitting next to him. Afterwards, in the crush of the green room, Henry bypassed the pleasantries and whispered his lust.

It was Jess's first affair in a long time. She was overwhelmed, euphoric, anxious. She could make no sense of it. She tried not to be herself. At first she lay still, disbelieving, and let him find his way around her flat, her life. But then he started to move things, to rearrange things. They collided. When words were needed she couldn't find any. The last day was laden with hurt, the last hour bruised by fists of anger. Her fists. He left. She locked the door. It was worse then than it had ever been. She sank again, only further, much further.

The thoughts send a numbness through her veins. She feels weak and closes her eyes. She drifts for an hour, then suddenly looks around her as the brakes screech and the train stutters and slows. A guard is walking through the carriage towards her.

"Where are we?"

"Just coming into Diss, madam. Last stop before Norwich."

She gazes blankly out of the window for a while, then looks again at Rudi's bag. She lifts out the fat, brown envelope, sees the words "Anna's Journal" written small in the corner, and tears it open.

4

My dearest Anna,

This most precious and most memorable of days is yours forever, my child, and it is my sincerest hope, in all the continued happiness I wish for you and your dear husband, that these empty pages will be filled by you with a vital record of something of the months, and the years, that follow.

Amongst gifts this journal I give to you is nothing when compared to the multitude of things you have given me these past fourteen years. My own journals are so much richer for your eyes, your counsel, and your tireless encouragement, and it has been a joy to work with someone whose thoughts are so full of the charm of existence, the glory of our world and the very elixir of life.

I now have a multitude of treasured memories on which to draw, of what is, without question, our very special friendship. Anna, you so richly deserve the wonderful world that awaits you, and I must confess to a seed of envy at the opportunity to study nature in such a rare and wild place. However, I would urge you to begin with something of life's journey thus far, for this path is well known to you and, thus, the first lines may prove a little easier. Indeed, I firmly judge your stories to be worthy of record and, as one who will greatly miss your accounts of your life, it gives me great pleasure to think that you may now formally transcribe your many thoughts and notes into this volume. Further, it may assist you to consider this undertaking to be not just for oneself, but for dear Jacob too, whom I am certain will take great pleasure, and pride, from reading it, when you have lovingly taught him how.

With my heartfelt gratitude and sincerest love, Thomas Brazington.

Swanton Rectory, the Second of February, 1873

Swanton Rectory, Sunday, the Sixteenth of February, 1873.

My name is Anna Farrow, and this is my Journal.

Two weeks have passed since my joyful marriage to Mr Jacob Farrow, in the Parish Church of St Mary's, Swanton Morley, Norfolk, the parish in which I have resided since 1860, that being the year in which I came to this house in the service of physician Dr Thomas Brazington. This journal is Dr Brazington's wedding gift, and I am seated, somewhat uncomfortably I must confess, at his desk as I begin the task. For certain it is a time of confused emotions in my heart, for while I so happily dream of the new life that lies before me, it is with great sadness that I shall leave this house where I have learned so much and have so enjoyed the company of both Dr Brazington and his daughter, my dear friend Constance. I continue to reside here for a few weeks more, though not in service, for Jacob has journeyed to the Fens where he is expected. He will return after Easter, as he has always done, and it is then that we will make our way to our new home in the wetland to the east. Dr Brazington resists me working further for him, though I still accompany him on his visits whenever I can, and almost daily he has been urging me to begin my journal. Now the good Doctor has brought me to his study, where he has dictated the first sentence and then departed. I owe it to him to attempt the task, yet my situation, and my emotions, leave me somewhat at a loss.

Hickling Heath, Sunday, the Sixteenth of May, 1873

Three months have now passed from my wedding day and, with the gentle encouragement of my dear husband Jacob, I have, finally, summoned the courage to begin this journal once more. I wish it could be possible to erase my first words entered herein, but Jacob argues against this, saying there is an openness and truthfulness to them that points the way. I cannot be so certain. Now Jacob has settled me upon a chair in front of our table, which he has carried from the kitchen and placed in the sunshine upon the rough grass that lies between our little house and the dyke. Some minutes past I watched him row out to the Duchess, the wherry he works upon with his uncle, Mr Jack Nealon, and I can see them now, far off on the water of the Broad, preparing her for tomorrow's journey to Martham, to collect more bricks to be carried down river to Thurne Mouth where a new wind pump is to be built.

This volume, as is recorded well enough from the first page, is the gift of Dr Thomas Brazington, a person whose absence, along with that of his daughter, the now Mrs Constance Baker, are the only shadows to dim the colours of my blessing. So, it is for them, too, that I am driven to begin, and in doing so shall heed Dr Brazington's bidding and commence with some knowledge of who I am.

I was born a pauper in the Year of our Lord 1847, at Gressenhall, in the Mitford and Launditch Union, the workhouse where my mother was to seek shelter, and where I was to be orphaned when but a few days old.

Should any person reading this know of it, or of such places as Gressenhall, then I will ask them not to judge me. This Union house was to be my dwelling for almost fifteen years. The people within were all I possessed by way of relatives, and I am bound to say I owe those walls, and some of those voices, which I still recall with some clarity, my gratitude. Since departing that place and learning of other such institutions, I can only consider myself most fortunate to have found the company of people who were not without kindness. Indeed, while my thoughts are also of the sadness and cruelty I encountered therein, I am bound to say that I have found life, and many souls beyond the walls of Gressenhall to be no different.

Any such account of this must begin, of course, with my mother, whose name was also Anna. She gave no other name and spoke so few words during her few days at Gressenhall that I grew up knowing almost nothing of her. It was not until my twelfth year, when I was departing that place for the first time, to enter service at Temble's Farm, Bawdeswell, that I was told something of the true extent of my mother's despair. The women who cared for me as an infant could only tell of my mother's fever and her death, which came so swiftly after I was born. As for the master and matron of Mitford and Launditch Union, Mr Horace Sullivan and his wife, Mrs Juliette Sullivan, they made no reference to her, save once, in stern answer to my persistent questioning on the matter, when they informed me they had examined the minute book which recorded her name to be Anna and that she died four days after arriving at Gressenhall.

It was the porter at the gatehouse, an upright, serious man of few words whom any young child was bound to respect, who cast the most light upon the darkness of my family history. Of all my memories of Gressenhall it is among the strongest.

His name was Mr Walter Copperdin, a former soldier with handsome whiskers who seemed to tower over all other souls. He lived alone and had been custodian of the gate key for many years. His steady eyes watched over all who entered and departed, while his undoubted strength enforced both the laws of the land and of the Union. It was not difficult for the children to look upon this giant of a man they dare not speak to, with his straight back and stiff walk, and to imagine his place in battle. Some of the men did not like him, for reasons of their failings I fear, not his. But I recall with great clarity the respect in which he was held by many bound together at Gressenhall, both officers and paupers, with the unwise ever mindful of his justice. The punishment book was filled with the crimes and the punishments handed down by the guardians, and I can record, whether the task was taking reluctant men to the board room for judgement, or transporting inmates to the court of the Swaffham Magistrates, that it was Mr Copperdin's duty to be their escort. I can remember him in every aspect of life in the Union, from espying him placing wildflowers on a fresh pauper grave to enforcing the silence at mealtimes, or, indeed, his careful preparation for visits by the chaplain and medical officer. That the master relied heavily upon his good offices cannot be doubted, both in the running of the workhouse and also in his judgment of the souls therein and what was best for them. Much later in my life a guardian told me that the porter's astuteness was known to the whole board and so widely understood.

To this day how clearly I remember that day Mr Copperdin spoke to me, in the autumn of 1856. It must have been the

September or October for the leaves were falling and blowing about my feet as I waited inside the gate with my bag. The year is clear to me because it was when I was to leave the Union for the first time, and I was waiting to be collected by someone from Temble's Farm. I had been instructed in what was expected of me by the Master and the Matron, and also the Schoolmistress and some of the women who had been in service, and I was reconciled there was no alternative and I would be leaving Gressenhall. When I had said my farewells, stating both my reluctance to leave my friends and my firm intent to visit and see them all again, I made my way to the gate from whence I was to be collected. Any confidence fell away as I sheltered from the wind in the shadow of the wall and watched the clock that looks down from the front of the workhouse upon the well and main gate. I recall how tears overwhelmed me, and I must assume the porter heard my crying, for he appeared through the entrance to his lodge. He collected up my bag and, placing his large hand to my back, kindly urged me to enter.

Therein Mr Copperdin guided me to a small chair by a fire, settled opposite me, and solemnly questioned my despair. He advised it was right and proper that I move from the workhouse, and there was no doubt that the person would arrive to collect me, for that had been the arrangement. I told of my fearfulness and I remember his smile and gentle words of encouragement, saying that my mother had not sought the shelter of Gressenhall so that I might remain a pauper all my life.

I asked that Mr Copperdin tell me what he knew of her. Mr Copperdin recounted how my mother had arrived on a hot summer's day, saying he could recall it quite well, for the air had been full of insects and heavy with the terrible smell from the open sewer which runs from the workhouse to the river. He said she must have crawled up the hill past the ditch to the

46

gate, for the front of her skirts were torn and her knees and hands were scratched and bleeding. When he opened the gate she fell with it, one hand still clinging to the knocker, which, I later observed, was in the form of a human fist holding a short bar. She begged to be allowed shelter and in answer to his questions told him of her journey from the Beadon Park estate, some six miles to the east, where she worked as a maid in the great house. Mr Copperdin considered she could not have been more than eighteen years of age. She had smiled at him as he had carried her in and he said he could remember her polite whispered words of gratitude. These remarks by the porter were delivered quietly, more tenderly than anything I had ever heard him say, but as he sat by his fire and recounted this to me to comfort me, I did not readily appreciate the importance of it. Yet his few words, still so clear in my mind, have since fostered so many precious thoughts and discoveries that I thank him to this day. Whatever his intention, he ensured that I would care for my dear Mother and discover, quite recently, more of her.

Just before my marriage I was greatly surprised to be told by Dr Brazington that he had gone to Beadon Park without my knowing and had spoken with two long-serving members of the household who remembered my mother. He told me that her name was Anna Packman and she was the only daughter of a gardener on the estate and his wife, both now long dead. She was indeed a young maid, remembered as a flower of spirit who had grown up upon the estate, and who had been shamed by a cruelty it grieves me to dwell upon. I may, however, in time, recount more of my learning and my love for her.

That I know my maiden name to be Packman is irrelevant, for I am now Anna Farrow, and so glad of it. How I came by my mother's first name is simple enough, as the Master and Matron of Mitford and Launditch Union decided upon it after the mothers of the bastard children, who had cared for me during the first weeks of my life, had persisted with the name after my mother had passed away. The Master then chose to give me the second name of Hall, after that place, and so fulfil the needs of the records of the workhouse.

I was one of nearly two hundred pauper children born in, or carried to, the Mitford and Launditch Union. Some forty of the children therein had both their father and mother in the workhouse, but the vast number were born out of wedlock, orphaned or abandoned. Knowing the course of things for certain souls of Gressenhall I must reflect that my mother's passing was a blessing, God rest her soul. For her part, life wearing a jacket, for if you do not know jackets marked the sinners who were the mothers of bastard children, could not have been bearable, such was the unforgiving nature of many within those walls. Two fellow jacket women were with my mother during the four days she was there, that is to say caring for her during my birth and at the painful end that followed.

Their names were Peace Kettle and Mary, whose last name I do not know. They helped me into this world and took pity on me, each taking their turn in putting me to their breast. Peace, so stout of heart and arm, who had three bastard boys including one just a month older than I, later told me of the feeble cry I gave as she held me in her arms that she was sure I would die. Her gift was to pass on a fortitude which has carried me to this day.

Mary was to follow my mother before I had reached four years, leaving a daughter, Alice, to fend for herself. Alice was six months older than me. We shared a straw mattress and I, it seemed, was her only friend. I revisited Gressenhall a year ago and learned that Peace remained there until her death. She was a simple, great-hearted soul, a certain part of that place, a round figure and red face that would fight when need be, press her case to the highest council, and open her arms to any child.

She knew of the punishment cell and was not afraid. Peace taught me so much and encouraged me to learn far more, and I remember her happiness at my accomplishment at learning to read and write. The schoolroom was near to the room of the jacket women, just beyond the place laid with straw on the floor where vagrants slept. Our teacher, the spinster Miss Charlotte Thorne, would admonish Peace for standing at the window, and on one occasion she was taken before the guardians and punished for refusing to move. She sowed in us a love of natural things, taking what chance there was, often on the day of the Lord when we were allowed, to lead us down beyond the workhouse farm to the river and along the hedgerows to gather wildflowers. She encouraged us to consider which were our favourites. For me it was the yellow irises rising high along the water's edge. For Alice it was the poppy, so strong of colour and so plentiful, and for Peace it was the pretty daisy white petals and yellow hearts, and at night she would whisper us to sleep, knowing by heart a poem, telling us to count the petals of her beloved moon daisy.

Jess lifts her head, stunned. A long-forgotten chord chimes back to childhood. She reads the words again. She looks out, unseeing, at the countryside flying by and remembers, hears her mother's voice. Her eyes fall hungrily back onto the words again and she reads on.

After Alice and I were moved to the women's ward on the other side of the workhouse, we were discouraged from speaking to the mothers of bastards. Peace continued, however, to watch over us, whether it be during the silence of mealtimes or the labour of the laundry work. That place forbade her any dignity at all and yet she lived with it. I remember one Christmas, when I was about ten years of age, the cold could not be defeated by the fires and the genuine misery was lifted on Christmas when we were treated to a feast of roast beef, plum pudding, and potatoes. The men had ale and tobacco, the women were given tea, butter, and snuff, and we received nuts and oranges. But the unmarried mothers were excluded and were mocked.

I do not ever recall Peace being removed from the workhouse for punishment, for I sensed a silent regard for her judgement if not her spirit, but there were those who taught the children a great deal by poor example. Often it was the tramps. For failing to pick oakum in return for a night's lodging one man was taken before a magistrate and committed to Swaffham prison. For how long I cannot say. I remember his twisted face. Another suffered the same punishment after he burned his coat, waistcoat, and trousers, for what reason I do not know, but I well remember the incident beneath the master's window.

I should, perhaps, now tell of the unhappiness that befell Alice. While we shared a straw mattress and spent a great many of our moments together, I often slept alone and could not see her because she was to find her way to the punishment cell more often than any child within those walls. Alice would not accept her fate, nor the advice of others, and whilst she remained tolerant, indeed kindly, towards me, she would not obey either the rules or any judgements. By some enormous fortune I was reunited with her some four years ago and made the acquaintance of her husband, Walter Breeze, a farrier, and a fine one by her account, and learned of their two young sons. She was living close to the town of Holt, on a great estate beside the road to the port of Blakeney, where it seemed her past was little known and much forgotten. It is true to say I found it incredible to consider her salvation given the past depth of her despair. Dr Brazington's work had taken us to Holt whereupon I encountered her in the street, or rather she approached me, for her appearance had changed such a great deal I barely recognised her. Such joy! We walked upon Holt

Hills and sat beside the spring while she told me of her experiences, and, to my amazement, her news that within the month she and her family were to sail to begin a new life in Canada. Another estate worker had made the journey and it seemed that Alice and Walter were inspired to follow his example. We sat in that beautiful place on the Hills for some considerable time as she then relayed to me what had happened to her after I left the poor house for the final time in 1860, aged fifteen years.

To my distress Alice explained that her ungovernable temper and disorderly conduct led to five periods of confinement, sometimes for over a month, in Little Walsingham Prison. She told me that her frustration then turned to violence and she was deemed by the prison medical officer to be insane, and she was bound and removed to the County Lunatic Asylum at Thorpe. She found herself confined with people without a mind to recall their own names. I remember how she said that it chilled her, and I thank the Lord I have never seen this place. Alice recounted how she was only there a short while before being discharged as sane and she was returned to Gressenhall where another year passed, but her troubles were not yet over. She told me that, when outraged by her exclusion from a meal for speaking out, she attempted to set fire to the workhouse, and, while waiting in the House of Correction at Wymondham for her trial, she was again thought to be insane. For a second time she was held at the asylum but, thankfully, the medical officers of that institution never deemed her to be of unsound mind. If you had met her when she was young you might have judged her mad, but she was not. Alice was blessed with an intelligence and spirit that would not accept her circumstances. She was a bastard child in a pauper house, and her heavy frown, coarse looks, and evil tongue could inspire thoughts of insanity. She would not listen at school and yet she could read. She would refuse to speak when asked to, refuse to stay silent when demanded, and she would smile her defiance at anyone who sought to control her. When outraged or overcome, Alice would bellow her anguish to the heavens, a raw cry that seemed to come from the depths of her soul. It was a sound I heard but twice, yet it has stayed with me always. It is a miracle that she should have found some level of happiness. Indeed, I was truly astonished to discover her so reconciled and obviously contented. As we sat beside the spring and recounted our experiences she told me that she missed me a great deal when I left Gressenhall, that I had been her only comfort and that it was thoughts of me that had helped her to find some way out of that life. We both shed a great many tears that day, understanding that we would almost certainly never see one another again.

I returned to Gressenhall last year and found it much changed. Peace was with my mother in the paupers' grave and it also grieved me deeply to learn that Mr Copperdin had perished in a fire at the farm while bravely seeking to save livestock from the flames.

Within the walls of the workhouse I discovered that there was now a chapel and an infirmary, and there seemed to be many fewer children. It was, in so many regards, a very different place from the one I left for the farm of Isaac Temble so many years ago.

I must, as briefly as possible, relay my unhappy experiences at Temble's Farm. It is not a difficult task, for I made a record of my clear memories of that time and many other happenings in my childhood just a few years later when I was first in the service of Dr Brazington at Swanton Rectory. Miss Thome had kindly made Dr Brazington aware of my interest and progress with reading and writing and soon after my arrival in his house he kindly offered me one of his old metal pens, some ink and sheets of paper, and also ensured that there was a table in the room I was to share for a short while with another young maid by the name of Ella West.

The worker from Temble's Farm who came to collect me from the workhouse was a frightening man with grey hairs upon the cheeks of his face and hanging from beneath his torn and dented brown hat. He was seated upon a small, dusty carriage pulled by a young black horse which he did not spare. We raced past woodlands and then came upon a river where a beautiful woman and a young girl, both with long dark hair and dressed in white, were walking along the bank. I watched them for as long as I could, until their bright clothes were lost behind the trees, and felt certain that I had seen the woman before. It was only after we had travelled a little further that I was struck by the realisation that it was the woman who had come to the workhouse and questioned me some months earlier, yet I could not know at that time that I would never see her again or that the young girl would later become my dearest friend.

As for that journey, I shook with cold and was gripped by both a fear of falling and great despair at what awaited me. The worker, who forced the horse to wheeze in pain, seemed, for the most part, to be addressing some other person. I was to learn his name was Richard Borrow, also known as Dewy, though I know not why. His rounded shoulders, bitter face, and contorted hands bore witness to a life of service on the land and, I can but conclude, to a man with little pity. I was told Mr Borrow had been the herdsman, but after the years had overtaken him had been set to doing chores in addition to tending the fowl and the vermin that preyed upon them.

It was my teacher at Gressenhall, Miss Thome, who informed me that I was to be employed at Temble's Farm, although I am bound to conclude that this most dedicated of women, so correct of deed and thought, was in no way aware of the exact

53

circumstances awaiting me. She had taken particular care with my education in letters for which I showed aptitude, and some months prior to my departure to Temble's Farm she brought a woman to the Gressenhall schoolroom, the same person, I am sure, whom I saw beside the river that day upon the cart, who paid great attention to my work and asked me many questions about my interests. The meeting had neither significance nor consequence for me at that time, but that hour was later to prove to have the most profound and valuable bearing on the course of my life.

The reason for my leaving the workhouse for Temble's Farm was a simple case. The Master and Matron had been approached by Isaac Temble regarding any pauper children of an age to be suitable for domestic and farm work. Miss Thorne told me herself some months later that she had initially declared her objection to this, but as her endeavours to find work for which she felt I was more suited had brought forth nothing she had but to cease her protests.

As for that terrible journey, Temble's Farm was not visible until we were upon it. Narrow woodland of no great age surrounded much of it, and only the front of the house looked out across meadow. I did not appreciate that I was looking at my future place of employment until we turned sharply onto a track between the house and trees, where chickens scattered before us and the wheels sank into the mud. A boy, little older than me it seemed, as thin as a sapling, opened the gate into the yard and shielded his face with his arm. There was a hole at the elbow of his jacket, one of the clear pictures still in my mind to this day. I was left to stand in the yard and exchange stares with the boy before Mr Borrow stepped up behind me and pushed me towards steps rising to a door at the rear of the house. He barked for the boy to get on with his work. A large woman took me in and asked my name. She told me I was to call her Mrs Ferris and that she was the housekeeper. I was to

54

do her bidding in the afternoon and evening and work upon the farm every morning. I was to sleep in an attic room. She also informed me that Mr Temble was in East Dereham, for it was market day, and I was to be presented on his return. Until then I was to wash the steps at the back and front of the house.

So I began. The few possessions I had, namely a shawl given by Peace and a cloth bag with a spoon, a knife, needle and thread, and nightgown from the workhouse, were taken from me and left on a chair and I was handed a heavy apron. I had barely commenced upon the bottom step at the front of the house when a mighty grey horse, half lost beneath the heavy coat of its owner, stopped so close to my side that I could smell its laboured breath. The gentleman did not seem to notice me as he dropped from its back and walked heavily up the steps. And so it was to be, for I was never presented to, nor spoken to by Mr Temble. He did me no ill or kindness in the few months I resided there, and I remember a coldness in everything and everyone. Perhaps it was those winter months, but I felt I never lost the chill of that carriage ride.

I took my leave one night when, by the Lord's good grace, the moon and stars were bright enough for me to see my way back to Gressenhall, a journey of some hours. I was decided upon leaving after witnessing the boy, known only to me as Kemp, suffer a dreadful beating for overturning a bucket of milk. Mr Temble took a broom handle to him, caring not if he hit his face or hand, a terrible deed he fulfilled in silence before he turned and walked away in the manner he walked everywhere, head bowed with hands behind his coat. I could only guess upon his unhappiness for no one spoke of it, and as for my efforts to comfort Kemp and tend his wounds, these were spurned. Indeed, all of those farm souls looked upon me with suspicion, although I laboured with them from every dawn before returning to household duties in the afternoon and evening, and the only answer I could conceive of for my exclusion was my domestic station and nightly isolation in the attic room. I still have dreams about that place and the people there, for the brooding darkness of it all seemed a deal more desperate than the workhouse.

On my return to Gressenhall there was some consternation at my running away from the farm, and the Master and Matron reproached me severely. However, to my relief, they decided not to settle upon any sort of punishment, and I was grateful also that no one from the farm came seeking me. I settled again among the people I was familiar with, working in the laundry, taking a little responsibility for some of the younger children and helping in the schooling of needlework, reading, and writing. The next two years passed without great incident, save the ordeals of dear Alice which distressed me greatly. For my own part I refused any talk of my leaving to enter service again, but in time it was made clear to me by every person that it was without question, and that I must be reconciled to it.

I hesitate to call it my good fortune that Dr Brazington should approach the Guardians at Gressenhall regarding myself, for two terrible tragedies had a bearing upon his decision. Following my introduction to others residing and working there, namely maid Ella, whom I have mentioned, cook and housekeeper Miss Nan Frere, and the elderly groom and gardener Mr Charlie Blyth, it was Dr Brazington's daughter Constance who told me in hushed tones as she guided me around the house that a maid called Catherine, God rest her soul, had been tragically injured after tripping on her skirts and falling down the stairs, an event witnessed by Ella. The injuries were such that Catherine could not be saved. It was an unthinkable thing for them all to bear, for I also knew, having been advised by Miss Thome before I travelled to Swanton, that Mrs Emily Brazington had passed away that previous winter. She also told me at the same moment, to my considerable surprise, that it had been Mrs Brazington who had come to the workhouse and taken such an interest in me the previous year.

There was, indeed, a deep sorrow among them all at Swanton Rectory that prevented me from questioning much at all, save being clear on the tasks I needed to fulfil. I wondered, though, how it was that Mrs Brazington had died, a question I was to have answered a short while later.

One Sunday morning, as Ella and I–

5

"Excuse me—"

The words make Jess start. She looks up from the manuscript and stares at the woman standing over her.

"Only, this is Norwich. Train doesn't go any further. Just wasn't sure you knew. You looked so engrossed."

Jess glances out the window, then, embarrassed, hurriedly bundles everything up and throws on her coat and scarf.

Norwich Station echoes with the announcement of the late arrival of the 11:25 from London. Jess has fifteen minutes to make her connection. She stops, drops the bags, and puts the manuscript she's been clutching to her chest back into the brown envelope. She walks to the iron gates in front of the platforms and looks for the Sheringham train.

She asks a guard, who points to a dirty green, two-carriage diesel puffing grey fumes into the air. Platform three. Jess asks when the next train to London is.

"You've just missed one, love. Next is at 2:20."

Jess takes a deep breath, shivers, then heads for Platform Three. She struggles with the heavy door and looks both ways along the open carriage. Ranks of empty bench seats sit close together like on a bus, gently vibrating as the train idles. It's very warm inside. An elderly couple at the far end stop talking and watch her. She drops the two bags onto a seat, takes off her coat and scarf again, sits down, and is about to light up when she sees the red NO SMOKING sticker in the window, on all the windows. She watches her hands vibrate with the train, then rubs her eyes and looks down at the empty track, the oil-coated stones and river of litter beneath the lip of Platform Two. The sky has started to clear, and for a moment the sun shines on her face. She fishes her sunglasses out of her coat pocket, stands, and pulls at the small sliding window. A woman with a toddler in a pushchair peers in, then walks further along the platform before boarding. Two teenage girls in burgundy uniforms climb aboard, slam the door, and sit in the seat behind Jess. They talk about skiving off sport that afternoon and about another girl called Katie – what a slag she is and how they hate her.

Jess looks again at the carrier bag, thinks about reaching for the brown envelope, but remembers the second train journey is short. She fishes instead for Rudi's letter that she never finished.

Gordon is a really decent chap and he knows who you are, very keen on classical music. Obviously excited to meet you. His wife left him many moons ago and he has brought up their daughter on his own. Nice girl. The hotel keeps them afloat, as Gordon puts it, and they get by. Quite good at it, actually. But don't get the wrong idea he's a gentle soul. He loves his sailing too and exercised Otter for me last summer, otherwise she would not have been sailed at all. It shouldn't take more than ten minutes to get to Ludham. Womack

59

Water is very close to the village, just at the end of a pretty lane, and you will find Otter at the county sailing base, the old Hunter's Yard. We have had a mooring there since about 1982. Francis used to sail Hunter boats as a boy, and that is where he taught me to sail. We used to hire from there for many years. Then Francis got it into his head to buy a new boat a pretty Thurne class thinking, rightly, that we were spending so much time in Norfolk and so much money on yacht hire that it made sense. Anyway, I pressed for something more comfortable, and so Francis bought Otter four years ago. The train moves. She's a Sparkes design boat like new. Helen and Ted will show you the ropes! I am just glad Francis had a chance to enjoy her for a couple of summers at least. Diane runs the office at the yard, and Ted maintains the fleet with the help of two other boat builders. It's a wonderland. They have a fleet of their own of about sixteen wooden boats, many with two or four berths in traditional cabins, which were built by Percy Hunter and his sons just before and after the war. None of them have engines. (Don't panic Otter does.) The whole setup is owned by the county council now and used for school parties as well as private hire, with the private fees paying the bulk of the bills, basically. The whole scene probably hasn't changed in fifty years. There's usually someone at the yard until about 5 p.m., so you should be OK. When I spoke to Ted, he said he would be happy to get you under Potter Heigham bridge, and if all goes to schedule, the evening low tide should be perfect. From Potter Heigham, follow the river and then, just past a busy boatyard and just before a windmill, bear left. This will take you through to Hickling. When you get to open water, stay in the channel, i.e., between the posts red on the left, white on the right.

There will be another channel, signed to Horsey, on the right beside a post which has been painted yellow at the top. Do not turn here. Keep straight on, and about 100 yards later you'll see another, smaller channel, also to the right, but marked PRIVATE. This will lead you to Swansong, a very remote thatched timber lodge built in the reed beds some ninety years ago by the Didbury family. Don't turn in there, although by this time you are getting close to our dyke, so be *prepared. When the river bears right again, hug the edge of the reeds on the right and head for the small coppice of trees that should be in view by now. You will then see another (even smaller) channel and, hopefully, Whispering Reeds at the end of it. There is a staithe at the end of the channel where Otter fits snugly. Pop along to the farm and give me a ring when you are installed. Margaret won't mind. Good luck. And thank you so much.*

Much love,

Rudi

P.S. You'll know by now that I've lobbed in a couple of books you may find of interest. Could you put them with the others on the shelves by the fireplace? That's where they belong. And there's the large brown envelope too, of course. It is Anna's Journal a diary kept by a woman who lived there a hundred years ago and was found in the cottage long before we had it. Winston gave it to Francis, who in his last year decided to set about making a copy of it, painstakingly working through it and retyping it. It gave him something, a focus, right to the end, and I'm just glad he managed to finish it. You may like to read it.

"Be there in a second! I'm coming! I'm coming!"

Jess can make out a figure through the frosted glass of the front door. The man's voice is eager, but he seems to be moving very slowly. A lock turns, the door opens, and a man in his early fifties in a navy cardigan with a walrus moustache and steel-framed glasses beams at her, his face pink with embarrassment.

"So sorry to keep you waiting. Ruddy ankle. Just twisted it about five minutes ago chasing a cat out of the garden. I put scraps out for the birds, you see. Sorry, you don't want to hear all that. Hello. I'm Gordon, Gordon Crang. So very pleased to meet you."

Jess holds for a second the hand that shoots towards her. Gordon reverses back into the hall and opens the door wide.

61

"Won't you come in? Can I offer you coffee? Have you eaten?"

"Er–yes, I have." Jess lies.

"Coffee then? Or–"

"No, thanks, but no. Actually, I'd be grateful if we could get moving. Only…"

"Yes, yes, of course. Of course. Absolutely. Rudi rang last week and again this morning. I'm delighted to be of some use. The ankle's easing already, so I should be fine to drive. Er… right. I'm sort of ready."

He pats his trouser pockets as if looking for keys.

"I've put some bits in the car. Hang on, I'll get my coat."

He turns.

"Janey, darling!"

A young voice calls back. "Yep?"

"I'm off now, sweetheart. May stop off in the village and pick up some supplies as well. If any of the guests come back in and need anything, or anyone arrives, you know the score."

"OK!"

"I'll only be about an hour!"

Gordon pulls the door shut.

"Just getting over a cold, but she's on the mend. May be back at school tomorrow. Right."

He gestures towards a cream Morris Traveller parked on the opposite side of the road.

"There she is. Can I carry anything for you?"

Jess shakes her head. She picks up her bags again and follows him.

Through the rear window of the car she can make out a lumpy blue nylon sail bag and a cardboard box. Gordon opens the back doors.

"Rudi said you might need some gear. May I ask what you've brought with you?"

"Um… warm clothes. Trainers…"

"Well, in there–" Gordon points at the sail bag. "You'll find some yellow waterproofs that were, er, Jane's mum's. Should fit. Some waterproof sailing boots too. May I ask what size you are?"

"Fives."

"They should be fine too, then. Great."

He stalls for a second.

"Um… oh yes. There's also some sailing gloves–and an old baseball cap, which you probably won't want, one that Francis always left on the boat. I took it home to stop it rotting over the winter. Washed it. It's something very familiar–we can all remember him wearing it. Take it back to the cottage, if you don't mind, though you can wear it if you want. I admit I have. Good for keeping the sun out of your eyes while helming. The sun can get very bright out on the water, but, of course, you know all about these things, being a sailor. Sorry. In the cardboard box you'll find some of the other things I retrieved from Otter in October–tea towels, river map, bird book, binoculars, tranny, that sort of thing–and I've added some tea bags, sugar, and a carton of milk. There are new batteries in the tranny too. Hope I haven't forgotten anything. OK, shall we go? But can I make a suggestion? You're very wise to be wearing jeans–better for sailing, for sure–but it might be better to change your shoes now. Put the trainers on, I mean. They give you better grip than normal shoes. Safer."

Jess hesitates. "Actually… if I gave you money for petrol, could you take me straight to the cottage?"

The question seems to panic him. "I'm sorry, but no. Sorry, I can't.

63

Truly I can't. I—I've got to get back to cook dinner, my ankle is very sore, and, to be honest, I don't want to drive that last mile along the track either. It'll do untold harm to the old girl." He taps the car roof. "And I can't drop you in Hickling Heath because… well, there's far too much to carry the last bit to the cottage."

Gordon is making his way to the driver's door as he answers. "The boat's the best way. Honestly."

Jess watches him get in. More bloody lies. She looks up at the clouds, then over her shoulder at the railway station, before tugging her trainers out from the bottom of her holdall and opening the passenger door.

The Morris Traveller pulls up a hill, crosses a main junction, then weaves its way out into the countryside along a winding road. Jess swaps her shoes and looks out. The gearbox whines. They don't talk. Jess doesn't want to talk. Gordon doesn't know what to say. He senses she knows he's not being honest, and he feels very uncomfortable. He hopes Rudi's right, that he knows what he's doing.

Jess looks sideways. There's some sort of military radar station and signs for staithes and boatyards. They pass through a couple of villages, and then suddenly the car drops down a hill and they are on the dead flat of the wetland. Jess can make out round towers, the remains of what once must have been windmills. The tops of a few yacht sails betray the wandering course of the river through the middle of the pastures. As they cross a bridge, she can see there are more motor cruisers than yachts, and scores of them are moored nose to tail along the banks. By the bridge there is a pub, a shop, a few boats on trailers for sale, and a handful of houses. The road starts to rise again and they pass the Ludham sign, following the road round two sharp bends in the village, then slipping off to the right down a narrow lane.

"In case you're wondering about bedding—" Jess isn't. Her mind is a blank. "I took the mattresses, blankets, sheets and stuff to the yard

64

yesterday. Helen's got them in the office. Shouldn't be a problem. We've rigged her too. Right—here we are!"

The old car pulls up on deep shingle, slotting in next to an old cream Land Rover in front of the first of two large adjoining wooden sheds. The sun breaks through again and Jess notices that the sky is now a muddle of blue and grey. The place looks closed. Jess pulls herself out of the Traveller, looks up at the Norfolk Sailing Base sign, then peers through a small, dusty pane of glass. There is a workbench to the left with wood shavings on the floor. Most of the building seems empty. Light is pouring in from a wide opening at the far side, and she can make out the silhouettes of two people talking. Beyond them there is water and a couple of boats with creamy-white covers on.

"Come in. I'll introduce you. Leave the stuff. I'll get a trolley later and bring everything down to the boat."

Jess looks at Gordon limping heavily towards the door and thinks what a ridiculous thing it is to say. She follows him through a small door. Inside it seems as cold as a church. Now she can make out three other people. Two men are sitting and drinking from mugs by a pot-bellied stove in the far corner. An older woman is washing up at a sink beside them, chatting as she works. Jess can see a few boats in the shadows of the other shed. Poles, masts and other bits of rigging are strung up in the eaves above her head.

"Look." Gordon is pointing at the name of a boat hung high on the wall. *"Teasel."*

The word is painted on a panel of wood the shape of the stern of a boat.

"They used one of the Hunter boats to film Arthur Ransome's *Coot Club*. Have you read it?"

Jess shakes her head.

"One of the great children's books. Set in the Broads. *Teasel* was the boat Dick and Dorothea stayed on during their run-ins with the motorboat tourists who Ransome called the Hullabaloos. Filming was a big excitement at the yard."

They turn again and slowly make their way towards the large open doors and the ribbon of silver water. Jess hangs back and stops just inside the shed beside an old dinghy full of red and white lifejackets. One of the men turns and greets Gordon. A small woman in her twenties with red hair emerges from behind a door marked "office." She waves a greeting to Gordon, then makes straight for Jess.

For much of the next hour, Jess doesn't know quite what to say. She hadn't really thought about the sailing before, but now she's apprehensive, worried about looking an idiot, terrified about the responsibility. The woman–Helen–has guided Jess into the warm office, introducing her father Ted and giving them both a mug of tea. Between telephone calls Helen keeps urging her not to worry about anything as she presses on with office work. Ted chats calmly, seemingly weighing Jess up. All the time Jess is desperately seeking a way to say she isn't sure about any of it. But Ted keeps talking, his soft Norfolk voice gently probing. Occasionally he breaks off to go and speak to the other people in the yard, leaving Jess to look out of the office window. At last he returns and says, "Best we go and have a look at her, all right?"

They walk out along a grass staithe towards the river. The four boats near the shed look identical. One has its cover off and the wood–mahogany, she guesses–shines like glass.

"They're… beautiful."

"Not long been back in the water. We repair 'n' revarnish o'er the winter. Quite a few went out Saturday. Season's kicked off now. Busy time for Helen 'specially. Paperwork. Y'know the sort a thing."

"What sort of repairs?"

"Everything. This here's river sailing, gal, with the added challenge of bloomin' motorboats zigzaggin' about. We expect a few knocks–fact of life with the ol' Hunters, what with no engines on 'em. Takes a bit of skill to handle them and everyone tries to avoid coming to any harm, o' course, but they're built to stand a knock or two. Bound to get clattered now and ag'in. Anyway–" He points ahead. "Tha's Otter. Four along."

They are close to the end of the staithe. There is a small cut into the reeds to the left, close to the river. Five different yachts, more modern boats, are moored there nose to tail. Ted is about to climb aboard when he stops abruptly and faces Jess.

"We don't have to do this. I sense you're not sure. I don't take too kindly to people telling me what to do, 'n' if you're not happy about it, tha's OK by me. I'd as sooner run you out to Hicklin' in my ol' Land Rover. Frankly, Rudi made no secret of his excitement at getting you afloat ag'in, but tha' int fair if you're not for it."

Jess is staring at *Otter.* Her white fibreglass hull gleams as if polished. Her cover is off and her rich red timbers look as if they have just been varnished. She seems huge. Untouched. Jess's heart is thumping. She doesn't answer.

"How about you 'n' me take 'er out on the ol' Thurne now? Get a feel. Nice gentle breeze. Forget your gear for now. Then we'll see. Plenty of time."

Jess nods and smiles nervously. She likes him. He speaks with the calm confidence of her Grandpa and has the same weathered, brown skin. He steps onto the stern and the boat rocks gently.

"Gorgeous, in't she? If I weren't so tied up with the Hunters–and so poor–I'd be tempted." He reaches out an arm to Jess. "Watch your step now."

He tells her to sit by the tiller and then slowly explains the rigging and general layout. Then he points out the engine controls by Jess's knees and tells her to check it's in neutral and to turn the key. The engine fires immediately.

"You got 'er."

Ted speaks a little faster now, but assuredly.

"I'll release 'er, we'll get 'er turned 'round, nose to wind, maybe at the end of the staithe, then get the sails up. Get 'er out into the river, tickle 'er round gently, then back to me. No other boats about. You're OK."

Before Jess can think, Ted pushes *Otter* away from the staithe. Jess puts her in gear and nudges the throttle. *Otter* glides forward. Jess reaches over the side to fend off the boat moored in front as *Otter*'s stern swings towards the staithe. Then she stands up and steers her into the river.

Twenty minutes later all is quiet but for the sound of water slipping by and the occasional gentle slap of the tan sails as Jess teases the rudder to find the wind. *Otter* is tilted slightly and moving gracefully down the centre of the river Thurne. The river is about fifteen to twenty yards wide with reeds on the left and a high grass bank on the right. Poplars beyond the bank gently sway in the cool easterly breeze. The reeds, the colour of sun-bleached straw with fresh green shoots at the base, are reflected in the dappled water by the broken afternoon light. Jess looks up at the sky. The clouds are massing again. Two motor cruisers pass and a man waves. Jess raises her arm. The cool, fresh air on her face feels good, and for the first time she feels glad.

"Predicting a spot or two of rain later, but should be clear by mornin'." Ted is lounging by the cabin door, one arm resting on the cabin roof, looking back at Jess. "She feel OK?"

"Yes."

"Bring 'er around ag'in then. We'll get back in."

Jess suddenly thinks again about what she faces. "What if I did any damage? What if–"

"You can sail, I can see that. Bit like riding a bike, I always say. Once you've learned how to feel the wind, tha's it. Don't need to learn ag'in. So stop you worrying. She needs to be used. As long as you've got a feel for her, and you have, and can stall 'er when you need to, she's a manageable single-hander. Just take your time. If in doubt, don't carry too much sail. If in trouble, run her nose into the reeds 'n' get the sail reefed or down altogether. Use the engine. There're enough people afloat to give you a hand if you need it. You'll find somebody to give you a tow if you get in a pickle. Sit and wait, someone'll come by. Then, if you've had enough, just get to a phone and give us a ring. Right? Now then, Womack comin' up. Ease the main. Push the tiller over."

Otter sweeps round and Ted and Jess move to the starboard side.

"Don't expect I'll be hearing from you, though."

Jess smiles back. She feels better. Strangely excited, even. Otter doesn't seem so large now. She can handle her. They turn into Womack Water. Jess lets the sail out into a broad reach and the softening wind pushes them back the short distance to Hunter's Yard.

Her bags, the box and sail bag are on a trolley at the end of a path by the river. The bedding is on the grass in the fold of a large piece of plastic. Jess takes Otter past the yard, turns her nose into the wind, and the boat settles gently against the end of the staithe.

"Nicely." Ted secures her. "Get those bags stowed. I'll go 'n' see my Helen. I was goin' to take the tender 'n' outboard, but it's four o'clock now, so she may as well pick me up from Potter Heigham after lockin' up. Back in a min."

He starts walking towards the boat sheds, then calls back.

"Actually, might as well drop the sail. We'll motor up. Save time the other end!"

Jess is still grappling with the mainsail when Ted returns carrying *Otter*'s cover and a flask of coffee. He helps her finish wrapping the sails, then they pile the bags, bedding, cardboard box and boat cover into the cabin.

"What boat's that?"

Jess points to a huge mast sticking up behind bushes about fifty yards further along Womack Water. The top of the thick wooden mast is painted blue with white and red hoops. It looks familiar.

"Albion. She's a Norfolk wherry. Last of the ol' sail traders. Tha's her base. Big black sail. Quite a sight. Which reminds me—tell Phil and Margaret that our day out on her is booked for September the twenty-first. A Sunday, as normal. Meantime you may get very lucky 'n' see her, but unlikely above Potter, to be honest. She don't often go through there. Bit of a squeeze under the bridge 'n' the skipper has to mind the tides. Not a big problem for us, though. Right. Fire her up."

Jess stares at the vast mast for a few seconds, thinking about the journal.

Ted gently puts his hand on her shoulder. "Come on, gal, time to go."

This time they turn left when they reach the main river. Ted pours the coffee and then puts his feet up across the cockpit.

"Meant to say earlier. You don't really look the part in that coat."

Jess grins, blushes. She wishes she'd dug out the gloves Gordon had given her. She is standing with the tiller between her legs, like she used to on her Grandpa's little wooden yacht, and is cupping her cold hands round the warming beaker of coffee.

The wave carved by *Otter* laps into the reeds. The wind is strengthening. The blue sky has all but gone. Ahead Jess can see what must be the start of Potter Heigham. There are little timber buildings on both sides of the river, and as they draw level with the first of them, she can see they are summer homes, each different from the next, but all with their narrow piece of lawn and clear view of the river. Some look tatty and damp. Others are painted and cared for, with armchairs that look out through double-glazed French doors. Several are as large as bungalows with boathouses and verandas, and a few show signs of life with lights on or smoke rising. Jess eases back on the throttle, but Ted tells her to press on. He says the bridge is some way off yet.

Jess points into the cabin. "Oh—nearly forgot. I've a letter for you. From Rudi."

"Right."

"If you don't mind digging it out, it's in the plastic bag."

Ted puts his coffee down and crawls inside.

"And do I owe you anything for this? Today, I mean."

Ted reverses out through the doors with the bag and sits down with it between his feet.

"Nothin'."

"But your time."

Ted ignores her. He pulls the old book out of the bag.

"Well, I'll be blowed. Ellis's Broads book. Don't come much finer than this. And signed! Rudi give it to you?"

Jess remembers where she'd seen the tall mast before.

"Yes. And on the cover's the sailing barge with the big mast we just saw, isn't it?"

"Tha's a wherry, but not Albion. But don't you let anyone hear you call them sailing barges. They in't."

Ted puts the book back into the bag.

"Try 'n' read it if you can. Depends how long you've got. Ah, right, here's my letter. Should be a cheque. Ta."

Ted kisses it and stuffs it into the pocket of his sailing jacket.

"So what d'you reckon?"

"Think?"

"Time, I mean. Reckon you'll stay a while at least?"

"Just a few days. For Rudi. You know. I've only brought a few things with me and, well, I really need to get back to London. Can't say exactly when. Wednesday. Maybe Thursday."

"Let me know. I'll be using her moorin'."

"I was thinking, Ted, could I ring you to help me get her back? Through Potter Heigham bridge at least?"

"Got to get her under today first. Ease off a bit now. See the bridge?"

"Christ."

Jess is already reaching for the throttle. There's a large grey building, a boatyard of some sort, on the left and a marina packed with yellow and blue holiday cruisers. Motorboats and yachts crowd the riverbanks too, and just beyond them is the old stone bridge. The rounded central arch seems desperately small.

"Can we get under there?"

"Make for that temporary moorin' on the left. Where the ducks and swans are. We'll get the mast down then go through. Some of these bigger boats may be waiting for the tide to drop a bit more, but reckon we'll be fine."

As soon as Otter is tied up, they stand on the muddy staithe and Ted points out a food store across the road.

"There is a chip shop on the other side of the river too. Here's a good place to stock up. But you can do that when we're through 'n' I'm off home for my tea."

He takes Jess slowly through the routine of dropping the mast. He puts it up again and, arms folded, smiling, tells her to do it. Then they cast off. Ted warns Jess to get the boat into the middle of the river, to line Otter up and then ease her forward.

"Last of the tide's still against us, so it's vital to keep her movin'."

Otter edges slowly towards the medieval bridge. Holidaymakers and people who are feeding the ducks stop to watch.

"I can't do this. You take her."

"Nope. Give her a little more now."

Ted is standing at the bow looking forward, hands on hips. Jess leans out to one side then the other, trying to get the boat into line. The gap under the bridge looks too small.

"There's not enough room."

"There's enough. Tickle those revs up a bit, I said."

Otter's nose is at the arch. Ted kneels and reaches out for the bridge. He shouts.

"Right—give her a bit more."

Jess feels for the throttle without taking her eyes off the bridge and then ducks as Otter shoots forward. For a second she pinches her eyes closed and clenches her teeth. The engine noise echoes and then they are clear. Someone claps.

Ted looks back at Jess.

"Nicely."

She glances over her shoulder at the bridge and then stands up. They pass a boatyard that is a muddle of old yachts on the right and then glide under a new, much higher road bridge before mooring again on the right bank. By the time Otter's mast is up and the rigging sorted, Helen is walking along the path towards them.

Jess wants to ask before she gets to them.

"Ted?"

"Yep?"

"You asked me earlier if I was sure."

"You blummin' well better be by now. We're 'ere. And I'm off for my tea."

"No—I'll press on. May not sail, though."

Jess stretches out her hand.

"Just wanted to say thank you. I wasn't sure. Still not. Still worried. You know, damage, looking stupid, all that stuff. But it's been OK."

"You'll be all right. Just don't hurt them there fingers."

Jess watches Ted and his daughter stroll back along the bank, talking—about her, probably. They turn and wave and then are gone. Jess suddenly shivers. She feels cold and hungry. She grabs her bag and the boat keys, locks the door, and makes for the store. As she gets onto the old bridge, she sees Ted's Land Rover pulling out of the car park. She waves. They don't see her.

Jess crosses over to the public toilets, and when she comes out she hears the anxious exchanges between a man and woman tentatively approaching the bridge in their small motor cruiser. She remembers being aware of them earlier, moored on the right bank, the man loudly summoning his wife to watch Otter tackle the bridge. It is obviously a private boat. The red ensign flag hanging out the back looks so large. Jess senses they need more speed to counter the tide. There's a scraping sound as the man loses the line and the cruiser brushes against one side of the arch. The stern then swings across and clatters into the other side.

"Shit!"

The word is amplified beneath the stone arch. Jess winces. Then the outboard roars and the cruiser appears on the other side. A yacht is waiting in the middle of the river to go through in the other direction, and the little cruiser, now charging along, almost hits it.

It is starting to spit with rain as Jess reaches the store door. She buys bread, butter, marmalade, instant coffee, peanuts, bacon, toilet roll, cigarettes and a large box of matches. She grabs a bottle of vodka too. Then she heads for the fish and chip shop. There is a queue of eight people, and when she emerges with her cod and chips, the rain is pouring down. Puddles are growing. The path back to Otter is slippery, and just beyond the new bridge Jess falls hard onto her hip and elbow. Cursing loudly, wet hair across her face, she limps to the boat, fumbles with the lock, and then collapses onto the bags and boat cover in the cabin. The rain is thundering on the roof. The light is fading.

Anxiety drowns her. She starts to talk to herself.

"What the hell are you doing? This is insane."

She lies there and wonders what to do. Then she hears another engine and there are shouts as a boat moors close by. Too close. Hurriedly she clears a space in the chaos, takes off her muddy coat and squats, pulling first at the newspaper wrapping then at the cod, pushing the fish and chips into her mouth. Then, still chewing, she searches for the yellow all-weather jacket and trousers and struggles to get them on. She finds the boots, the gloves and Francis's cap too.

With the hood of the coat up over the cap, she climbs out into the rain, starts the engine, leaps onto the bank to release Otter, and then clumsily leaps aboard before pushing the boat out into the middle of the river with her foot.

6

One Sunday morning, as Ella and I assisted Nan in the kitchen, Dr. Brazington entered and asked if I would accompany him to his study. I followed him and he asked that I be seated in the chair facing his desk. He seemed unclear in his thoughts, then after a moment of silence began by apologising for not formally welcoming me to his house on my arrival. He asked that, given the tragic circumstance of Catherine's accident, I might understand, which indeed I most certainly could. He then hesitated again before stating it had been suggested to him some years before by Miss Thorne that I should be employed within his household, but that this had not been possible for reasons he did not offer.

He then began speaking with startling frankness, rising from his chair and pacing back and forth, his head down, his face grey with shadow. He said that since the tragic death of his dear wife Emily, he had taken responsibility for their daughter's learning but had grown increasingly troubled not only by the difficulties this presented him given the pressures of his work as a doctor, but also by Constance's isolation and lack of companionship. He had sought to foster contacts with other families but declared that, in all honesty, he found those he could seek out in that remoteness of Norfolk to be utterly foreign to both his and, indeed, his daughter's character and opinion. It was most peculiar, as if he were preparing a speech for some other person and not addressing me. He then looked at me and stated earnestly that Constance was the mirror of her mother, and here, for the main part, lay the reason for him seeking that I join them at Swanton Rectory. This made no sense to me at all, but given his obvious distraction I did not deem it sensible to question him.

I returned to my duties and at the earliest opportunity confided in Nan what had been said to me. She took me into the garden that afternoon, and as we walked I learned so much more about why I had come to be there and what Dr. Brazington was trying to say to me.

Nan explained that Mrs Emily Brazington was herself an orphan, and as a newborn infant had been found on the steps of the dowager's house on the Bembroke Estate some thirty miles to the north, three miles from the coast where there are great sand dunes and pine woods. Lady Crofton, who resided there, had defied her son, the young Lord Crofton, and refused to give up the child to the poorhouse, instead seeking that someone working upon the estate might care for her. A coachman and his wife, who were childless, took her in and raised her as their own daughter. As to the real mother, her identity was never known, though some surmised she lived in the port of Beckmouth some three miles away and that the father was most likely to have been a person from the estate.

The orphan girl lived among the people within that park until her twentieth year, during which time Lady Crofton took particular interest in her care and education and was much taken by her character and amused by her spirit. Nan said that Mrs Brazington had talked often of Lady Crofton with the greatest fondness and would recount how they grew to value each other's company so much, often taking a carriage and enjoying long walks along the beach, a habit which was to bring the young woman even greater fortune.

Dr. Brazington, newly appointed at Swanton, first encountered his future wife when he had travelled to the north coast and marshes and was staying for a few nights at an inn while he pursued his study of ornithology. Their meeting was a most unusual one. Dr. Brazington had returned to the inn one afternoon to discover that his notebook had dropped from his pocket. He retraced his path through the pine woodland behind the sand dunes and came upon a young woman in a white dress with long, flowing black hair, reading to a distinguished lady of far greater years, who was listening attentively while resting upon the low bow of a tree. The young woman stopped as soon as she saw him, but he had heard enough to know she was reading his words. The older woman asked if he could be Dr. Thomas Brazington, as was written within the cover, and he stated he was. Lady Crofton then introduced herself and also her young companion, Emily, and commended him for his most enlightening observations. Dr. Brazington had felt embarrassed, but the young woman had spoken up.

"Indeed they are, they truly are," she had said as she handed the notebook to him. "Please forgive us."

Some years later, when I heard this account again from Dr. Brazington, he told me how he would never forget those first words or that moment. Lady Crofton then declared she was feeling tired and, asking for his arm, invited him to return with her and Emily to the estate for tea. Hence a wonderful romance had begun.

Dr. Brazington and Emily were married the following year, in the chapel at Bembroke Hall at the insistence of Lady Crofton, and for twelve years they shared their love of wildlife and nature, with Mrs Brazington helping her husband in both his work and his studies of flora and fauna. They moved into Swanton Rectory and shortly afterwards were blessed with Constance, although the birth was exceptionally difficult and Dr. Brazington was deeply concerned that his wife might not recover. But she sustained, and the following years were full and happy in so many ways, until that last, particularly cold Christmas when his wife accompanied him on a visit to a sickly child in the village and shortly later was herself taken with a terrible fever. She died on the first day of the New Year. Nan said the Doctor's will and spirit seemed broken beyond repair.

Nan herself became distressed at the memory of her mistress. She went on to say it was well known that it had always been in Mrs Brazington's mind that she should seek to help others less fortunate, that she despised prejudice against the poor, and that she had implored her husband with increasing resolve to seek a child they could offer sanctuary to, and perhaps someone who would be a companion to their daughter. Miss Thorne, whom Mrs Brazington had been familiar with through her projects to offer chalks and boards and sometimes paper, pens and ink to teachers in the poorhouses, deemed it appropriate to visit the Rectory concerning me, saying that in her judgement I was a child who, though two years older than Constance, was most suited for what they had discussed. To this end Mrs Brazington had accompanied her to the Union house and was the woman who met with me and asked me questions and spoke with me on several occasions.

I did not join them at Swanton Rectory at that time, however, because Dr. Brazington deemed it was not possible to add further costs to the household. The good Doctor told me many years later that his main reason for resisting my employment, other than finance, was his hope for them to have a second child. He was, he said, both deaf and blind to his wife's wishes and, indeed, to her open resignation that she would not be able to bear another child. Her death cast a dreadful veil across their lives which, with the subsequent tragedy of Catherine, had pushed Dr. Brazington to the edge of this world, for sometimes I heard him muttering bitterly as he walked through the house.

He did not, however, to my eternal gratitude, forget his wife's beseeching, and following Catherine's accident he decided to ride to Gressenhall himself to inquire if the same orphan Mrs Brazington had spoken of was still seeking a means whereby she could leave the poorhouse.

7

Jess stirs from her fitful sleep with a start, and for a second she can't understand why there's the sound of an engine. The motorboat chugs by. Otter rocks and then bumps hard against the staithe. The vodka bottle on its side rolls back and forth close to Jess's face on the shelf beside *Anna's journal.* Jess pulls her arms from under the blankets and rubs her right elbow, now stiff as well as sore after her fall. The air smells damp and of fish and chips. She yawns and pushes her fingers through her hair, shivers, and feels the need to pee. Light pours into the little cabin from round the patches of cloth hanging in front of the four tiny oval windows. Her coat still lies across her feet, and the yellow waterproofs are on top of her holdall on the other bunk. The cardboard box next to it is on its side, and some of the contents, along with the carrier bags with her food in them, have spilled over the crumpled boat cover that almost fills the narrow floor space between the two bunks. The fish and chip papers are wedged into the shelf on the other side of the boat beside the red fire extinguisher.

Jess pushes herself up and rubs her upper arms She has no idea what time it is. She crawls through to the toilet at the front of the cabin, then scrambles back. The cold and dampness are too much, and she climbs under the covers again, pulling the blankets up to her nose and ears. She blows warm air under the blankets and tries to close her eyes. After a few minutes she hears another boat, only this time the flap of canvas, the slap of waves, and raised voices are very close. Otter bumps again, harder this time. Jess throws off the blankets and sits up, the back of her head clipping the paraffin lamp on the panel behind her. She moves quickly on all fours along the bunk towards the back of the boat, struggles into her coat, looks at her wet trainers, then finds and pulls on the sailing boots that Gordon had given her. She pushes open the door and cold air stings her face. She can see a yacht tacking away towards a windmill standing at the turn in the river that leads back to Potter Heigham Bridge. Above the grass bank she can also see the tops of two more sails, both moving swiftly in the other direction, towards the turn, towards her. She looks down at her coat, the arm and side stained by mud and grass, then quickly takes it off and reaches into the cabin for the yellow waterproof jacket. She scrambles up onto the old staithe where, in a mist of drizzle and dying light the evening before, Otter had clattered into the oak beams and Jess had felt round on her hands and knees in the long grass for a place to secure her. Both lines have held, but one of the two soft rubber fenders she hung between the boat and staithe has vanished. She pushes the boat away from the staithe to look for it and rubs a wet finger across the scratches in Otter's varnish. Then she sees the missing white fender, twenty yards back along the river towards the mill, trapped in the reeds where the staithe ends.

Jess, the retrieved fender lying between her muddy boots, draws hard on a cigarette and swings her hip to push the tiller. The pop-pop rhythm of the engine is comforting, and Otter's nose follows the river as it twists left past a tatty windowless hut on stilts jutting out from the bank. A flaking red and white sign warns of eel nets, so Jess gives it a wide berth, nudging the throttle forward to gain speed in case a holiday cruiser sweeps round the next corner just a few yards ahead. The river turns sharply to the right, and on the corner, just a few feet from the water's edge, stands a solid, squat timber building and a boathouse, both with walls as black as tar and weighed down by thick, dark grey thatch. The windows are boarded up, waiting for summer. *Otter*'s wake rolls along the staithe in front of it, and Jess eases back on the throttle. Now the river blurs into a wilderness of wide water and reed. Posts mark the channel as it stretches ahead across the rippling graphite surface. There are no more buildings and no other boats, for now at least.

Jess pushes hair from her face and drags a hand across her stomach. She puts the engine into neutral, leans over the side to wet her cigarette stub, then drops it beside her feet. She waits until Otter has slowed, then quickly reaches into the cabin for the peanuts. Seated sideways, resting her forearms across the tiller, she pulls at the packet with her teeth, then, slowly chewing on a few nuts, stares blankly across the water. She is floating in the middle of a lake. She watches what she thinks is a grebe disappear beneath the little waves just a few yards in front of her, and she scans the surface until it appears again ten yards away.

Breathing deeply, she thinks back to her struggle the night before, when, cold and wet, she had finally managed to light the paraffin lamp; how she shed her wet things, rolled out the bedding, kicked her legs beneath the blankets to warm them, then drank from the bottle. She had felt bewildered lying there, listening to the wind shaking the rigging and the rain falling on the roof just inches above her head. She hadn't slept on a boat since she was a child, that last autumn on the Cape with Grandpa. She couldn't sleep, so she got more pillows from the other bunk and reached for *Anna's journal*. After a few pages she tried to increase the brightness of the light, but turned the wick the wrong way and the flame had gone out. In the blackness she managed to find her lighter on the shelf, but the wick had dropped too far and would neither rise nor light. She gave up and lay there until sleep finally came.

Jess glances ahead along the channel and can see a holiday cruiser in the distance heading towards her. She takes another handful of nuts, thumps Otter into gear, and stands up. The boat surges forward. Jess suddenly feels determined. *Get there,* she tells herself. *Just get there.*

Away across the heads of the reeds, a couple of hundred yards to her right, Jess glimpses the terracotta tiles of a small cottage amid the cover of trees. The two small top windows are open, their white frames partly obscured by the leaves of a creeper. It must be Whispering Reeds. She feels sure she has followed Rudi's directions, but she can't see how to get to it. The channel ahead is swinging back towards Hickling Broad and away from the cottage. Then, as she draws level with the front of the building, there is a sudden break in the reeds, a narrow channel. There looks to be barely enough width for Otter, but Jess instinctively pulls hard on the tiller and the boat tilts as she sweeps right, the wooden sprit jutting from the front of the bow swishing through the reeds on the corner. Jess straightens Otter again, and now, dead ahead, she can see a staithe patterned with old car tyres. Grass rises gently to French doors and a wooden bench against the cottage wall. She glances over her shoulder at Otter's wake in the dyke. If She's wrong and this isn't Whispering Reeds, there is no way she can turn round now.

Jess puts the engine into neutral and lets the boat glide. She reaches down and picks up the cigarette butt and empty packet of peanuts and stuffs them into her pocket. She shuts the cabin door too. Then she stares ahead. It's a pretty place: low, with weathered red bricks and mottled roof tiles that ripple down to the two small upstairs windows and a riot of ivy. She can now see that on either side, two single storey rooms with pitched roofs butt up against the end walls. The one on the left has a small square window like those upstairs and is half covered by the climbing ivy. But the other, on the right, although built from the same sort of old bricks, looks recent, the mortar neater and unweathered. It is much narrower and has a deep window with a round top, and Jess can see books and some binoculars on the windowsill. She guesses there could be three downstairs rooms, three or four, and maybe one bedroom, possibly two.

The staithe is drawing close now, and the channel starts to widen. Jess sees there is space to turn and is about to swing *Otter* round when a black Labrador runs out from behind the cottage and bounds towards her, barking. A woman in a chequered shirt and jeans appears, waves, and walks purposefully across the lawn.

"Calm down, Biba! Stop that noise now. Don't worry. She's completely harmless! Just excited. Hang on, I'll lend you a hand."

She is a short, stocky woman with a round face and shoulder-length wavy hair, once blonde, now streaked with grey.

"Th...then this is Whispering Reeds?"

"It is. Shove her into reverse for a second to stop her, then throw me a line."

The woman has her feet on the staithe now, fists on her hips and a huge smile on her face. Her skin is soft brown like Graham's at the boatyard. The dog is standing beside her, tail wagging.

"The old tyres'll cushion her until we get the fenders on, so don't worry."

Otter settles against the staithe. They secure her on iron rings, then rise and face one another. The woman rubs her hands down her shirt, then offers one. Her eyes are shining. "Well, here you are. Welcome to Reeds, Miss Healey. I'm Margaret. Margaret Bunn from North Bank Farm away back down the lane."

She points over her shoulder but doesn't break her gaze. She speaks fast, lyrically.

"I was just here checking things over. Graham rang to say not to expect you yesterday. Lit the Rayburn stove last night and it's kept in, I'm glad to say, so the place is cosy for you. You got here good and early, which is just great. Have you a bag now?"

"Er..."

Jess glances down at the boat. She doesn't want her to see inside. Margaret understands. "Oh, not to worry. You can get it later. All in good time. First, come into the warm." Margaret turns, and Jess, bewildered, slowly follows, nervous eyes scanning.

"Will you be needing a cup of tea? Oh, I must shut those windows.

Was giving the bedroom a bit of an airing. It needed it."

They walk up the gentle rise of the lawn, and Jess looks left at a long shed with a fibreglass dinghy propped up against the back of it. The shed timbers are stained black like the thatched wooden chalet she saw earlier, but the sagging roof has weathered tiles the same as the cottage. It's split in two. The end nearest the water has a little window and white padlocked door, and the far end is open and stacked with logs beside a coal bunker.

Between the shed and the cottage and at the back of the house, Jess trails behind Margaret across compacted shingle locked with weeds. There's barely enough space for a car. A few yards further back there is a green mass of wild hedge, bramble, and trees either side of a wooden gate. The gate is open and Jess can see a muddy track running left and right, then a ditch, a barbed wire fence, and a huge water meadow where black and white cows are grazing.

Margaret waits for her by the back door, a tiny dark green wooden porch wrapped in a climbing rose and honeysuckle and shaded by tree boughs that reach out over the roof of the house. Just past it, cocooned in undergrowth, there is an old bird table rising from a patch of deep grass. A bicycle with a basket at the front is propped against the wall of the cottage next to stacks of old upturned plant pots.

"Come in. Come in."

The kettle on the Rayburn whistles. Jess is sitting on the edge of one of two wooden armchairs facing it and can feel the heat on the side of her face. She looks at the profile of the woman, her certainty as she warms the pot, the dog stretched out at her feet in front of the stove. Lost for words, Jess remembers what Rudi told her to ask.

"You're from Ireland?"

Margaret puts the pot on a metal trivet on the side of the Rayburn. "I am, with a little bit of Norfolk thrown in now. God knows what my dear ol' Gran MacLaughlin or my dear Da' would say."

"How, um, I mean…"

"How'd I get here? How long have you got? Ha, now that's a story. Oh it is that, and it's a few miles from Kerry I'll tell you that for nothin'. We Irish are scattered all over this planet like stars in the sky." She scoops loose-leaf tea from a small wooden caddy. "Simple really. Pip, my Philip, and I met when I was in London. I was a trainee nurse at Charing Cross Hospital. He was an airman, from a family of farmers right here. Stationed in Kent and up in London on a jolly. Hurt his stupid self walkin' in front of a car trying to get to the middle of Trafalgar Square. Said he was looking at the statue. Drunk more like. Hardly a hero. Real handsome though." She laughs. "I'll maybe fill in the gaps when we've more time. You don't need me witterin' on now." Margaret takes a china mug from the cupboard under the draining board. She puts it on a wooden tray, along with a blue jug which she fills with milk from a bottle she takes from a small fridge. She then adds one of three round tins stacked at the end of the work surface.

"Sugar?"

Jess raises her hand. "No."

"Oh, while I remember, cutlery's in the right-hand drawer of the dresser. I'll not be joining you if you don't mind. Phil will have a pot of tea on the go about now, and, besides, I've a hundred and one things to be doing. There's chicken stock festering on my Aga stove for starters."

Jess stares out of the window at the vast sky.

Margaret studies her as she carries the tray to the table beside the Rayburn. Jess is just as Rudi had told her.

"You'll be all right, I know you will. You can explore on your own, better that you do it without me. You must be hungry, and sick of the sight of me already. Right, I'll just nip upstairs and shut those windows while I remember. Or would you do it?"

Jess nods.

"Great, because I must be getting back."

Margaret pulls on a worn waxed jacket. "I think the weather's going to be patchy all day and chilly, but at least it isn't raining at the moment and we've a few bits of blue to let the sun through now and again. Now, anything you need, anything at all, just walk down the lane. Out the gate and turn left. Five-minute walk "tis all. I'm usually about. If not, leave a note inside the porch round the back of the house." She points at the fridge. "I've left you some lamb chops and some eggs and milk from the farm, and a bit of bacon too. You're not vegetarian, are you?"

Jess shakes her head. Margaret turns and points.

"Thank God for that. There's leek and potato soup in that green saucepan on the side. Not much in the way of vegetables in my garden yet, I'm afraid, but I've bought a little, bottom cupboard, below the shelf, along with some tinned bits and bobs."

She taps the tin on the tray.

"And there's some of me homemade biscuits in there. Now, what else? Rudi told me, and has no doubt told you, You're to use the place as your own. Francis would want that too, I know. Use whatever you need now. Oh, and you'd be wise to keep an eye on the Rayburn and keep it topped up. Fuel's in the bunker next to the logs in the shed. You'll soon get the hang of it. Should it go out, use paper and kindlin'. Plenty in the shed too. Logs for the wood-burner in the lounge as well, as I said. Anyway, if you need anything just ask, OK now, Miss Healey?"

Jess nods and tries to smile.

"Right then, I'll be off. Oh, Rudi told you, right, about the electricity, in so much as we're at the end of the line here and the wiring is a bit out of date, to put it mildly."

Jess looks at her blankly.

"What I mean is, should it go off, a reasonably regular occurrence, particularly if there's a storm about, don't worry yourself, 'cos It'll come back in its own sweet time. If the trip switch goes, wait 'til things blow over, then flip it on again. It's in that cupboard by the door. You'll find paraffin lamps and candlesticks all over the place and quite a stockpile of candles in the left-hand dresser drawer, along with the matches too. I've topped up the lamps and checked the wicks, and there's more paraffin on the shelf in the shed should you be needin' it. Actually, I quite like it when the power's off. Tend to get back to living by the sun and not sittin' up late staring at some stupid programme on the box. Oh, while I remember, there's no telephone, but we've got one, so pop down should you be needin' to use it. And as for the tap water, I wouldn't be drinking it unless You've boiled it first. It's collected off the roof and runs into a quite a big tank above the bathroom and then, when that's full, into another big tank outside at the other end of the house. There should be plenty for what you need, so don't be frettin'. When this place was built a hundred and fifty or so years ago, the river water was clean enough to drink, but not now. Nothing like. I've put some bottled water in the fridge too. Rudi and Francis would come and get it from the farm when they needed it, along with milk. If the power's off and you want hot water, you can always heat it on the stove. There are a couple more big kettles in the cupboard over there. Three's just enough for a bath, unless you like to wallow like me. Right, maybe I'll pop back tomorrow and see how You're getting on, OK? Right. That's just about everything for now. I'll be on my way. Alright?"

Jess nods. "Thank you." She looks anything but certain.

"Nothin'. Nothin' at all. Pleasure. Keep warm. Bye now. Come on, Biba dog. You're not stopping this time."

Jess stands and watches Margaret through the window as she pushes her bike to the gate, climbs on, turns left down the track, and vanishes behind the bushes, followed closely by the dog. She checks the back door latch is shut, then, arms folded, starts to drift through the cottage. Up until that point she hasn't taken much of it in, but now Margaret has gone, and with her the worry of what to say, Jess begins to see Francis's heaven.

The kitchen is quite a large room, but there is little space. It has a high, angled timbered ceiling, old pamment tiled floor, and warm walls the colour of dark sand. Just inside the door, in a recess to the left below the high cupboard with the electrical switch in it, an assortment of hats and coats hang down above shoes and boots lined up on a worn doormat. To the right a wooden work-surface, seasoned with watermarks, runs to a deep butler sink with brass taps under the window that looks out towards the gate. Both the windowsill and the work-surface that continues to the biscuit tins in the corner are lined along the back with old bottles, little china saucers full of shells, and candlesticks heavy with wax. There are three little wooden elephants facing the door. Jess stares for a second at the hot and cold taps, worn by Francis's and Rudi's hands. Her head turns slowly. Along the windowless end wall of the cottage, on the north side close to the woodshed and dinghy, there is a shelf with a few paperbacks propped up by a bust of Schubert, some framed photographs of the cottage, and, at the far end, a brass carriage clock with no hands. Further along, in the other corner, several gold stars of different sizes have been painted on the wall and ceiling above the tall, narrow pine dresser whose top shelf is a pretty muddle of china figures of different sizes, with just two floral mugs hanging from hooks. Below them are cookery books ranked neatly in order of height, largest on the left, smallest on the right, with pieces of coloured paper sticking out of the tops of them. Beneath the front window a little drop leaf table with two small chairs either side of it is all but covered by the combination of the tea tray, an oil lamp, and a pile of wicker mats on top of a piece of lace. Then there are the two Windsor chairs, with cushions on the seats, facing the Rayburn on the inside wall and crowding the middle of the room. Pans hang from meat hooks above the stove.

Beyond the chimney breast, in the corner, there is a recess and another door. Jess pours some tea, then walks slowly through it.

The lounge walls are burgundy. It is dominated by the fireplace at the far end, with dusty logs stacked high either side of a wood-burner beneath a smoke-stained hardwood mantle and a red brick chimney breast. There's a gilt-framed mirror above the fireplace with a fan of mottled brown feathers wedged behind the top of it. The room is patterned with framed photographs and paintings, and there are tapestry curtains of gold, greens, and reds at a small window at the back of the cottage and, to the front, the wide wooden French doors. To the left of the little window an aged, elegant walnut upright piano waits with a small pile of music scores on top of it. The keyboard lid is unlocked. It is a Hoelling & Spangenberg. She plays a chord, then carefully closes it again. Beside it, just to Jess's left, is a bookshelf with cupboards along the bottom. It fills the wall warmed on the other side by the Rayburn.

Jess bends and opens one of the cupboard doors. It's crowded by glasses of varying sizes. She closes it and quickly opens the next one. Five or six bottles of spirits, some almost full, are lined up on the shelf. She lets out a long breath, closes the door, and looks round the room again. Like the kitchen the lounge has a timbered ceiling, but it is low, with two main, slightly bowed beams She wonders if they have come from a ship. The floorboards, the grain lifted in places out of the darkness of age by the polish of feet, run towards a large deep red sofa, the back, seat, and cushions of which hold the forms of those who last rose from it. It is angled, looking both at the fire and French windows, its high back shielding the piano from both. There is a small pile of magazines on a low wooden table in front of it and a stool beneath that.

On either side of the chimney breast there are two more doors. The one on the right is slightly ajar, and beyond it are the first narrow, high steps of the stairs that turn and spiral. The door on the left is wide open, and Jess can see the high end of a white bath with clawed feet, standing on floorboards painted the same pastel blue as the walls beyond. Before she walks in, she knows this is the room with the deep, round-topped window. Jess sits on the edge of the bath and looks left out onto the wetland. There is a ditch at the side of the grass, full of wide, grey-green leaves that fuse with the reeds beyond. Then there is the band of water, a thin seam of distant trees, all layered beneath the vastness of sky. She flickers a smile, for the toilet faces the window, where the binoculars and two dog-eared bird books also sit. She turns her head. Facing her is the sink below a square mirror in a frame decorated with pieces of smooth driftwood. Near the door there is an old tiny wooden chair draped with towels. Three wicker shelves hanging on the wall are filled with folded flannels and assorted soaps in a bowl, a basket of bath cubes and little bottles of essential oils and, on top, two china candlesticks and an incense burner. Between the mirror and the window the wall is a mosaic of photographs and pencil sketches. The drawings are of the wetland. The photographs are mostly of Francis and Rudi, alone or together, and at the heart of them is a large black and white picture of the two men sitting on a park bench, laughing, their shoulders pressed together, their heads tilted towards one another. Their faces radiate harmony. Jess thinks it must be about ten or fifteen years old. Rudi, in his waistcoat and tie, cane between his knees, looks so well and happy. Francis, his wild hair cut quite short, has his shirtsleeves rolled roughly to the elbows and there is the familiar jumper round his shoulders. He's wearing shorts, and the curly hairs on his arms and legs look especially thick and dark. One of his arms is clutching a folded newspaper to his chest, the other is resting on Rudi's leg. In the bottom of the wooden photo frame, wedged in one corner, there is a small, folded piece of paper with "READ ME" written across it. Jess wonders for a second, then takes it and gently opens it. She starts to read. A smile flits across her face again. Then come tears.

> *For Rudi*
> *With my body clock ticking loudly by the bed,*
> *Next to a sinful pint of bitter*
> *And blue cheese on bread,*
> *I've decided to knock on the door in my head,*
> *To the box room of things I don't need*
> *But can't forget,*
> *And tell Pythagoras, Fred, Bill and Roy,*
> *–Messrs Quimby, Haley and the Melchester Rovers wonder boy–*
> *To pack up the old hats that crowd my mind,*
>
> *And while they're at it*
> *To take any poetic seeds they can find,*
> *For this is the last*
> *Of Francis's rhymes.*
>
> *I want to think only of special times,*
> *Our lives,*
> *Our world,*
> *Our wicked crimes;*
> *The here and now, this house with you;*

To smell the air and drink this view.
Nothing more
Than to know
In every minute
In every way
What I care for more than all
Until my calling day.

8

So it was that Swanton Rectory became my home and, in time, Constance my dearest friend. These beginnings at the Rectory were, however, as I have stated, times of uncertainty, for there was a constant anxiety regarding the well-being of Dr Brazington, who forever seemed lost in his deepest thoughts and had neither appetite for food nor company, so much so that we often brought meals to him in his study in the forlorn hope he may eat more. He forsook all his studies of nature for beyond a year, and no one could be sure that his profound grief and despair would ever leave him. It was obvious to all, also, that his own health was weakening.

For young Constance to witness such things following the loss of her dear mother was dreadful, and I firmly believe that were it not for the steadfast resolve and care of Nan, and with it the support of both Mr Blyth and Ella, matters may well not have changed. Nan was as much wedded to that house as she was to the family, for prior to the arrival of Dr and Mrs Brazington, both she and Mr Blyth had been in the service of the retired clergyman, Canon Wentworth-Toft, who had resided there for some ten years until his death. Certainly, Nan was very much inclined to treat the Rectory as her responsibility, but in a manner that was endearing not vexing, and she seemed to relish the duty of caring both for the dwelling and anyone who resided therein. She was a stout person, both in heart and body, God-fearing and with a boundless vigour and a motherly countenance that brought her to speak freely, when she judged it appropriate, to anyone, regardless of their station. I sometimes pondered if she was in some way related to Peace but never dared to put this to her, should she in some way be offended. Some time later, in far happier times, Dr Brazington once remarked in humour, after one of the many occasions when Nan chided him for not eating well enough for one so active in his work, that she ruled us all with a rod of celery. She had left the room when he said this, but she undoubtedly heard him, for there came her familiar laugh from the hallway.

We called her Nan and not Miss Frere at her insistence, and she taught both Ella and I, and, indeed, Constance, a great deal not only of domestic matters and the preparation of food, but also the satisfaction of growing both vegetables and flowers. She would say to Constance that it was to her advantage to know these things for, with the Lord's blessing, the day would come when she would oversee a home of her own, which indeed it did.

But Constance did not need any encouragement. For all of us, even Dr Brazington who, when time allowed, would come and sit on a kitchen chair by the door, it was a pleasure to be with Nan in the kitchen garden on a clear day, whether it be to undertake some planting or to harvest some of the many things she would grow. She was assisted to some considerable extent in this endeavour by her brother, Mr Jeremiah Frere, who lived in the village and had a large family. Mr Frere was a worker at the forge and took it upon himself to offer his help to his sister and Mr Blyth as often as he could, for Dr Brazington had regularly provided, without charge, care for his children at times of sickness.

His eldest son would often accompany him as a gardener's boy, but he was sullen and idle, and if he did not receive encouragement to do otherwise, his favourite work was chasing snails off the garden paths.

As for the flowers within the garden of the Rectory, these Nan persisted in referring to as Mrs Brazington's, for everyone told me the borders of the main garden had indeed been the Mistress's joy. While Mr Frere and Mr Blyth worked upon the lawns and helped with the heavier duties, Nan continued the work of gardening that she had once shared with Mrs Brazington, remarking during the most colourful season that her mistress would be greatly pleased. Indeed, it was only during the darker months of the year when you could only find dried and not fresh blooms within the Rectory.

As for Mr Blyth, whose bed was in the room adjoining the stables, he was a man of very few words, though it was clear from his mellow face and ready smile that he was a person of a gentle disposition. When he did offer comment it was frequently short, except on the matter of horses, and without any question he was at his most contented when tending to his duties as groom. It was said of him that he possessed the ability to calm the wildest of animals and was celebrated in the locality for his knowledge, something that brought other grooms to the Rectory in much the same way as people came seeking the assistance of Dr Brazington. He was a small, thin man who had seen far more years than those that awaited him. He had pointed features, distinctively large ears, and legs that bowed outwards at the knee as if he had spent many years astride a steed. He was slightly stooped and could never be rushed, but nor was he idle, and rarely would you see him sitting unless it was at the kitchen table at mealtimes or cleaning a bridle. Nan explained to me that he had been apprenticed as a tailor in his youth, in Norwich, that being the trade of his father, but had run away and sought work as a groom on a large estate in Yorkshire where, many years later, a certain Canon Wentworth-Toft, another exile from Norfolk, learned of his expertness and offered him employment. I enquired of him once why he would choose to leave a grand house and stables for somewhere as simple as Swanton Rectory with only one or sometimes two animals to care for, and his only reply was, with telling Norfolk frankness, "It suits me well."

In truth, that house suited us all very well, and it is perhaps pertinent to record a few words regarding both its aspect and position. It had been built some twenty-four years earlier on the instruction of Canon Wentworth-Toft, whose family had been landowners within the valley of the River Wensum, and who had been countenanced by his only surviving relative, his spinster sister, to return to his native soil upon his retirement, and there to erect a house where they could both reside. The house stood upon a slight hill close to the lane that led north to Two Bridges and the turnpike road from Norwich to Deepenham, and south past the ancient church of St Mary and into the village of Swanton. The forward outlook was to the east and upon the winding course of the river and the meadows and wood-cloaked rises of the valley. To the south and west lay much of the formal garden, and if one followed the path through an arch in the beech hedge, you entered the kitchen garden. My room offered this southerly view, encompassing also the large lawn that ran to a small wood of ash and oak where could be found Constance's swing and her secret paths. To the north were the stables and laundry, against the south wall of which, within the kitchen garden, Dr Brazington had constructed for his wife a glasshouse for the tending of young plants.

The house had rooms on three floors with two staircases, one leading from the main hallway to the first floor and five main bedrooms, the other to the rear of the house rising from the kitchen lobby to both the first and second floors where Nan, Ella, and I had rooms After a few months my wish to leave the bed that had been Catherine's was made known to the Doctor, and a room that had been set out for the repair and storage of clothes and materials was cleared for me. That room with its fine view of the rear garden was to be my bedroom for more than thirteen years, and it was at a table beneath that window where, in those following months, I was to begin to make my notes.

Looking back on this account of my beginnings at Swanton Rectory I recognise that there may well be confusion as to my exact position within the house, and I can say I was equally uncertain. My initial expectation was to fulfil the duties of a maid under the supervision of Nan, work I willingly and regularly undertook. Yet the lack of any severe regime such as I had previously been accustomed to, coupled with the young Constance's almost immediate desire to take me with her on what she called her adventures to the river, the Two Bridges and the Bramble Wood, meant the significance of my being there turned most sharply from maid to companion. I still fulfilled my duties, but after Constance's eagerness for my companionship became apparent, it also became clear to me that both Nan and Dr Brazington were more than content that my priority lay in this most pleasant of responsibilities, and both would question me regularly on the child's well-being, together with earnest reminders of my need for alertness regarding her safety and care.

That I could read and write undoubtedly had a significant bearing on our new friendship, for reading to one another upon the riverbank or beside the fire in Constance's room became one of our fondest pastimes, and there was an almost immediate accord and understanding that bridged the two years between us. I was overjoyed, also, at the invitation to join her in her studies under the tutelage of her father, and to be entrusted with books from the library. I remember quite clearly that one book we would read again and again was the novel entitled David Copperfield, by Charles Dickens, for we loved the vivid account of Mr Peggotty's wonderful house upon the Norfolk beach and the young David telling of the smells, sounds, and sights of Yarmouth's South Quay. We spoke of what it might be like if we journeyed there, for it was not so far off, two days" travelling at most, and promised ourselves that we should attempt it one day. In those many moments together we shared a number of things and, in time, our innermost thoughts as I imagine sisters might.

To say it was an unusual circumstance would be to understate it, for the Rectory was a place where, notwithstanding the respect we all had for our master, there was little sense of formality or division, but rather a great amount of openness and a bond it is hard to explain. I grew to love them all, and such reflection always touches me deeply. I shall stop now, for my hand aches, and so too, a little, does my heart.

I have picked up the pen once again, for the rain is falling and I cannot continue my work of several days, clearing the space in front of the cottage and freeing the glorious yellow irises that had almost been overwhelmed by a binding weed. My heart leapt when I saw their yellow flowers on first coming here, for they grew in considerable numbers too along the banks of the Wensum and were something so familiar to me. The garden, if I could presume to call it that, is slowly returning from the wilderness, and it has enchanted me with its music of birds, the lapping water, and the wind in the reeds and rushes. There is not so much land, but I have set aside some space in the shelter of the trees and cottage where I have sown some of the seeds I brought with me from the kitchen garden at Swanton Rectory. As for our home I have begun that task too, and the three rooms are a great deal more organised. The weather may prevent it, but Jacob has said that on his return from Norwich this week on a wherry he will attempt to bring a bed so we no longer have to sleep upon the floor.

Now I shall apply myself once more to my account of life at Swanton.

There was one occasion at Two Bridges when a grand gentleman in a fine tall hat and riding upon a trap pulled by a wild-eyed grey horse stopped to enquire the whereabouts of a certain manor house beyond Swanton. Constance left the riverbank to answer him. Then he deemed to offer her and her sister a ride to the village, should that be our home. His confusion must have stemmed from the fact that we were similarly dressed, both had black hair, and I was some way off. As one might imagine, this story was the cause of much merriment during all our years together. It was to lead too, when once we had savoured that happy memory yet again, for Dr Brazington to declare that to witness Constance's general happiness at that time had served in his own re-awakening. I had, he said, unconsciously stepped partly into the void left by her mother, but rather in the role of an older sibling. What had transpired was far beyond his faintest hope, and he declared truthfully that we were all blessed that the wisdom of his dear late wife should have spawned such vital attachments.

With such familiarity and discussion I grew to feel that I knew Emily Brazington, not least because the common remark was how similar Constance was to her mother in appearance and character. The young girl was both daring and inquisitive, to the point of filling me with much anxiety regarding her safety, and she was little interested in society's expectations regarding how a young lady should both dress and behave. Her remarks to the gamekeeper at Braddington Park who discovered us within the walls of that estate just to the north of Swanton were to cause Dr Brazington some embarrassment, for she'd readily admitted being there to liberate animals held in traps. I had first followed her when it was clear she would not be persuaded otherwise and must confess that after several such excursions I shared her zeal. On being discovered by the fearsome man we were taken home by cart and admonished by Dr Brazington and made to apologise in person to the frail Lord Chettington, who seemed somewhat amused and easily charmed.

Nan would constantly despair at Constance's wildness, as she called it, for even if her hair was combed and held at the beginning of the day it was invariably loose around her shoulders by the evening, and the hems of her white dresses and her sleeves would often carry marks of water and soil. She was unquestionably beautiful, slim and fleet-footed, and ever eager to discover something that would delight her father, whether it be a butterfly specimen, a river insect, a moss or fungus, or a passage from a book.

With the passing years Constance grew also to display her parents" capacity for compassion and a contempt for injustice, for her father saw merit in assenting with increasing frequency to her requests that she might travel with him and seek to help him in his work. I went too on occasions when I was not needed within the house, and it afforded me knowledge I have much thankfulness for. Indeed, after Constance's marriage it was I who became Dr Brazington's regular companion on those visits when he deemed he may need assistance or, in his weariness, to accompany him upon the journey.

Before I tell of Constance's marriage I should perhaps tell of my own, or at least the beginnings of it, for the story is long.

When I was twenty-one years of age and Constance was eighteen, we were passing along beside the Wensum and had reached the point at the end of the meadow where it passed through a copse when we were astounded to discover a youthful man bathing in the shallow water, his clothes upon the branch of a small tree and his worn boots on the ground beneath it. He too was much surprised. As we retreated along the bank we heard a cry of pain. We returned a little distance and shouted if he was hurt, and he replied that he was. We waited for several moments, then he came from behind the trees, now clothed, with one hand held up in front of him that was cut and bleeding. He was quite short but of a solid frame, and we could tell from his appearance that he was probably someone who worked upon the land, for his clothes were rough and simple. As he wrapped his neck scarf around his hand he said he had not meant to alarm us, and that he would leave, for he did not seek trouble. We asked him how he had cut his hand and he said that in his hurry to leave the river he had pulled on a branch of thorns. Constance said her father was a physician and that the house was close by. We urged him to accompany us, a suggestion he resisted at first. Then on the short journey we told him who we were and we persuaded him to tell us his name, which was Jacob Farrow.

I'll edit this continuation of the historical narrative, maintaining UK English conventions and the Victorian voice.

It transpired that Jacob was a waterman and not a farm worker as we had first surmised, and that he lived among the rivers and lakes of the great wetland some thirty miles to the east between the city of Norwich and the coast. As Dr Brazington tended his wound we all questioned him eagerly, for it was an extraordinary discovery, with the doctor declaring he had visited it on a few occasions some years before his marriage and had found it to be a wonderful expanse of wilderness.

With encouragement Jacob began to speak to us with a little confidence, saying he worked cutting reed and keeping the dykes clear while sometimes helping too upon wherries, large boats with black sails that carried all manner of things. He did not know his age, but later, as he rested upon Mr Blyth's bed after hungrily eating the food offered to him, Dr Brazington said he thought this must be about twenty years, adding that Jacob was, by all accounts, one of the water gypsies, the altogether different people of the wetland. This point left the question, put by Mr Blyth but in all our minds, as to how he came to be such a distance from that area. On his waking some hours later we offered him more food and drink, and Dr Brazington advised that he should stay for a few days to ensure the wound to his hand did not become poisoned. The Doctor said he could sleep within the stable, and once this was agreed we pressed him to tell us how it was that he was so far from his home. Jacob said he was making his way west, just as his father had shown him, to the Fens of Lincolnshire where at certain times of the year there was the chance of labour in the Fenland dykes and helping to clean land. It was not a necessary journey, but one his father and grandfather had made and one he wanted to continue. He said the knowledge of the journey, made by following the courses of certain rivers and streams, was something important, and that he understood it and enjoyed it for he saw something else of this world.

Jacob stayed at the Rectory for a full week, in which time Dr Brazington took what opportunity he could to question him about the creatures he had seen on the wetland, and we listened in wonder as he spoke of vast clouds of birds in the sky and told us of the haunting call of something he and Dr Brazington knew to be a secretive bird called a bittern. This had the doctor scurrying to his study in search of his notes, and Jacob whispered that to hear such a sound at dawn was to know that the spirits were watching you. Constance was enthralled too, though her studies were as much of the man as they were of what he was telling us, and afterwards she would share with me her observations of the other scars on his hands, the darkness of his rough skin, and the obvious strength in his body. I, too, had noticed these things and we also agreed, with much blushing and laughter, that, although he was not of great stature, Jacob's thick fair hair and blue eyes gave him a most pleasing appearance.

His departure came all too soon, but to our delight he appeared within the garden two months later, bringing with him two different species of waterfowl tied to a string across his shoulders, saying that we may eat them. He said that he was returning home and, having once again offered in simple words his gratitude for our kindness, he was gone. Constance and I climbed to Nan's room that offered the highest of views of the river, and we watched Jacob as he made his way back across the meadows until he disappeared into the trees not far from the place where we had first encountered him. Hence began a most unusual friendship, for in the following seven years Jacob would come and go again every spring, staying for a few days each time, and relaying to us his adventures as well as his misfortunes, on one occasion being much saddened at the recent death of his father. Constance, however, was not present for five of these years, for by the summer following her nineteenth birthday her life had taken an altogether different course, with a young gentleman taking first her heart and then her hand in marriage. While her beauty always dictated that there would be no end to the line of suitors, I felt certain that our somewhat remote existence, together with Constance's unbridled spirit and her attachment to her father and the way of life at Swanton, would make the challenge facing them most difficult. It proved not to be so, for one autumn day Dr Brazington was invited to luncheon by another physician who lived at Dereham and who worked within that town, an invitation that was extended to Constance also, and it was clear to me from the moment of their return that something within her had changed.

The physician in question was Dr James Baker, who had a house within the village of Hockham. Dr Brazington had made his acquaintance at a meeting in Norwich at which a shared interest, namely the somewhat controversial theories of Charles Darwin, were the matter for discussion. It was a new friendship that pleased the Doctor, for the two men were so very clearly of a like mind, but for Constance the invitation to luncheon was something she did not wish to undertake and only did so out of duty. We had been told that Dr Baker had two sons, the elder of whom was an officer in a regiment, while the younger had the responsibility of the care of land and livestock, chiefly sheep, cattle, and horses, on a large Breckland property that had been his grandfather's, Breckland being an area of heathers and twisted pines further to the south in the county of Norfolk.

On her return Constance seemed much distracted, and I was told in whispered tones by the Doctor that both the sons had been present at the luncheon and that the officer had paid Constance a great deal of attention. For some days Constance would not talk of it, then one night she came to my room to wake me and ask for my help. She led me to the laundry, where I had noticed she had spent a large proportion of that afternoon, and said most determinedly that it was her intention to carry out the ceremony known as the "Wake of Freya". I had not heard of this, and she said it was a means by which she might discover her future, for if she washed some of her linen in running water until it was white, as she had already done, and watched it drying before a fire from eleven till twelve at night, the Goddess Freya would, on the stroke of midnight, show her the face of the man she would marry. It was something she had read of as a child, it being a ceremony of Norse origin, and although I endeavoured to tell her of my unhappiness at such a strange ceremony, she persisted with an expression of the highest hopes. That nothing transpired was no surprise to me, but she was angered by it and took herself to bed again without further word. The following day I followed her to the meadows beside the river and encouraged her to tell me her thoughts. I had assumed, wrongly, that it was the officer who had captured her heart, but it was the second son, Edward, who had done this. It was a change that came upon us like a wind, for one day Constance seemed a child and the next she was a young woman, and for a while we were all somewhat troubled by the notion that she could leave us. It was most clear, though, that she had fallen in love, and not only did Mr Edward Baker subsequently charm us all with his bright character and obvious interest in nature and animals, but he also displayed an immediate appreciation of Constance's character and was not only a match for her sharp wit but saw amusement where others might find discomfort. He was a fine horseman and took particular care in the breeding of them for sale, giving Dr Brazington at the announcement of his engagement to Constance a most striking mare newly in foal that Mr Blyth declared was one of the best he had seen.

So it was that dear Constance left Swanton Rectory, but not before the most wonderful of weddings at the Church of St Mary close by. Under the Doctor's and Nan's direction we all shared very happily in the work in preparing for that day, and we were rewarded with the most enchanting of occasions that passed far too swiftly. After the service the two families and their guests returned to the Rectory and enjoyed the garden on what was, thankfully, a bright and beautiful summer's day, *and Mr Blyth delighted all by bringing out the mare and her young chestnut foal.*

As we said our farewells that day and watched the new Mrs Constance Baker leave with her husband I knew that my life was bound to change too, and was foolishly taken with a dread that I might not be able to remain at Swanton Rectory. I say that I was foolish because the matter was never raised, and almost immediately Dr Brazington made it quite clear that if I was willing there was an equally important task for me to fulfil, namely supporting him in his work and with his notes just as Constance had done. So began a new chapter in my life, one that transpired not to be great in length but one which was full of learning and contentment.

9

Jess rubs her eyes, pulls herself off the bed, and goes to the window. A gangly teenage boy in jeans, black muddy wellies, and a blue sweatshirt is pulling the dinghy across the grass towards the staithe. Biba, Margaret's dog, flops down on the lawn close by and pants contentedly, watching. The boy pushes the boat into the water, ties it to a ring, then walks back towards the shed. Jess thinks for a second what to do, then wraps herself in a blanket and goes down the narrow wooden stairs into the lounge. She looks out of the French doors but can only see the dog. She goes through to the kitchen, watching the windows, then just inside the back door bends to put on her trainers.

"Hello."

Jess recoils, shocked. The boy is standing in the porch.

"You made me jump."

"Mum told me to get the dinghy down for you."

"Oh. Right. Um. David?"

He nods.

"What time is it?"

"About five. Mum said to say she'll be down in a while. Bye."

"Bye."

Jess stares after him. She must have been asleep for hours. She remembers eating the last of the soup for lunch, then taking *Anna's journal* upstairs with a glass of scotch.

She fills the kettle, then wanders outside. It is a clear, still end to the day. Biba hasn't followed David home and comes towards her wagging her tail. Jess squats and makes a fuss of her. The dog's shiny black coat is soft, her eyes bright and kind. They walk down to the staithe together and Jess pulls at the corners of Otter's cover, checking her knots are still tight. She'd put it on two days before, that first afternoon after Margaret had gone, once she'd carried her bits to the house and cleaned out the cabin. The second day had been a blur of grey and wet and she had lit the wood burner and lay on the sofa, reading, smoking, sleeping, drinking. Time is already slipping.

Standing on Otter she feels quite pleased. The cover looks neat. Otter looks good.

She yawns and looks down at the dinghy. There are two wooden oars in it. It crosses her mind to try it, but instead she steps off Otter and walks slowly back to the cottage with Biba beside her. She makes coffee and is about to light a cigarette from her last packet when she hears footsteps on the gravel. Margaret is carrying a basket under her arm. She pops her head through the open doorway.

"All well?"

Jess smiles and nods.

110

"Can I come in?"

"Of course."

"You look tired. Don't worry, quite normal. You'll find the fresh air up here will knock you out to start with. Blows straight down from the North Pole." Margaret puts the basket by the sink and takes out a loaf and then a saucepan wrapped in a tea towel. "Got some of my fresh bread and some stew. Made more than we need. Right, David tells me the dinghy's in, so if you'd like we'll get the outboard on her, then you can use her. What do you think? There's a shop away across the broad, by the Ferryman pub at Hickling Heath, if you want to, that is."

"Yes."

In her head Jess shouts the word. She was wondering how the hell she was going to get more cigarettes. She feels strangely elated. With the dinghy she needn't be dependent on Margaret or anyone, or have to take the cover off Otter. The notion dispels the one thing that weakened her growing appreciation of the cottage and the easy isolation. A few days have already passed and there are no more thoughts of leaving so quickly.

"Come on then. Have you the key to the shed?"

The inside of the small shed is full of cans, pots of brushes, tools, and sailing gear, including rope and old fenders hanging from the roof. Margaret and Jess carry the outboard and a can of fuel down to the dinghy. The engine is small but heavy, and Margaret asks Jess to steady the boat against the staithe as she clamps it into place. She then tops up the tank, turns on the fuel feed, checks the motor is in neutral, and pulls sharply at the cord. At the third attempt it rattles into life.

An hour later Margaret stands at the attic room window of the farmhouse, watching, waiting. From there she can see most of the broad, a ribbon of gold laid across it by the setting sun. A couple of holiday cruisers go by, and several sails stand becalmed on the far rim of the water near the village staithe. Then the dinghy appears from behind the reeds to the left, cutting a line across the still surface. Jess sits hunched at the back of the boat, one hand on the outboard. She glances back towards the cottage and Margaret instinctively steps away from the window. Then she lifts binoculars and watches the boat as it turns right and follows the channel posts that sweep in an arch to the west.

"Margaret? It's Rudi. How're things?"

"Everything's fine. How are you?"

"I'm not too bad. She settled?"

"I think so. Yes, I think so."

"Do you think she'll stay? She said she'd head back to London by the end of the week."

"I reckon a while longer at least. She's only been here a couple of nights, Rudi, and the air's knocked her out. I've left her in peace, but we did get the dinghy sorted this afternoon and She's already used it to get some shopping."

"Which might suggest She's in no hurry?"

"Don't know. She may have just been to get cigarettes, but I think You're right. It doesn't look like she's going to shoot back to London straight away like she said."

"Has she mentioned anything, talked about anything?"

"No, she hasn't. Very quiet."

"Right. Good. I'll be there on Sunday as planned."

"D'you want us to pick you up?"

"Kind of you, but no. Gordon's coming, and I'll be staying with him. Don't say anything, of course."

"You asked me not to."

"Right."

"See you then. Call by at the farm afterwards. It would lovely to see you."

"I will. Thanks, Margaret."

"Nothin'. Bye."

"Bye."

10

Constance's marriage was in the summer of 1868 and I had been at Swanton Rectory for nearly seven years. That autumn I travelled with Dr Brazington to visit Constance at her new home, a journey of some two hours, and found it to be a quite grand and delightful farmhouse surrounded by many stables and flat pasture that had been neatly fenced and which contained Mr Baker's horses. We delighted in each other's company again, but it was all too brief, for it was a long journey and the need to travel home before nightfall required that we depart in the middle of the afternoon. It was agreed that on the next occasion we should stay more than a day and afford ourselves time, and Mr Baker advised Dr Brazington that on his return he would escort him to some area of the Brecks nearby where he might see all manner of wildlife. So it was that we grew to know that rough highway well, for we would journey along it three or four times a year, on one occasion at some speed in our excitement and haste to greet the doctor's first grandchild, Rupert Thomas Baker. Before I myself was married and departed the Rectory, Constance had two more children, twins whom they named Emily and Alice.

As for life at Swanton Rectory, it grew strangely quiet, and some time after Constance's departure there was a melancholy which we could only counter with routine and labour, of which there was ample. Dr Brazington was particularly burdened in the course of one month, firstly with a dreadful fire at Cookerson's mill in which three men perished in the disaster and three more suffered considerably, and subsequently by an outbreak of cholera among the families in the village of Merridock, three miles to the west. I accompanied Dr Brazington on both occasions in order to offer assistance where I could, and it was at Merridock that I committed myself to provide all support possible to his campaigning to improve the pitiful life of the land workers. The foulness of what I saw, and the manner in which the squire dismissed the Doctor's demand that the dwellings should be much repaired or replaced, stirred my blood to the point where I too spoke out. The road was much neglected and there were dust and ashes everywhere, and the thatch upon all of the clay cottages was torn and rotten and overgrown with weeds, and in a few cases almost open to the sky. We visited all of the hovels one by one, and in each we found souls stricken with sickness. Three people, two of them children, had died in the days before the pastor, the Reverend Proctor, had ridden to the Rectory to declare his fear that the cause may be typhus or cholera and not the common fever. In one house we found a woman holding a dead infant before a wretched fire that she was trying to keep alight. The window was broken and patched with rags, rain was falling down the chimney, and the room was full of smoke. In another place we counted ten people in the two rooms, there being two families living there, and in all the dwellings the walls were cracked and stained with damp. Some people, several of them children, were stricken with cramps and crying, while others were all but taken by the fever and were lying still. At the end of it the Doctor's exhaustion was most apparent, but his anger would not allow him to sleep before he had made his opinions regarding the state of the houses well known both to the parish and the medical board. His views on this occasion, and, indeed, many others, made him unpopular with a considerable number of landowners and farmers, but he would not forbear, declaring openly his support for the new Association for the Defence of the Rights of the Poor, and also any workers who organised themselves to seek better circumstances for themselves and their families.

During the years before my marriage to Jacob I learned much about the treatment of illnesses, and of what the Doctor called the worst malady of a society, where the distance between the classes was the breeding ground of so much persecution. It was his habit to come into the kitchen garden or wherever Nan or I could be found and to speak out to the ceiling or the clouds, venting his delight or deep frustration at something, whether it be an article in the Norfolk News, or correspondence from either a supporter or detractor.

There was one matter, a long endeavour on his part to persuade one goodly but unbending magistrate farmer to build a school for his workers" children, that serves well to illustrate his toil. When, finally, his arguments were accepted and the gentleman did indeed pay for the building of a school, it was so ill attended because the parents of the children continued to send them to work on the land. The building was there, but so too was the farmer's need of child labour and the parents" need of money. This situation was not helped at all because there began at that time a crisis regarding the dropping value of wheat, leading farmers to cut the wages of workers, something that in part prompted many to gather in Dereham in a protest that quickly turned riotous. I recall seeing many people walking along the road past Swanton Rectory and they confirmed to us that they were travelling to a meeting. We also were aware, for Dr Brazington had read to us from the newspaper in his normal manner, that the workers had also been much enraged by the enclosure of the heaths, a great injustice that prevented commoners from keeping animals. The Doctor decided to travel behind them to witness this, refusing my request that I might accompany him, and on his return that night he told of how the crowd had quickly erupted into violence and he was forced to seek shelter in the home of another doctor, Dr Chinery, where that afternoon and evening the two physicians had to tend to many injured people.

Such a life of medicine for one so blessed with a deep conscience and a readiness and determination to both act and speak out might be considered a certain path to despair, and indeed there were days when he seemed to bear the world upon his shoulders. But Dr Brazington's character is such that he will never be bowed for long, and every positive matter, however small, will charge him with renewed optimism and inspire another outpouring of letters, some of which he would dictate to me. If, however, no encouragement was forthcoming for a time, such as occurred during the bleak year of the riots, then he would take himself off and seek it through his study of nature, and, as was often the case, if I was not with him when he encountered something rare or delightful it was his habit to return and take me to it. As with his letters I was also called upon on occasions to write down the Doctor's observations in his nature journals, for he would jest that I had a steadier hand and he liked to discuss and then dictate his thoughts as he paced his study holding his notebook. This joy at nature had such importance, and following his joining of a new Norfolk society of naturalists there came to the Rectory a succession of the most interesting and like-minded people. I can say with all honesty that these were moments of my greatest contentment and learning in the years following Constance's marriage.

That time saw other changes at Swanton Rectory, for Ella was herself married, having very much fallen in love with a young man called Nathan Brindid who was apprenticed to the smith in the village and who would come to bring the shoes for the horses. Their friendship was an amusement to us all, for neither seemed able to speak when they saw the other, and it was Nan who finally broke this silence when she instructed Ella to fetch Nathan from the village because, falsely, Mr Blyth was not feeling well and therefore needed his assistance.

So there came another maid to the Rectory, a woman from the village with the name Edith whom the good doctor had treated for a fever and whose brother kept the general store. She was known to us all and, though much different from quiet Ella, it proved an uneventful change. Ella was a constant visitor and when she had children they too became well known to us.

Throughout this time dear Jacob continued to call on his journeys, and we all took delight in listening to his stories and learning of the things he had seen and done. I confess I grew to hold him in the highest affection, but not being certain of his thoughts and also being so settled in my life at the Rectory, I could not conceive of there being any more than a special friendship. That he should, last year, ask me to walk with him to Two Bridges and thereupon say that it may be his last journey to the west, and then to declare his love and to seek for me to agree to marry him, came upon me like a bolt from the heavens and sent me into a turmoil of joy and uncertainty.

118

He said that he had secured a small marshman's house for rent and that there was now regular work upon a wherry so that he could provide for me.

Jacob continued to Lincolnshire the following day, promising to return within the month when he would seek my answer. When I told Nan of this she said she was not at all surprised, for it had been obvious to her for some considerable time that Jacob's visits had not been inspired by her cooking alone or, indeed, the questionable comfort of the stable. She asked if I had advised Dr Brazington of this, and I said I was uncertain how to attempt it. Nan then told me that he too was aware of Jacob's intentions, as they had discussed it, and while the possibility of my leaving had clearly somewhat shaken him at first, he was also much delighted for me. So I entered his study, where he had first welcomed me to his house so many years before, and we talked of what such a marriage might mean for us all. I told him that I had not seen any life for me other than at Swanton Rectory, where I so willingly and happily fulfilled all manner of tasks, not least supporting him in his endeavours. He looked so kindly upon me and said that although it was another very significant change in their lives, it was, in his firm opinion, a wonderful moment for me and he would willingly and most happily give his blessing should I decide to marry Jacob. He said that he considered Jacob to be among the sincerest of men, and although there was some uncertainty of what lay before me, he entreated me to follow my heart.

We were to talk at much length during the weeks before Jacob's return, the doctor stating most clearly that all would be well at the Rectory and that I should not consider his own situation at all; yet, in all honesty, I was unclear on my answer for some while. Perhaps this was due in part to the familiarity and security of my surroundings and Jacob's absence once again, a normal circumstance. But more than all it was the concept of forsaking such strong attachments. It seemed *impossible to reconcile, yet this eased with every passing day. When Jacob returned I was certain and, with Dr Brazington's blessing, agreed most readily to be married.*

So it is that I come to be sitting in our cottage writing these words. I have done the Doctor's bidding and told both of who I am and the path of my life. Now I may keep my journal.

11

Jess sits on the garden bench in the morning sun, shielded from the east wind, her head tilted back against the wall. Her eyes are closed and her hands nurse an empty mug on her lap. Francis's transcript of the journal lies beside her. She can feel the warmth through the long T-shirt she has been sleeping in and her bare skin tingles. She opens her eyes and shades them with a hand to follow a line of noisy geese flying high above the reeds, then closes them again and takes a long deep breath. She thinks she may take the dinghy out again today, going on from the shop to explore the far quiet corner of the broad where she has seen several swans feeding. But first she must eat. She stands and stretches, then freezes. She can hear a car, definitely a car, getting closer. She walks to the corner of the house and listens again. It is bumping down the track. She dashes round to the back door, shuts it behind her, and waits. There is the crunch of tyres on shingle. The engine stops.

Jess creeps to the kitchen window and peers out. It's Gordon's old car.

121

He's getting out and, God, Rudi's with him. She pulls back and hides, panting.

She hears Rudi say, "You wait with the car, Gordon. She may still be in bed."

Jess looks round in a panic, then hurriedly puts on her coat. There is a knock at the door that makes her jump. Then another knock. She takes a deep breath and opens it.

"Hello, Jessica."

Rudi is standing there, round-shouldered, tired, smiling, leaning on his stick.

"May I come in?"

Jess moves back, a look of shock and puzzlement on her face.

"W...why are you here? I thought..."

"Meant to give you something, and I've brought you this." He lifts his violin case a few inches. "It's mine. Not as fine as the one you played, but it has a good voice. I thought you might want to work again, and I figured a week was long enough without an instrument."

Jess takes it and puts it on the table. She reaches for a towel thrown over the back of a chair to dry, but Rudi lays his stick on her arm.

"Leave it. Glad to see it. Now then," he turns, "I think it's much too nice to be in here. Let's go round onto the grass, shall we?"

He shuffles out. Jess looks at the washing-up piled in the sink and the full ashtray beside it. She pushes her fingers into her hair and pulls at it, pressing her temples with her fists. Then she follows him. Outside she looks sideways at Gordon, who is standing by the car. He smiles nervously and raises a hand. She blanks him. He lied.

Rudi is in the middle of the lawn, eyes shut, his head tilted back, smiling at the sky. She waits beside him, then he turns and calls for Gordon to come and help them.

"Would you be so kind as to lift the bench away from the cottage, help him, would you, Jessica? And carry it down to the staithe."

They walk slowly towards the lip of the lawn. Rudi taps the grass with the point of his stick.

"Somewhere here. Ah, there's one. There're some old bricks set in the lawn. Francis put them there. Stops the bench legs sinking. And the other one is just there."

Gordon offers to make tea. Rudi tells him to bring some cushions. They watch him go, then sit down.

"So good to be here." Rudi says softly. "Thank you."

"Thank you?"

"Yes, Jessica. Thanks to you. If you hadn't have come I may never have come here again. Until I am dead."

"But I'm going soon."

"Are you, are you really?"

"Yes. There was no need for you to have come all this way with my violin. I don't need it."

Gordon comes out with two cushions from the lounge, arranges them for Rudi, then trots back to the cottage again. Rudi pats Jess's arm.

"That's not the main reason why I came."

They fall silent and gaze out across the broad.

"We'd sit here for hours, you know," Rudi says finally, "watching the dragonflies dance. Reading. Not talking much. Drinking on occasions."

Jess stares at Otter. Her cover has come loose.

"Glad You've got the dinghy down. Take it You've got the hang of the outboard. Oars are best though. Peace. You really must. Wonderful late evening, or early morning..." Rudi's voice falls away. He is still looking out across the reeds to the open water.

"Francis would row. He'd make a nest of cushions in the back of the boat for me and then we would drift, dreaming, eating chocolate, or drinking a bottle of wine, or dozing, sometimes until the sun had dipped below the horizon. One time, not long before he fell ill," Rudi lifts his stick to point and then lets it drop again, "we were out there. I just said it. I said "I don't need you. You understand, don't you? I don't need you, Francis". Well, Francis put down his book, looked at me, smiled, and said "That's wonderful. It means that you choose to be with me". He understood. He always did." Rudi falters, whispers. "Came here after he died. Stayed for nearly a month. Thought it would be a comfort. Even thought I could move here. But I couldn't cope on my own. Not on my own."

Jess turns her head and looks at Rudi. There are tears in his eyes. She puts her hand on top of his. He closes his eyes and lifts his face as if scenting the air.

Gordon returns with a small camping table and folding chair, then fetches the tray of tea. He sits to the side of them and pours. They say nothing, drinking the tea in silence, looking out onto the reeds and water.

Gordon gets up again and says he wants to check the car's oil level. "Got to keep a close eye on it. It needs topping up regularly. I...I'll just be over there, so call if you need anything, all right?"

Jess watches him go.

"Rudi..."

"I'm glad You've settled, Jessica. I was worried you'd be unable to relax here. It's not really a holiday cottage."

"No."

"More like being in someone's home, I suppose."

"Yes."

"I didn't want that if it made you uncomfortable. Yet there is a deep sense of Francis here."

"Yes."

"I know how deeply you loved him too."

Jess feels like being in a timeless dream world, but one that can't last. All she says is, "Maybe I shouldn't stay any longer."

"Why? You've been here a week. Surely..."

"I don't know. I honestly don't know."

"You like it, though, don't you?"

"Yes."

Rudi twists his face towards Jess and looks at her anxiously.

"Glad you came?"

"Yes. Yes, I'm glad I came. You're right. It's a very special place. Very beautiful. But I'm not sure I should be here."

"So what would you do, Jessica? Go home? To what, mmm? Stay a little longer. Give it time. A little more time." Rudi looks away again. "And, well, there are some things I would like you to do for me. Things that need time. You see, there's a piece of music, wonderful music. Herbert Howells. It's just come to light after seventy years. Can you believe that? Amazing. Anyway, I want you to look at it. Tell me what you think. Not many people know about it yet. Only a few of us."

Jess lets the words sink in. "What is it?"

"*Three Dances*. For violin and orchestra. Written when he was a student in 1915. Performed once and then locked away. It was forgotten. It's breathtakingly fresh and alive, Jessica, and I suddenly thought I'd show it to you; that you might appreciate it here. Written with his native

Gloucestershire in mind but fits somehow, I think. I'm seriously interested to know if you like it."

"But Rudi..."

"I've brought my violin, and Suzy kindly helped by packing some more of your things. Please forgive us. Oh please, please. And don't be angry with Suzy. She just wants you to have a vital time, a break. She made me promise to give you her love. And, you know, coming today, I know for sure now that this is right. Francis will love you being here, that there is life again at the cottage. It has waited far too long to be lived in again. And I sense that a little time here will be so good for you, Jessica. Time to gather your thoughts about what you think of it."

"I don't understand."

"I mean to give it to you."

Jess looks at Rudi open-mouthed.

"If you want it."

She is speechless. She looks round her, and then again at Rudi, her expression and mind a muddle of shock and confused thoughts.

"Just think about it, Jessica. Don't hurry. Please don't hurry. We all need space, nature, a chance to breathe."

Rudi starts to push himself up off the bench and Jess moves quickly to support him. They walk slowly back round to the car. Gordon shuts the bonnet of the Morris when he sees them and wipes his hands clean on a rag.

"Oh," Rudi suddenly turns and makes his way towards the back door where Gordon has left a case. "One other thing."

He disappears inside, returning a few minutes later with the photograph and poem from the bathroom under his arm.

"The real reason for my journey."

He eases himself gingerly into the passenger seat.

"The music, by the way, is in the violin case."

The swans circle the little boat as it rocks in the rippling shallows. Jess sits still watching them as she glides slowly towards the bank of reeds. The cottage looks a long way away across the rough water and a few dark clouds are hurrying by above it on the pastel blue sky. She is far beyond the channel posts that are lined across the broad. The nearest boat, a yacht tacking into the east wind and which keeps heading towards her, never strays far into the vastness of the shallower water. The dinghy settles against the reeds that hiss softly in the breeze. Jess leans, and beneath the shiny surface of the murky water she can see the pattern of weed. Her mind continues to drift. As she tears pieces from one of the loaves she has just bought and throws them out onto the water, she feels that familiar numbness, but not with the ache in the pit of her stomach. "Did Rudi really say that? Does he really mean it? He must do, he must. But do I want this? Do I? Yes, maybe I do. Maybe. It's so strange. I don't know. I don't know."

Ducks hurry along the reed edge to join the feeding. One of the swans grows impatient and stretches its neck into the boat, tapping with its beak at the crumbs on the wooden seat beside her. Jess hurriedly tears at the bread, throws all of it out as far as she can, then uses one of the oars to push the dinghy away from the reeds, far enough to start the outboard.

There is a note wedged behind a jar labelled "APPLE CHUTNEY 1987" standing on the mat in the porch.

"Michael rang. All's well, but asks that you ring. Should catch him about six tomorrow. Come for a cuppa then. Welcome to stay for a bite. Margaret."

Jess tops up the Rayburn with coal, brings logs to the wood-burner in the lounge, and lights it. She pours a drink, runs a bath, and lies there listening to the wind building outside, her mind a muddle of thoughts. She pads through to the kitchen, makes a sandwich of cheese and pickle, and sits eating in front of the Rayburn, her bare feet on the warm rail. The light outside has suddenly gone. She smokes. A heavy squall sweeps by, rain drops knocking gently at the windows. She flops her head sideways and looks at Rudi's violin case.

It rains all night and for much of the next day, but by late afternoon it has stopped. The track is slippery. Head down, Jess picks her way carefully between the puddles until she finds herself standing next to a white picket gate in front of an old farmhouse. There are three worn stone steps up to the gate that is set in an old flint and red brick wall. She climbs the steps. The gravel path leading to the dark blue front door is lined with box hedges and the squares of lush grass on either side are surrounded by deep borders of flowers and shrubs. The garden, about the size of a tennis court, is protected by the wall and is detached from the track and wilderness in front of it and the rough hedgerows to the sides.

Jess decides not to open the gate. She drops back down to the track, walks to the corner of the wall, and then turns on a muddy concrete drive that leads to the back of the house. A muddle of farm buildings gives off the scent and sound of cattle. There is a light on in the barn. Heavy steel gates and fences section the space between the buildings, and a dark trail of hoof marks and straw converges at the entrance to a long, lower building on the left. At the far end of the yard there's an open-ended shelter with slatted sides, and the black and white faces of the milking herd look back at her. She walks round the corner of the house to where a muddy Land Rover and old Volvo estate are parked close to the back wall. A light springs on and dogs start barking.

"Can I help you?"

A man in blue overalls and flat cap steps out of the long building.

"I'm Jessica, from..."

"Oh, right." The man raises his hand. "I'm Phil. Go in now. I'm nearly done here an" I'll be over. Margaret's inside."

128

Phil Bunn turns and disappears into the low building.

The door behind Jess opens a fraction and Margaret's flushed face peers round, smiling. There is the sound of scratching and a struggle.

"Come in! I've got the dogs. They won't hurt you."

Jess pushes the door open and Margaret is holding Biba and another older black Labrador by their collars. She is in a large lobby lined with coats, boots, and hats. The dogs are wagging their tails, pulling hard to get to Jess.

"Shut the door, then I can let these pickles go. You know Biba, of course. And this old girl is Tammy, her mum. Now come on, you two. Bed now. Bed!"

The dogs greet Jess, then obediently go and sit on a large blanket against the wall.

"They're soft as fudge, but make a noise if someone's about, which is important. Wouldn't hurt anyone. Lick you to death more like. Hang your coat up there."

Jess follows her through into a huge kitchen with a long refectory table and a range on the inside wall like the one at the cottage but far bigger.

"Coffee?"

"No. Thank you."

"Tea?"

"It's almost five and..."

"Oh, have something. How about a nip of something a little stronger? Have a drop of Irish. Yes?"

Jess smiles. She feels at ease with Margaret.

Margaret walks down a hall towards the large front door and turns left into a room.

"Come through!"

An old brown-and-white spaniel lies sprawled in the middle of the sitting room sound asleep. Margaret is standing behind a large floral sofa by a dark oak sideboard, pouring a whiskey.

"Irish. Can't beat it. That's Charlie Boy, by the way, the old man. We let him in here now for a bit of peace and quiet away from those two. Knocking on fourteen, which is good going for a Springer. Deaf as a post, though, and his eyesight's going too, bless him, poor old boy. But he's happy. Been a bloody good dog. Oh, mind my French. The family reckon I swear far too much, but I'm a bit long in the tooth to change."

Margaret turns with the glass in her hand.

"A little early, but what the heck. You're on holiday. Sit yourself down here now."

She puts the glass on the table beside an armchair, next to a telephone and lamp.

"Quieter in here. Be as long as you like now."

Jess sits for a moment, drinks, and stares at the phone. Then dials.

"Michael?"

"Mum? Hi. You OK? How are things? Is everything OK?"

"Fine. You? How was your trip?"

"Really good, actually. Good audiences, and we did OK I think."

"Good."

"Thanks for ringing back, Mum. Margaret sounds lovely."

"Yes. She is."

"So what's going on? I think it's wonderful You've got away for a while. The place sounds amazing. Rudi had left a message on my phone and I popped round to see him this morning. He's looking much worse, don't you think?"

"Yes. So, tell me about America. I want to hear."

Jess sits half listening, looking round the high-ceilinged room. There is a large painting above the fireplace, a hunting scene with people in red coats on horseback charging across a field with a pack of dogs racing ahead of them. Beneath it, on the mantlepiece, there is a carriage clock and several framed photographs, some black and white. She can make out a bride, possibly Margaret. Yes, definitely Margaret. Phil is there beside her. She looks so small against him. They look so happy. Then Jess sees the seed of those expressions in the faces on other photographs, of people who must be their children and relatives. There is a black upright piano against the wall behind the door. The leather seat of the stool, partly hidden behind one of the two fat floral armchairs that face the fire, is cracked with age. Her gaze slides to look at the brass door handle, then the ceiling rose. She feels the deep carpet with her toes. The whiskey is warm in her throat. The scrawny dog's stomach slowly rises and falls. Only some of what Michael is saying sinks in. He's been away for three weeks. New York. Boston. Syracuse. Her old world.

"But, Mum, guess what?" "What?"

"We're coming up to Norfolk at the beginning of July. No sooner had I got back than we got a call from our agent. There's something called the Summer Classical Suite at stately homes up there and, well, The Frendle had to cancel and, to cut a long story short, we got the gig."

"That's wonderful."

"I was wondering if I, maybe all four of us, could come and see you. If you are still there, I mean."

"Um –"

Jess hestitates. She sounds negative. She doesn't want to sound negative. Not to Michael.

"Er, yes – yes of course. If I'm still here. Where are you playing?" "Somewhere called Bembroke Hall."

"Where?"

"Bembroke Hall. Have you heard of it?"

"Yes. Yes I have."

"I looked it up on the map. About thirty miles away from where you are, along the coast, isn't it?"

"Don't know. It was just mentioned in something I'm reading, that's all."

"They want Dvorak's *American Quartet* which, of course, we've just been playing, so when the Frendle Quartet had to pull out for whatever reason, someone suggested us. We get to stay in the hall and everything. Apparently there's a large chapel – more like a small church – where they put on concerts. Rudi says they lay on a supper and –"

"Rudi?"

"Told me today, when I went to see him."

"Oh."

"Said he'd been going there off and on for years, ever since the Lady Crofton started the series. Knows her quite well, in fact. The place sounds intriguing."

"When is it?"

"Hang on a tick." Michael lays the phone down for a few seconds. "Got my diary. Right, Saturday, July the fifth. We were thinking we'd make a trip of it. The US thing's been great and everything, but it was knackering and things are full on through the rest of May and all of June, so we thought it would be good to plan some sort of break. We'd come up to Suffolk and stay a couple of nights with Dad at Aldeburgh, then come on up to you for a couple of nights. Thursday and Friday if that's OK. Margaret has kindly offered to put the guys up and I could crash on the sofa with you. If you're not there then we'll stay on at Aldeburgh. What d'you think?"

Jess agrees. They talk a little more. Michael says he hasn't seen his father for a few months either, so it would be good to spend a little time with him too and maybe catch up with some old mates as well. Jess half listens again. She thinks about Aldeburgh and that little townhouse where Michael grew up without her; the big bay windows with the flaking paint that look out across the shingle where, on the rare occasions early on when she found any courage to visit him, they would sit and look at the sea; the cycles in the hall; their lives; the smell of the salt air; the way it hurt to be there. She thinks about Tom; always gentle, always careful with his words; urging her to visit them more; how he moved out of London all those years ago when he took the job at the Britten Pears School at Snape. That safe job, that safe, sensible place to raise their son. And he's still there, still there, long after Michael has grown and left.

Michael and Jess say their goodbyes. She puts the phone down, empties the glass, then sits for a moment more, feeling the alcohol run through her.

She goes through to the kitchen. Phil is leaning against the sink, mug in hand. He stops talking in mid sentence, steps forward and greets her warmly. Margaret is bending over in front of the range, taking a large pot out of the oven. The table is laid for three. They make her sit with them. Phil's accent is like Graham's at the boatyard, and he urges Jess to stay and eat. Margaret lifts the lid of the casserole on the table and smiles at her. They push past her uncertainty. Phil opens a bottle of wine. They eat the beef casserole with large flour cakes floating in it, which they tell her are Norfolk dumplings. Then there is apple crumble and coffee. Their manner is relaxed and easy. Jess listens as they discuss the herd and their children, planning the next day. Jess asks where David is. Margaret says he's staying with a friend. Jess helps to dry the dishes, then they sit again at the table with coffee.

"Heard you playin' this morning."

"Phil!"

Margaret glares at her husband. They had agreed no questions, no probing, just let her be.

"What? Oh, give over woman."

Phil looks at Jess again.

"Don't mind me asking do you? Only I'd like to know what it was. Crack of dawn. Was walking the dogs round the far meadow, came back down the ol' track and heard you playin'. Bewtiful. I stood awhile. Really, really bewtiful."

Jess glances down into her coffee, then looks at them both anxiously.

"It's by Herbert Howells, *Three Dances* by Herbert Howells."

Jess had looked at the music then gone to bed. But she couldn't sleep, so got up and started playing the *Dances*, again and again, until dawn. She had then slept all morning and half the afternoon.

"Only I'd like to get it."

"Leave it now, Phil. We'll get it sometime."

There is a moment of loud silence. Jess wonders what to say, then remembers a question.

"Where – where's Gressenhall?"

Phil looks puzzled. "Thas a fair ol' hike. Dereham thereabouts. Why?"

"Because …" Margaret leans back in her chair and smiles at Jess "You're reading Anna's journal, aren't you?"

12

Today I ventured with Jacob in a small boat to meet his uncle aboard the Duchess, whereby he left me by some meadows to return alone, learning as I must the art of the oars. It took some time, for my progress was slowed not only by my being a novice, but also by my wonder, for it was a journey through a wildflower garden with the faint scent of what seemed like new-mown hay upon the air. I stopped repeatedly to make sketches and notes of some of what I could see, and to watch butterflies, black and yellow swallowtails and red admirals, fluttering over the lovely flowering rush. The birdsong rose from every quarter and the sky was full of species of all sizes and colours. Cattle were feeding on the marshes, along with hundreds of rooks and jackdaws, and above the soft songs of the warblers there came the harsh call of the cock pheasants.

My journey home was also much delayed due to a most

unusual encounter. I was suddenly taken with the idea of following the channel which Jacob had said opened out onto a pool of water known as Duck Broad, and I had just passed the opening of a dyke when I saw an animal in the water carrying something within its mouth. I was most excited, because I could make out readily enough that it was an otter. It climbed into the reeds to devour its meal of a large eel, so I turned the boat as best I could and approached a little to observe it. It was then that I noticed the smallest of huts with a little chimney that was locked in the reeds just inside the dyke, from which a fearsome elderly man with a large grey beard appeared holding a gun and with the aspect of someone intent on murder. On seeing me he lowered the gun and shouted angrily at the otter that he would have it "afore long". He studied me awhile, then called to me. I could not understand what he was asking, so approached the dyke a little, whereby my clumsiness with the oars made him roar with laughter. He asked if I was Jacob's wife and I told him I was, and he shouted that he was his friend and beckoned for me to come on, for he was making tea before he went to bed. Jacob had mentioned this person called Pip, and that he worked as an eel catcher, so I continued, somewhat intrigued to learn a little more. As I drew closer I could now see that the boat was all but drawn out of the water upon the bank, and there ran from it into the river a line that sank beneath the surface. Beyond it there were some posts with nets hanging from them, and there was another boat, long and narrow, with small oars. The man lay down his gun and tied my boat to the rear of the boat with the hut upon it, then he rubbed his hands down his rough jacket before helping me to climb out. His face was all but covered with white whiskers and a brown hat was pulled down on his head almost to his eyes, which quite sparkled at our meeting. There were large gaps in his teeth, and his back was a little bowed, but he moved with extraordinary swiftness and agility for one so old, moving various possessions aside so that I might find it easier to stand. There was rope and netting, and also a fearsome-looking pole of some length, the end of which had four long barbed teeth.

He beckoned me into his warm hut, which was most cramped, much like a shepherd's night dwelling, and told me to sit at the far end upon a locker that clearly served as a bed. Beside it was a little round stove on which a kettle was almost boiling. I looked round me as he fetched his gun and hung it from a pair of leather slings hanging from the roof beside an open cupboard containing crockery, bread, some bottles, and several jars of fish that most likely was pickled bream. All manner of things were hanging from the walls too, including lines fixed with hooks, a pan, another hat, some clothes for rain, and a pair of long marsh boots such as Jacob owned. On another smaller locker facing me was some sort of sail undergoing repair and a large wicker-bound bottle.

It proved a most enlightening hour, for this man Pip told me of his work catching eels, and I learned a little of the art. He said he used something called setts, close-knit nets with openings into pods from which the eels cannot escape, and also lines with hooks, and it was from the latter that the otter had taken his breakfast. On a good night the eel catcher might take ten to fifteen stones, which he would carry to Potter for sale, but he lamented that the eels seemed to be less and less. I wondered if there was some new obstruction or other reason why the eels were not making their way in such great numbers along the rivers, for I told him that it was the opinion of naturalists that all eels were bred in the sea. He dismissed this as nonsense, saying they were bred out of the mud. Then, in whispered tones, said it was a fact that if you chopped horsehair, and this was cast into the river, it would turn into eels.

He complained, too, of the changes that were besetting the

marshes, for the wind and steam draining mills were turning the bogs into green pasture and the creatures were not to be found in anything like the number he remembered from his youth. He was clearly intelligent and observant and said with some bitterness how there was once a swamp at Horsey where many thousands of black-headed gulls nested every summer and the eggs were easy to harvest, but that the land was now dry grass. Nor too were the marshes still swarming with grebes, ruffs, bitterns, and avocets, a fact that he attributed also to the great increase in guns, for the fowlers were now better armed and far more in number. There were, also, he warned, some people afloat who were not watermen but rather yachtsmen from other parts like London, and that there were more and more of these pleasure trips, but that the north river where we sat was the quietest and that I was to promise not to tell a soul of its beauty. I left him with three fresh silver eels in my boat and as I made my way out into the main river he called to me to tell Jacob to show me how to get a line and to "bab" for them, whatever that was.

This meeting made me wonder yet more about these people of the wetland, for I am taken with a real sense that they and their distinct way of life, like their watery world, are diminishing, and it is already clear to me that it is a subject as worthy of study as the creatures we live among.

It is close to nightfall now and the mist is rising from the water. Jacob returns tomorrow when I shall tell him of my encounter and ask him the meaning of this word "to bab".

Now I may relay it, for last night was still and dry and we took to the boat in the darkness to attempt this babbing. Jacob had instructed me to find my darning needle and to dig for worms within the garden, ten or a dozen large ones, and this I had done in the course of my caring for our small crop of vegetables by the time he returned from his labours repainting

138

the Duchess. After we had eaten some broth and bread, he then cut some worsted wool and threaded this with the needle through the centre of the creatures before gathering them all into a ball which he tied firmly to a line, which in turn he secured to a stick. I was much amused and suggested that surely there was a need for hooks of some kind, but he merely tapped the side of his nose, lit a lantern, and led me to the boat. We rowed a little to enter the channel, and then he told me to lower the bunch of worms to the bottom and then to bab, meaning to bob, it gently up and down. Sure enough, within moments there was a strong tug upon the line and I pulled, but whatever it was had gone. Jacob told me to repeat this, but not to pull so hard, rather to lift the bunch of worms gently out of the water once it was clear an eel was feeding on them. This I did and to my joy a small eel emerged hanging from the line, its teeth entangled in the cloth. We continued for half an hour and I caught a further two which we will feast on tomorrow.

As for my meeting with Pip, Jacob was much delighted that I had encountered him, saying he was a former wherryman and reedcutter, but that the work had become too painful for his old bones, especially in the bitter winter months. He also told me that it was Pip who first took him aboard a wherry, the Diligent, to Yarmouth, when he was very young and still too weak to be of much assistance, and that he had slept in the hold that was loaded with many things, including fleeces, awaking to find himself in that noisy port.

It was a journey he was never likely to forget, for Pip had been the skipper and the hand was Snowball Wester, so called on account of being born on Christmas Day, and the two men had taken him to an alehouse. Pip and Jacob had returned to the Diligent and began to sleep when they were woken by shouts. This Snowball, it seems, was prone to fighting and had taken too much drink when he fell into dispute with a fisherman. He was injured with a knife and had been taken on a cart to the hospital, where they found him the following day with a bandaged arm and side, and a face that was barely recognisable as that of Snowball. It meant that Jacob, though still a boy, had to work as the hand upon the Diligent, helping first to unload the cargo and then to stock her again with timber bound for the new roof of Stackholm Church and to sail her back along the north river. He said that Pip, although his beard had long since turned white, undertook the lion's share of this labour and would leave Jacob to try and steady the large rudder while he raised and lowered the vast black sail. Pip had to do the quanting too, forcing the wherry on against the wind on the occasions when a turn in the river meant it was not with them. Quanting required lancing the heavy pole into the muddy bed of the river by the mast, and toiling back to the rudder, pushing with all his might, the pole pressed into his shoulder. I had seen Jacob doing this on the Duchess and it seemed dreadful toil to move a laden boat so large, even for a younger man.

I asked Jacob how old Pip must be, and he said it was not known, but that Pip would remark that at the turning of the century he was of an age to recall it quite clearly, and that he knew of the earliest victories of Lord Nelson.

I have asked Jacob if I might journey with him aboard the Duchess at some time, and he has promised to raise the matter with his uncle. I know that I will be of no use to them regarding the managing of the wherry itself, so it is bound to be a short journey, but I would be able to prepare food for them. I have yet to place a foot upon the boat, and have no idea how I may find it, but I suspect that it will be most enjoyable. And already I am wondering what it might be like to travel to Yarmouth in this way and, finally, to see that place that Constance and I so often talked of.

13

Jess reads and plays the violin.

She lies in the bath looking out at the yellow irises. She puts cushions in the dinghy and rows to the swans.

She sleeps late, then lies still, listening to the birdsong on the wind.

She wanders, leans on gates and watches cattle grazing on meadows. She sees the baby calves grow.

She walks further and further through the maze of meadows and ditches peppered with poppies.

She picks wild flowers, for the kitchen, the lounge and the bedroom.

Anna's Journal and *Three Dances* merge like the days and the weeks and take over her dreams

14

What wonder I found this day to ease my loneliness. Not so long after first light I made my way to the bank at the point where the river flows into the broad and where, close by, I have been studying the nests of reed warblers. It is, without question, one of my favourite places, for I have found an area of dry grass beneath a small oak, bent by the north wind, and this place affords me also a fine view of the river where I may observe both the creatures and the people upon the water. I confess I have not, for this one day, made my way to the Ferry Boat Inn to carry on my duties of cleaning and washing, for the work is without pleasure and I do not choose to suffer further the insults of some of those there. The decision may prove to be of some cost, for it is not the first time, but I do not care. I shall tell Jacob and make clear to him my hopes that I may soon be rewarded for my efforts in assisting Mr Caleb

Prior within the village school by gaining some employment there.

I was seated beneath my tree reflecting on this when there came close by an empty reed raft making its way into the warmth of the new sun, and I could see two people upon it. I waved, as I am often inclined to do, and on seeing me they turned their boat and came close, calling. They were both quite young, and I then noticed that the woman had in her arms a tiny infant. They asked if I was seeking to travel along the river, for they were making their way to Horsey to collect hay, and without any thought I said yes, for though I had no plans to do so the idea held great appeal.

I have been alone for some time, for the Duchess has once more made her way to Yarmouth to carry hay for the animals of that port and to return with the usual cargo of timber, and again there has been some cause to delay them. As for myself, I have given up all thoughts of travelling there, for Jacob's uncle, Mr Nealon, persists in refusing to allow me aboard the Duchess. It is some years now that I have ceased to petition Jacob, for he said his uncle had been at sea for many years upon the trawlers and was strongly of the view that for a woman to step upon the wherry would bring ill fortune. This is a nonsense and uncommon, for I know of two women who work the wherries with their husbands, and have seen families aboard them too. Yet, should he relent, I would not choose to go. He is a most unpleasant man, the like of whom I have seen within the Inn, for without drink he is of little humour and few words, yet when his prodigious thirst takes him he can shake the air with his voice and spout the foulest utterances. On first seeing him he seemed kindly enough, for he has an expression of one smiling, but I quickly learned that this is his habit and not a happiness. I was first taken by his appearance also, for the pork pie hat flattening his ears, and his red and white neck scarf, collarless shirt rolled to the elbows, and his blue trouser braces were somewhat comical, but I have long since tired of it. The fact that he is regarded as one of the cleverest wherry skippers is of no consequence, for his determination to work on when others might not, be it at night or in the coldest of weather, may please the Duchess's owners, the timber merchant Mr Ernest Cherry and his brother, the farmer Mr William Cherry, our landlord, but it means a dreadful life for Jacob, who has no say in it.

That Jacob should call this dreadful man his uncle is because he is the husband of his dead father's sister, Winnie, a sickly and much saddened woman whose two children work with her in the marshes. I have visited her but once at her cottage close to Horsey village, when Jacob rowed me there one cold autumn day in our first year of marriage to see the place of his birth, and I have reflected often on her misery. It has long been in my mind to visit her again, but the journey alone is too difficult for me, and Jacob has said he has no wish to labour so with the oars to a place where his work upon the Duchess often carries him. He assures me that he has visited her often, yet it is true that neither of us would choose the company of his uncle or to witness again his attitude towards Winnie. So it was that I took this journey to Horsey today and made the acquaintance of Billy and Ruby Breeze and their tiny son Albert, for whom I already hold such affection, and I had the good fortune of being able to repay their kindness by caring for him while his parents worked together loading hay. He is but a few weeks old, yet strong and bright-eyed with a contentment and smile to make me wish so hard for such a blessing for myself.

The water of Meadow Dyke was clear and I could make out below the surface the broad-leaved pond weeds. To the sides the meadow rue, willow-herb, and flowering rush were in full bloom, and the fragrance of the meadow-sweet was overpowering. With Ruby's encouragement I took pleasure *in naming some of the birds and insects we could see, and we passed some colourful wherries tied to staithes where, far off, marshmen were swinging their scythes among the long grass in the sun's glare. It was clear to us all that it was to be a very hot day, and as we came upon the large circular Mere its rippling surface sparkled with light and we fell silent with wonder. We crossed it and secured the reed raft close to a wind pump, where a blanket was laid out in its shadow and where Albert and I settled ourselves. To the north, beyond the trees shrouding the little village, I could see the long ridge of sandy marram hills standing between the country and the sea and drawing a strong sweep of gold between the blue of the sky and the green of the marshlands. There was none of the salt air I had tasted before, for the breeze was from the west.*

I had taken a little water and food with me for my time at the riverbank, and at midday, when the reed raft more resembled a small haystack, we shared our food and talked most happily. Billy and Ruby have recently taken a marshman's cottage at Hickling, and it excites me to think what further pleasures these friendships will bring. To my delight they are most content to let me accompany them again and to care for Albert, for although clearly it is to their advantage, it brings me such happiness and he is such a dear child.

There was also another meeting this day, for as Albert slept during the late morning the pump man, heavy-gaited, came along the path with a brown and white dog. He greeted Billy and I learned his name was, as he called it, "Jimma" Rudd, and that he was also in some way related to my Jacob, though exactly how he could not explain. He was of middle years, quite short and very wide, with no hair upon the top of his head but with side-whiskers that reached out some way. He had large, drowsy eyes and the habits of one who could not see well, and he carried a stick. He asked if I cared to see inside the high building with its sails just like a windmill and for him to explain the working of it. I left Albert with his parents and followed along the narrow path to the wind pump. The interior was strangely dark, and I had to take care in climbing the steep ladders which rose from one floor to the next, passing a long shaft and some large cog-wheels in which, to my horror, I was told a former millman had been crushed while staying there one dreadful night draining the flooded pasture. I also learned that the wind pump had been used as a storehouse by smugglers who ran cargoes along the coast. Had I been aware of these things before entering I might never have continued. However, the view from the top made this ascent most worthwhile and we spent some time there in discussion about all we could see.

This "Jimma" explained how the Mere had once been part of an estuary, long before the marram bank had been built to hold back the sea, and that there was then such a place as Horsea Island, spelled a little differently. He cast his arm in a large arch across the Mere and said there was a time when Roman ships floated there. Then he turned and looked at me and asked quietly if I knew of the hauntings. I said I did not. His story, if it is to be believed, is that in June there is something called Childer's Night. It was known to all thereabouts that, back in old times, Roman even, when a child died they brought the body out onto the water, weighed it down, and lowered it to the bottom of the pool. He said it was the spirits of these children that haunted the Mere, and on Childer's Night they all came to life again and for a while would sing and play.

Later that afternoon I took my leave of Billy, Ruby, and Albert for a short while once again and walked to the village to call upon Winnie, it being certain that her husband was not present. The cottage was empty, but I heard a noise from the garden and found her tending to her laundry. Even after I had called to her she hid from me behind the linen blowing in the wind, and then, when I approached, would not show her face. The reason became clear, for she bore the marks of blows. I beseeched her to talk to me, which she would not, instead becoming greatly distressed and telling me to leave. She shut me out of her cottage and so I did as she asked and made the journey back to the boat, pondering with every step what misery she must have to endure. I am so much saddened by her circumstance and will talk of it with Jacob on his return, and these thoughts continue to cloud what has otherwise been a most special of days.

For our return to Hickling it was necessary for Ruby, Albert, and me to perch quite precariously upon the bow, from where we could guide Billy, whose vision was completely blocked by the mass of hay. The sun was about to set when I was back alone upon the bank beside the oak tree. The light is all but gone now and I am suddenly taken with a heavy tiredness. I will to bed and pray that my Jacob returns tomorrow.

It is, perhaps, most unwise of me to tell of what has happened, but I must be truthful. Also, writing of all matters in this journal has become so important, a habitual undertaking for me that I cannot leave this matter unrecorded. So I will write it.

Mr Nealon is dead and I am thankful for it.

Six months have now passed and it would not have been possible to imagine the changes that have now come upon us. We have long since stopped wondering if the Excisemen will come, for everyone seems to accept Jacob's account that his uncle drowned in an accident and was taken by the Mere. Although I am certain there are some who know otherwise, none has spoken openly of it, for Mr Nealon was much disliked. While my Jacob is blameless with regard to his death, he could not admit to knowing of what occurred, for it would certainly lead to his imprisonment. For my part, although it now lifts my heart to see him as the master of the Duchess and for me to be able to journey with him, I was so much angered to hear of the dangers and labours which that most dreadful man placed upon my husband that I gave thanks for his undoing. I had long suspected that all that was taken upon the Duchess was not legal, yet I did not know of the extent to which this illicit trade was carried on.

It was in February when Jacob came home in the night, himself almost dead with cold and wet, having swum the water before making his way as fast as he could across the marshes from Kelder's Dyke. The Duchess had been placed in a channel in the reeds, for his uncle had arranged a usual meeting with smugglers. The men were much delayed, while his uncle had grown quite' drunk, and when they finally appeared out of the darkness, a disagreement began. Jacob said he leapt into the rushes when he saw the drawing of a knife, returning only when he was sure the men had left, to find his uncle dead upon the wherry. With good sense he decided to weight the body with stones and sink it in the Mere, for all other explanations other than drowning rightly seemed impossible. He then toiled to clean all traces of blood and to move the wherry out onto a staithe where it might normally be found, and then made his way home.

Jacob has told me that it was his uncle's habit to run goods such as gin, brandy, tobacco, and tea, all off-loaded illegally from ships at Yarmouth and hidden beneath her regular cargo of timber. These tubs of gin and packs of tobacco would then continue their journey from Horsey down the river Thurne as the wherry undertook other work on the wetland, stowed beneath reed for houses, or hay for animals. The habit was to moor up for the night in the same place on the Bure, where the goods were passed to wagons and taken to Norwich. It was a most dangerous undertaking, and one carried out without any regard for Jacob's wishes or well-being.

As for Aunt Winnie, she has been given shelter by the Parson who was in need of a housekeeper, and her countenance has much changed. It pleases me, also, to write that Jacob has taken Billy as his mate upon the Duchess and that, all being well, I may join them soon on the journey to Yarmouth.

This cottage continues to be filled with the sounds of children, for as well as visits from those in my care at the school, young Albert is now almost four years and so full of life.

15

Now. Now would be a good time. Michael studies his mother. She is leaning back, her arm lying along the tiller as Otter sails gently down the centre of the broad. Jess is calmer than he has seen her for such a long time, her face smiling into the sun as she keeps glancing up the sails.

"I went to the Cape."

Jess looks at him for a second. They both take some deep breaths.

"It's beautiful. Like here."

"Yes. It is."

"I was only there for a half a day, but ended up walking for miles. Asked about a bit. I found an old woman in a shop who remembered. She told me which house she thought it was, right on the sea. Had a porch with a heavy lattice pattern, at an angle, making diamond shapes?"

Where she would read with Nana.

"What colour is it now?"

"White."

Still white.

"Went out onto the beach. The tide was out and there were these people with buckets and rakes."

The clammers.

"I took some flowers to the graves."

"Thank you."

Jess bites her lip. Her back stiffens. They are getting close to the end of the broad. She is suddenly short of breath.

"Right, we are going to have to go about in a second. See where the channel turns?" She points. "Where the lines of red and black posts bear away? The one with the tern perched on it?"

Michael half stands, peering forward.

"We'll go about when we're level with that. Then you can take her, if you like."

"I'm not sure about this. You seem to know what You're doing, though."

"Don't be fooled. I've been practising. Been back and forth up and down this channel god knows how many times the last couple of days. I've had my moments. Now duck."

"What duck?"

"No YOU! DUCK YOUR HEAD!"

Otter sweeps round, back towards the other end of the Broad. Jess sets Michael by the tiller and tells him to fix his eye on a point in the distance and to keep the bow in line with it, just as she had dreamed of him doing, all his life. Now it's her turn to sit with her back against the cabin and to look at her son concentrating hard, both hands on the tiller, his bright eyes darting up at the sails and over his shoulder at Otter's wake. He's beautiful. She is so glad that she thought to do this, to practise sailing Otter so they might come out in her for a while. At first the notion was that it would be something to do, no need to worry about what to say, but it's more, far more. She'd thought he might have come to tell her he'd been to the Cape when he was in New England. It's OK. Still a shock, but it's OK. Feelings of relief and love overcome her. She loves him. He should know more. It's only fair he should want to know more. The last time they had seen each other, just before he'd left for America, had been so different, so horrible. She had been so horrible to him, had screamed at him.

"Don't tell me I shouldn't drink."

"But, Mum. I just want..."

"Think I'm an alcoholic, right? Well, do you? Do you? Well I do. I am. And I don't care."

"But your music..."

"WHAT? My music? The bloody music. Does it make you ill? Sick? Does it turn you into someone you hate? Does it? WELL, DOES IT? You're not like me, Michael."

"No, no I'm not. Mum, You're different. You have a gift."

"GIFT! God. It's a madness, Michael, that's what it is. Madness. The key to Jessica Healey, who could never manage two things at the same time: music and life. Well I'm not doing it any more."

"Doing what? Living? You're hiding. Locked away in this flat, this shitty flat. If you think what went before hurt me, then listen: it hurts me more to see you now. For the life of me I can't believe you want this. And why was music so important in the first place, Mum? Why? It was your way of coping, everyone knows that, understands that. Well, maybe you do need a break, but don't give up on it and replace it with booze. Please, for God's sake, please no. For me. Do it for me. Get your head together. Never, ever forget there are people who will always believe in you, love you."

"Who?"

"Me. All of us who care about you. Think about it. And there are the others too, thousands of them all over the world who love what you do, appreciate you for what you are."

"What am I? They don't know anything."

"Yes they do. They know what an outstanding musician you are. You just don't hear it anymore. We all need the applause, mum. You're no different. The difference, though, is that for you it's normally an ovation."

"Not now."

"No. But do you remember it? It's always there if you want it."

They sail the boat back and forth a few more times, then drop the sails and motor towards the cottage. Michael pours the last of the coffee from the flask and offers it.

"Rudi sends his love, by the way."

Jess looks at him blankly.

"Hopes You're alright and everything. I'll tell him."

"Tell him what exactly?"

Jess leans forward and takes the coffee.

"That You're OK."

They both look away. Michael wants to say more, to tell her what Rudi is planning, but he doesn't. She seems so much better, and part of him wants to prepare her. Maybe later, if it feels right. He hopes she can handle it, is strong enough to handle it. Either way, there's no going back now, and she'll have to know soon. Michael feels less guilty. Rudi was right about this place. It was the right thing to make her come here, wonderful to give it to her. It definitely feels right.

A young woman is sitting on the bench. She looks up and waves as they enter the channel, then walks down the grass to the staithe. Jess studies her. She is tall, slim, and square-shouldered; spirited. She keeps pushing her long, wavy blonde hair back over her head. Her white shirt is unbuttoned quite low, and her sleeves are rolled to the elbows. Her cotton skirt is thin and the light shines through it. She is bare-footed and as they draw closer Jess can see again the large eyes and full lips.

"She's lovely."

Michael watches Sally too, grins, and waves.

"Yeah. Listen, you don't mind, do you, me telling Sally and the guys to come here as well?"

Jess smiles weakly and shakes her head. She's not sure at all, but can't say it. Michael looks directly at her.

"Margaret and I sort of agreed it without your say-so, which is wrong. Sorry. A...and I've got another confession to make."

Jess waits.

"Said you'd have a listen if we rehearsed here. That all right?"

"Yeah."

"Sure? Because we can always..."

"Sure."

Music means fewer words.

Dvořák's *String Quartet No.12* drifts across the reeds and is carried away like scent on the afternoon breeze. Jess sits on the bench watching Michael, Sally, Sebastian, and Rachel. They are seated in a crescent on the grass, their backs to the sun and water, Michael and Rachel on the kitchen chairs, Sebastian on the one from the bathroom, and Sally on the piano stool, her cello between her bare knees, waves of hair hanging over her bowed face like a waterfall. She and Michael are lovers. Jess knew it before Michael told her on the boat that they were going out. The other three were together at college and formed the quartet with another student called Mark, but last year he was offered a full-time position as second cello in the Royal Philharmonic. Sally, who studied at the College of Music not the Academy, was a friend of Sebastian's. They had met when they were both playing for a touring opera company.

Sally plays well, very well, but is not as close to the others.

Sebastian, plump, already losing his dark hair, so alert, showing so much through his face, is a wonderful viola player. Jess has always thought so and watching him on the lawn of the cottage in his khaki shorts, socks, and sandals makes her smile.

Rachel's eyes, though, are narrow and keep flitting towards Jess. She's not comfortable, never has been with Jess. She plays well, fits well with Michael, and the two violins blend, but she is too timid. The others are beginning to outgrow her. Jess wonders if she still holds a torch for Michael.

Jess slips away and makes tea for them all. They have played through the whole piece and are just going back over the opening of the third movement. They stop as she comes out of the cottage with the teapot and mugs on a tray. Michael and Rachel continue to talk about the music, leaning and tapping the pages with their bows. Sebastian rushes forward and grabs a mug, beaming, then drifts off to stand by the irises and look at the skyline. Sally stays by Jess, sipping her tea.

"Wow, what a thing to be doing. Playing here. I love your place."

"Not really mine. Well..."

"Oh sorry. Only Michael said that it was now. That Rudi has given it to you."

"Sort of. You did well, by the way. It's coming together beautifully."

"Think so? Early days for me, of course."

"Yes. Look, Sally, Michael told me. I'm very happy for you both."

Sally smiles and drops her eyes. Jess feels able to say what she is thinking.

"Be good to him."

"I love him. I love him very much."

"I'm glad."

They look at Michael, who is still talking earnestly to Rachel, flipping through the score on the music stand in front of him.

Jess turns to Sally again.

"But, I've just thought. It's crazy for you to stay at Margaret's and for Michael to be here. You can stay here. Have the bed. I'll sleep on the sofa."

"No. No. Michael asked me. He wants to be with you, and I understand that. He's very happy to sleep on the sofa tonight and wants to have some time with you. I'll cope. Anyway, Margaret has offered to take the rest of us out tonight, to a pub by the sea. Actually, I think it will be good for me to spend some time with the others without Michael, you know, to get to know Rachel a bit better. Michael wants to cook for you and we stopped off in Norwich on the way to get some things, which reminds me, they're in the fridge at the farm. He's a good cook, but you probably knew that already."

Jess didn't. She watches Michael, who looks up at them and smiles. She smiles back, feeling weak inside again.

"Do you know about this music Rudi has found?"

Jess's question makes Michael lift his head and stop chewing for a second. This is it. He'd wondered if she would raise it, or if he would have to, somehow.

"Yes. He told me."

"Have you seen it, played it even?"

"Showed it to me briefly. I haven't played it." A lie. "Have you got it? Said he wanted to show it to you as well."

"It's here. He brought it."

"Really. Remind me, what's it called?"

"*Three Dances*. I like them. Early Howells; three miniatures; full of pathos. Yeah, I like the piece very much."

"Play it for me."

Jess smiles, shakes her head, and drops her eyes.

"No."

"Please?"

She looks again across the little table at her son. He has been so open and honest with her about his life, talking as they ate, about what he wants now, about Sally, about his dreams They haven't talked about Jess, or even Tom. Nothing that would hurt, not yet, and she feels safe. Michael's eyes are fixed on her above the candles, pleading.

"OK, OK. For you."

Michael follows her through to the lounge and eases himself silently down onto the sofa as Jess takes Rudi's violin out of its case and goes over to the music stand by the French doors. The music is already on it. He knew it was, had seen it when he went to the bathroom shortly after he arrived. He watches her as she tunes the strings. Then she takes a huge breath and begins. Almost immediately her eyes close. She knows it already. She knows it. Michael watches with butterflies dancing in his stomach. Her face changes as the music flows out of her. He closes his eyes too.

The last note crashes down like thunder. There is electricity in the air, an overpowering sense of energy, like that silence, that wonderful silence before the applause, when the vibration of the chord runs through you, when no one wants to break the spell. Michael waits for his mother to look at him, but she doesn't. She puts the violin back into the case and walks slowly into the kitchen. He waits a moment, then follows and finds her in one of the Windsor chairs in front of the cold stove where she has placed the candles. Her head is resting on the back of the chair, her eyes closed, holding her glass of wine.

"I keep seeing this person, a woman, here in the cottage, or outside. The *Dances* seem to have brought her to life in my mind. So vivid. Incredibly clear. I keep thinking of her, and Francis, and I think I sense him here too, you know?" Jess opens her eyes and rolls her head to look at Michael. "Strange, isn't it?"

Michael picks up his own glass and sits in the other Windsor chair. "The piece is evocative."

"I must write to Rudi. Must."

"What will you tell him?"

"The obvious, I suppose. That it is beautiful. That there's something about it. I'd like to hear it some day with full orchestra."

"I think he's already thinking about it."

"Good. Who? Where?"

"Don't know." Michael can't bring himself to say.

Jess looks at the candlelight reflected on the tiled wall behind the Rayburn.

"Michael? What are the graves like? I mean, were they overgrown?"

"No, they weren't. The place was very tidy. Grass cut. They keep it nice."

"Was it raining?"

"No."

"Wind blowing?"

"A little, yes. Why?"

"See any children on the sand with kites?"

"No."

"People with kids, dogs?"

"Yes, quite a few."

"Nice place for children, and dogs. Very nice. Flowers, were there lots of wild flowers?"

"Some. Don't remember. You don't mind, do you? Me going? You said you didn't."

"No, I don't mind."

She looks at him again.

"It's your family, Michael. They'd have loved you, you know? Oh yeah. And you'd have loved them, for sure. Oh yes. You don't know very much about them at all, do you? Never told you much at all, have I? I think I did a bit when you were little, but since then, well...sorry. I've been trying so hard lately to keep them in my mind, to think about them, instead of just the nightmare. I dream about them, about the crash, what happened, always have. After all these years it's still locked in my mind. It's always there. But it's such a long time ago I've wondered if it ever happened, or if it's just a terrible dream. But, you know, lately, strangely, they seem to be coming back to me. I see them more vividly, if that's possible.

"Tell me about them again."

"Mum, Nana and Grandpa? Oh. Goodness."

Michael tries to lead her. "Was there anyone else?"

"No, not really. Mum was an only child. Nana too, I'm pretty sure. At least I don't remember there being any. Your great-grandmother was from near Boston and the family was of Dutch origin way back, I know that much. Beatrice. Her name was Beatrice. I was very close to her. Mum had a job, was working on a newspaper like Grandpa used to, so I spent a great deal of time with Nana. A gentle person, quite tall, thin. She taught me to cook."

"Your Grandpa?"

"His parents were English, although he was born and grew up near Columbus, Ohio. He worked on the paper there, the *Dispatch*, before he met Nana. Gave me an old copy once, after we'd been talking, and I put it on my bedroom wall. Had his name on it. Really proud, I was. Wanted to be like him, like Mum, to be a writer on a paper. Not sure how or where he and Nana met, don't think I ever asked or was told, but I do know they went to live near her parents in Massachusetts after his first book was published. I remember, too, that he had two half-brothers, but they were quite a bit older and I only vaguely remember meeting them a couple of times when they visited. They still lived in Ohio. We never went there. Long way away. Don't remember much else."

"What did he write?"

"Novels, articles, and short stories for magazines and newspapers. His books were historical novels, and I think he wrote three or four altogether, honestly can't remember. I do remember, though, that his first was *The Sowers,* about a family of pioneers who crossed the Ohio River at the end of the eighteenth century and settled on the land to the south of what is now the state of Ohio. They were English, and the woman, just like Grandpa's mother, apparently, brought English wildflower seeds across the sea and over the Appalachian Mountains and scattered them. It's the story of their struggles, what happened to them, and it's all set around the area where Grandpa grew up. He gave me a copy of it for my tenth birthday.

Still have it. Read it several times when I was younger. It was like a comfort, I suppose, being able to read his words, imagining him writing it. It's a lovely book, very vivid, and poppies remind me of where I used to live too, with Mum, Nana, and Grandpa, because there were poppies in the garden there too, like there are here. There are so many here, aren't there? Everywhere you look. I'm sure Nana said that Grandpa's mother had given her the seeds. We all loved them. I've some stuff in boxes at the flat, a few things I've kept all these years. Just a few things. Long time since I looked, but I'm sure the book's there. I'm sure. You should have that too. I'll try and find it for you."

"And my grandfather? Your dad?"

"He was my father, but not my dad. Never was that. Put me in a boarding school, then moved to France. Think he and his partner ended up in America. Don't even know if he's alive or not. Never saw him much at all after I left school; few times, then nothing. Didn't care. He couldn't cope with me, for the obvious reasons. Maybe he felt guilty or something. I wasn't wanted and he didn't know how to handle my grief, my unpredictability, my anger, emotion. Oh I don't know. It just never felt like we were even related. Nothing remotely like I'd known, and to be honest I don't even think about him. Never have really, except when I was forced to live with him those few years, during the holidays anyway, and then we avoided each other. Literally. Horrible."

Silence. Michael softly breaks it.

"I'd like to know some more about my family in America, some time."

"Sorry. That's my fault."

"It's OK. I understand. But I'd love to read the book. Maybe go back there some day. Maybe we could both go. I'd like to go with you, Mum, if you can. If you want to."

"Yes, maybe. Never felt able to before, frightened I suppose. Always thought it would be too hard, too painful. Should have, though, shouldn't

I? Left it too long, way too long. Know that now. Even when I was playing in New York, I never went. Not that far, but I never did. Hard to explain. When something's taken from you like that, when everyone just disappears, it's a nightmare. I wasn't strong enough."

"I know."

"there's a ton of stuff I should have done."

Michael looks at his mum. For the first time, for as long as he can remember, she looks open, her clear eyes wide in thought, blinking slowly in the glow of the candle. There is the silence again.

"Listen, Michael." Jess lifts her head. "Tomorrow. I was thinking, d'you mind if Margaret and I come over to Bembroke Hall during the day?"

"Not at all."

"We'll stay out of your way. Just want to see it, that's all. Have a walk, go down to the beach, you know. I'm interested. I've read about it."

"You will stay for the concert, though, won't you? there's a supper. I know for sure Lady Crofton would love it if you showed up. I was really hoping you'd come. The tickets are sorted and everything."

Jess isn't sure. Michael can see it.

"Does she know I'm coming?"

"No. She doesn't have a clue who the tickets are for. You're probably the last person they'd expect to turn up. Not that many people know you're living in Norfolk now, do they? But go on. Shame if Margaret missed it as well. Come in at the last minute, if you like, and skip the supper."

"Where to first, do you think?" Margaret pulls over beside the lane just outside the gatehouse and the drive into the park. The cars that have been behind them since they turned off the coast road go by and disappear into the estate. They have decided to visit the hall first, and then to have a pub lunch down near the sea. "There's a lovely walled garden here, with a nursery, and I fancy getting some bits and bobs. The entrance to that's round the other side of the park. Or we can have a walk round the outside of the hall first."

"Hall first, no?"

"Right."

The drive dips down and swings to the right, past a pond surrounded by a black iron fence. Jess can see the start of a row of red brick estate cottages, partly shielded from view by a long privet hedge. They pass through another gate and the car shakes as it crosses a cattle grid. The drive sweeps to the left, through trees cropped at the base to a perfect line by deer, a large group of which is grazing on the fringe of the woodland where it opens onto an expanse of gently rolling grassland. Ahead there are more trees, and rising above them are the chimneys and grey slate roofs of Bembroke Hall. Margaret parks alongside other cars in the trees, against a wall and beside a gate to what appears to be the old estate stables and offices. There is a café and shop, and a sign telling of a collection of restored carriages. They walk on and out of the trees and find themselves standing at the back of the hall and looking at a lake. A few people are strolling or sitting on the rough grass. The towering back wall of the hall is made of the same red bricks as the cottages but is cast in shadow and is stark and lifeless.

They walk round to the front and stand for a while on the south side beside a large circular fountain surrounded by six yew trees the shape of cones, where formal gardens and four tiers of windows shout of wealth. Jess looks at the parkland round her and thinks it must have changed so little from when young Emily was here. They stroll further across the park, see signs to the nursery, and agree they'll walk to it. It's some distance, to the west, hidden by more trees close to another gatehouse. There is a steady flow of cars coming and going and the garden paths are full of people. Jess drifts ahead as Margaret stops to look at plants. It is like a maze. She finds herself standing by a long glasshouse looking up at a dovecot. She goes into the glasshouse, which is filled and shaded by the leaves and wood of a great vine. It's very warm. Bunches of green grapes, still not full, hang down above her head.

"Temptin" ain't they?"

A man in a flat cap is sitting motionless on a white wooden bench at the far end of the glasshouse beside an open window. His words make her jump. She hadn't noticed him.

"Not ready yet, though, not by a long chalk."

Jess walks slowly along the length of the glasshouse and sits beside him. The man is wearing the rough working clothes of a gardener, but they are clean. His cheeks are rosy and his face has a freshness, yet he is clearly quite elderly.

"They let me look ar'ter this, which at this time of year means parkin" me bum here, watching that nobody picks a bunch, and havin' a snooze. If it's not too hot in here, mind. I'm 84, you know. Worked here, man and boy. Not a bad life really, is it?"

Jess smiles at him.

"Visitor are ya?"

"Yes."

"One of them London folk?"

She nods.

"You'll be able to afford some of the things they're sellin' then. All a bit pricey if you ask me. Mind you, everythin' is these days. You weren't going to pick anything, were you?"

"No. Just wandering. Came with a friend."

"Here for the concert then? Few about that are, judging by all their finery. Makin" a day of it?"

"Yes."

"Your friend from Norfolk is he?"

"She's Irish...But yes. Married to a Norfolk farmer."

"That's all right then. Afore we know where we are you blummin" weekend folk will outnumber us others. And that in't right. Tell me," he leans towards Jess, but doesn't turn his head and continues to look along the glasshouse, "has she taken you down on to the sands yet?"

"No."

"Get yourself down there, gal, afore you go home. Lots of folk about this time of year, but you can out walk farther than them buggers. Head for the sea. Reckon that can be nearly a mile out some days. Take care mind, should it turn. Magical down there, it is, to hear the sea and wind in them pines. Right nice. I can here it now just talkin" about it."

Jess looks along the glasshouse too. Some people come to the open door and look in, but no one enters.

"Where's the dowager's house?"

"Next door, almost. Why?"

"I'd like to see it. Read about it. What's it look like?"

"Tha's a little hall, really. Where the old gal would live if the lord died first. Have to get out of the big hall 'cos to make way for the next lord. Rum ol' do, if you ask me. One minute You're the boss and the next you in't. Last one was a nice ol' bird. Spent a lot a time in the garden "ere. Helped her make the rose walk in her garden. She din't get along with her daughter-in-law, reckon. Tha's rented out now, 'cos the last lady died afore the lord."

"So, if I go out of the gatehouse..."

"Turn right down the Beckhill road, and you'll see it on the left. Some barrister fella there now. Retired, so they say, but I reckon he's just started. Full of 'imself and behaves as if he's bloody royalty. Can't say I like 'im at all. Twit. Thinks he's somethun" cos he live there. Well he in't no

165

dowager!"

Jess sees through the window that Margaret is looking for her. She gets up.

"Must go. Nice to meet you."

"Keep you a troshin', gal. Come back in September and I'll give you a bunch a grapes."

Jess makes her way to Margaret, who says she's done. She's holding a couple of green carrier bags with plants in. Jess explains that she wants to walk round to the dowager's house, to where Emily was left as a baby upon the steps, where Dr Brazington went for tea after that first meeting.

"I'd like to see that too. I've got to get out of here before I spend any more money. I've got a few bits and bobs and have just bought this little rose. That's enough. Can I come?"

"I want you to."

They go out of the gatehouse and follow the lane that runs alongside the estate wall. There are pink and white dog roses in the hedgerow on the other side and a field of corn stubble patterned with bales of straw. They come to another opening in the estate wall and turn in. A large house is just visible through the trees, with a Range Rover parked in front it.

Jess hesitates. Margaret turns.

"What? Don't you think we should?"

"I've heard he's not very nice."

Jess explains what the old man had said, about the dowager, the rose-walk, and the barrister.

"Well, leave him to me. Keep your sunglasses on then no risk of him recognising you. Come on. I haven't walked all this way for Nothin'. Can't beat a little bit of Irish charm now."

The front of the house has three pillars and a crescent of stone steps rising from the gravel to a large navy-blue door. They stand for a few seconds looking at it, then Margaret starts to climb the steps as the door opens and a cold-faced man in a cravat, tweed jacket, and corduroy trousers comes out.

"Yes? What do you want? This is private property. The main hall is..."

"To be sure." Margaret's accent grows with every word. "We'd be looking for the dowager's house. Would this be it now? Only we're come a very, very long way, haven't we, Una? You see, we're on a sort of mission, I suppose you'd call it."

"I beg your pardon?"

"You see, my cousin here and I are from Kerry and are sort of following an ancestor's trail while having a bit of a holiday as well. We're staying away down the coast at that pretty little town with a port now, and have just been to the lovely park, popping our heads into the nursery too, and..."

"What, pray, has all this got to do with me? Do be brief. I have house guests and many things to do."

"Well, to cut a long story short, our great-grandfather was an important man of the law, like yourself I believe, and came to England later in his life, to Norfolk in fact, after he was widowed. He was offered work, having been employed by the UK government before Ireland's independence. He'd met the then Lord Crofton in Ireland and, well, came and went to this estate. So you see, he was a close friend to not the current, not the previous but the one before that Lord and Lady Crofton, if you take my meaning."

"Really?"

"Much as you are with the current lord and lady, I wouldn't doubt. Anyway, after that Lord Crofton died our great-grandfather apparently would visit the dowager here and helped to plan the garden, that being one of his greatest loves away from the law. Would you still, by any chance, be having a rose-walk?"

"Well, yes, yes I do actually."

"All we ask is that might we be allowed to see it? I've bought a little rose at the nursery that I'd like to plant here in his memory. Would you be kind enough to let us do that? In a place where you'd want it, of course, this being your house now, and your rose-walk."

"Well, I...I don't see why not. Um, right. I have to go out very soon because I'm needed at the Hall. There's a concert tonight and I assist the family in such matters. There is, however, a little time. If you make your way round to the side, I'll meet you there at the gate in the wall. A lawyer, you say? Fascinating."

He goes in and closes the door.

"You fibber!"

They walk across the gravel to the side gate. Margaret whispers.

"Well, anyone who looks down his nose at me is asking for it. Toffee-nosed people who behave as it they are better than you always rub me up the wrong way. Old money usually knows better, but there are people that get some money or status and think they're Lord Muck. Found the best way to deal with them is to have some fun and massage their egos. Oh, come on, he loved it, and this is a good craic. We're havin' a giggle. You do want to see the garden, don't you? I sure as hell want to see this rose-walk."

The beams of the Volvo's headlamps weave along the twists and turns of the coast road, and Margaret and Jess happily keep their thoughts to themselves as they drive home after the concert. It has been such a full day. Jess feels tired, but content.

Getting down briefly to the beach after the rose-walk visit, breathing in the fresh salt air, reminded her so much of her childhood. The coolness and sound of the sea too; the mud and sand between her toes, the feel of the small stones and shells beneath her bare feet. And how strange the pine wood had been, set on waves of dunes. It had been silent but for the eerie, faint wail of the wind in the trees; the ground cushioned by millions of fallen needles. Here and there were low, curved branches where a person might rest.

She is so proud of Michael, so pleased to have found the courage to slip in just before the concert started. If anyone recognised her they didn't say so. Jess and Margaret went out into the dusk during the interval, talking about their day. At the end they had waited outside again for Michael to come to them.

16

This autumn night I cannot sleep for reason of my excitement, for I am in the small cabin, or cuddy as Jacob and Billy refer to it, of the Duchess and I have begun my long-awaited journey to Yarmouth. Jacob is sleeping on the other bunk beyond the warming stove, and Billy has given up his bed for me, saying he is most content to sleep beneath the hatch at the foot of the giant mast, in the little hold at the front of the wherry where are stored the mud weight and other items I trust he is not too cold and that the bed I have laid out for him is comfortable. It has not been the easiest of days for them, for not only could we not leave before noon, that being the lowest tide for our passage beneath the ancient bridge at Potter, but the wind was first against us and then fell to nothing. This was cause for Jacob and Billy to force the Duchess forward by means of the long wooden quants that they dropped to the river bed and then pushed with all their might, walking back and forth countless times along the long sides of her. To witness their tireless work today filled me with such awe, for after they first undertook the loading of a veritable mountain of sacks at the carpenter's yard, they then laboured so with those heavy quants, and also so skilfully and swiftly lowered and raised again the vast black sail and giant mast before and after the bridges. And how I have loved the task Jacob set for me, for I have steered the craft for quite some distance, pushing and pulling with all my might the heavy rudder to the point where my arms and my back are now quite sore.

We are out in the flats of the marsh pastures, not so far from a railway where engines go to and fro throwing their white smoke into the sky, and from where, at dusk when we stopped, I could stand on the hatches and see the outline of the port on the horizon in the east. I wonder if it will be as I have read.

This space within the cabin is quite confined yet very comfortable. Not so this afternoon when I struggled to make some tea, for reason of the vast length of fat sail rope that Jacob had kicked down into it, but now the stove warms the cabin quite perfectly for the doors are on once more and the night is shut out.

I am most pleased with my decision to bring my journal with me. I intend to write of everything I see, if my aching arms will allow. The wherry is loaded with sawdust for the floors of the inns in the port, and instead of returning with the usual cargo of wood Jacob has been instructed by the timber merchant to seek an assortment of goods including several barrels of herring.

Jacob has said we will run with the tide before first light and if the wind is with us too we may be within the port for *breakfast. What delight!*

I know not where to begin, for we are amid a great fleet of tethered craft of all shapes and sizes, and the sounds, smells, and noises of this day have overwhelmed my mind. Close by, towering above us, are a line of three ships set against the quay that are locked in by several smaller craft, including the Duchess who now seems so small. Further along the waterfront towards the sea there is a veritable forest of masts, rising from what Billy has told me are colliers, grain ships, and timber barques, and across the river are ranks of brown-sailed fishers. I have counted some twenty wherries but am told there are many more out towards the harbour mouth from where they take to the sea to unload the larger vessels that ride offshore. The water is never empty, there always being people rowing about and boats and wherries turning with their sails and rigging shaking in the wind, so much to make this place a feast for the eye.

Yet for all my dreams of what I might see, I never imagined what smells and sounds would shake the senses too. There is upon the air the constant odour of fish and sometimes with it smoke and tar, and above the din of voices and the carts over the stones there is a constant hammering from the shipbuilders where there are boats set on stocks amid small hills of timber. There came, too, a sudden roar of guns that quite frightened me, and Jacob, much amused, explained it was the Militia Artillery firing down on what he called the Denes, the sand strip lying between the river and the sea near the harbour mouth. I am sure this is where I will find Peggotty's house, if such a place exists.

We must wait for another wherry, the Fountain, to leave the quayside behind the fishing fleet before we can cross and unload the sacks of sawdust, and Jacob has said he will use this time to seek and purchase the things needed for our new

172

cargo. Billy will stay aboard the Duchess, but I am to go with my husband.

I am now once again in the small space of the cuddy and gladly so, for now that night is here I would not want to be wandering amid the maze of this place, fascinating as it most certainly is, for I feel sure I would become lost, or worse. I wonder if this is how London or any large place may be, for here are to be found such a great number of people living on streets so narrow that you can almost reach across from one side to the other. On occasions the quay is so thick with people and animals that you cannot walk, making it necessary to stand and wait for carts and trolleys to pass by. In this jumble of dwellings and yards, many of which were painted white for, I supposed, reasons of light, there were some finer houses too, and close to the new and very grand Town Hall there is a courthouse and gaol. I saw all manner of things being lifted from boats or waiting on the quayside to begin a journey, including coal, chalk, flour, and wheat, and even cinder ashes. On the river vast lengths of timber would swing out on ropes from ships to be stacked on wherries that all but sank under the weight, and Jacob said that further towards the sea were to be found many women busy at wet tables cutting and cleaning fish. Here and there were large pieces of wood with figures and names carved upon them, and Jacob said these were from ships that had been lost upon the shallows or beach during storms, which I could well imagine, for Dickens has described such violence with clarity. My husband's progress would, no doubt, have been swifter without me, and once he had completed his business and we returned to the Duchess we found Billy in a state of some agitation, for the Fountain had left and another wherry, the Jackard, laden with firewood, had swiftly taken her place at the quay and her skipper and mate were lifting the hatches in readiness to unload. There was some disagreement, both among Jacob and Billy and these men, and also among other people on the quay, but circumstances were not to change, so I sought to make recompense by preparing food and tea within the cuddy.

While Jacob ate I asked that I might have time to explore yet further this port, and he said I undoubtedly would, for the wagon would not return for the sacks of sawdust until the following morning.

My intention was most clear, namely to make my way to the sea and then to the sands by the harbour mouth to find the place where lived Peggotty, Ham, Little Emily, and Mrs Gummage. That there actually existed, as David Copperfield had espied from Ham's shoulders, that black barge with an iron funnel sticking out of it, I very much doubted, but this journey was one Constance and I had talked of so often and at first I almost ran where the crowded quayside allowed me. Beside the Town Hall I decided to take another, perhaps less difficult and less crowded route, hoping that this Middlegate Street would bring me to the sea. But it did not, and on both sides of me were endless alleyways that left me in some confusion. I asked for guidance regarding the direction of the sea, and then would not believe it, for it was not the same as the course of the river, so I turned back and rejoined the quay as best I could.

It was a far longer journey than I had thought, for as well as long it was at first impossible to walk at one pace in a straight line through such was the throng. I found myself closer still to the frightful sound of the guns I had heard before, and ahead along the river there came into port an armada of fishing vessels to join the many already lined along the quay. A great many herring fish were being put into baskets, the rows of which filled the quayside and drew people who seemed to be judging them and bartering. This activity slowed my progress yet more, so I turned to the north towards a towering pillar that had a figure of Britannia grasping her trident upon the top of it. Beneath her there were six smaller statues and behind them, in an open space, I could see people moving and arms pointing. This monument I noted bore four names, Aboukir, Copenhagen, St Vincent, and Trafalgar, and yet more people were gathered at the base of it, clearly waiting to climb inside it. I was informed by a man who claimed to be the Keeper of the Pillar, that it had been erected in honour of the Norfolk seafaring hero Lord Nelson, who had come ashore close by. I considered what a fine view of the port could be gained from such a climb, but given the number of people already there it was certain to take some time, and I was both determined to make my way to the beach which was now not far off while also being mindful that this journey had already taken longer than I had first thought.

Amid the dunes beyond the monument were laid out many nets, and there I encountered the women Jacob had spoken of, busy packing the fish into barrels, raising a great din with their talk which I could not comprehend. I continued on across the sand dunes before standing at the highest point from where I could see all. Far off at sea lay all manner of ships, and running back and forth from them to the port were small craft of different sizes, their number including wherries with their distinctive black sails. The sea was quite rough and waves were crashing onto the sand where several people walked. In vain I looked all round me for sight of the old boat that had become a house, but saw only small pieces of wood and other matters that looked like broken boxes. To the north, where the town met with the sea, there were large brick houses and a jetty reaching out onto the water, and I could make out horses and carriages and people in fine dress. But around me the sand carried nothing that looked like it may have been that most unusual dwelling described in such detail by Master Copperfield, save a pile of rotting timber. I returned towards

175

the monument again and dared to ask the man who called himself the Keeper if there had indeed been a house such as Peggotty's close by, and to my delight he said that there had, but that it had long since been broken and taken for fires.

So I returned to the high point and sat upon the sand a while, wishing that I had with me that book so I might read once more that which delighted Constance and I so.

By the time I had made my way back along the quay to the Duchess it was growing dark, and with the coming of the shadows I found the mood was much changed, for the inns are now full and I sense it is a place you would not want to be if you did not know it well enough.

I found the Duchess pressed against the quayside as Jacob said she would most likely be and while I prepared food for them, Jacob and Billy continued to work with the aid of lanterns.

We have long since eaten and Billy has taken himself off in search of ale. Jacob is outside with a pipe and I am snug within the cuddy. What a day it has been! Tomorrow I will write to both Constance and her father to tell them of all I have seen.

All is set for our return along the river, but the weather holds us here, having turned to blow a strong breeze from the west. Jacob says that before we make our way back along the Bure we are to sail across Breydon Water, for he has been instructed to collect from a trader at Burgh Castle a new gun punt for wildfowling, that being a pastime of the Duchess's owner. But as we wait here this westerly wind brings more and more wherries to port and matters are getting crowded. Amid this vast assortment of craft I have today seen one wherry that was somewhat smaller, but none the less of thirty feet or more in length, where a tall boy was working alone unloading corn. As we had no further work to do save to wait for the wind to change, Jacob and Billy offered to help him, already knowing him to be John Gauntlet and telling me aside that he was just fifteen years of age and sailed and managed the wherry *Charity* without a mate. I was somewhat stunned to learn this and for a while could not be sure if I was being misled for their amusement, but learned soon enough that it was true. I sought to help in the labour, and when the task was done young John's face beamed and he made tea for all of us. I listened as Jacob, Billy, and he talked of trade and where the wind might take them next, and for this boy it meant returning along the north river to Stalham Staithe with a cargo of coal, and then on to Horstead marl pits, his smaller wherry being best suited for such a difficult journey.

I am home once more, and have just written to my beloved Constance. I am both tired and elated, for it has been such a journey, and while I might be glad to have seen that port of Yarmouth and to have sought the world of Master Copperfield, it is so pleasing to be here again amid the reeds and trees. Of all I have seen and done I must write that it has been the journey itself just as much as the days within Yarmouth that have enchanted me so, and it is my hope that it will not be too long before I'm again able to be upon the *Duchess*.

While I am much tired, there is one occurrence I must record while I think clearly of it, for it was a spectacle of wonder. When, finally, the westerly wind that had held us in Yarmouth for a further two days abated and freed us, there was a considerable excitement within the port and the river filled with wherries seeking to leave. Jacob and Billy were prepared for this and we were among the first to get away, and after a very few moments were at the head of a fleet of black sails crossing Breydon Water, a huge expanse of estuary with gulls and terns filling the sky. It became something of a race and we were overhauled by two much larger and, I think, much younger wherries whose brightly painted sides and cuddies *shone so. Jacob asked that I climb upon the hatches and count the black sails behind us, which took some while, but when done I declared that the number was sixty-one. This was a sight I will never forget.*

17

"Rudi?"

"Jessica. What a lovely surprise. So good to hear you. Are you..."

"I can't do it. I've got your letter. You'll have to find someone else...or cancel. I can't do this."

There is a breath.

"So, how's the cottage? Have you got all you need?"

"Will you bloody well LISTEN!"

Margaret hears the shout. She was half expecting it. Jess had looked so grey when she appeared at her back door, her shoulders hunched and her head slightly down, her troubled eyes shining with tears. All she said was that she needed to make an urgent telephone call. Rudi had called Margaret twice in the last two days asking if Jess had said anything since

179

she'd passed on his letter. Now Jess had come. Margaret had shut the sitting room door, but Jess's words still reached the kitchen.

"I CAN'T DO IT!"

"Then leave it."

"AH!"

"Don't look at it."

"For Christ's sake. You bastard. You bloody bastard."

Jess starts to cry.

"I'm sorry, Jessica. I'm sorry."

Rudi listens to her sobbing, his head racing. He must choose his words so carefully. He must wait, let her speak, let her anger out.

"How...how, how can I just forget it? How? Ignore the fact that you have arranged for me to play these pieces? Without asking, Rudi? Without bloody well asking? My God. You've planned this all along, haven't you?"

"No. No, Jessica darling, no. I merely hoped..."

"What? That this place of yours would change me? I don't believe it. I just do not believe this is happening. I trusted you. You were one of the few people I felt I could trust. I came here because you forced me to. And yes, yes, I do like it, I do, but..." Her chin buckles again. "That just makes it harder."

Rudi stays silent.

"I...I thought you were going to ask me, I did. I was convinced you'd brought the music so you could ask me, then dismissed it as paranoia. But I never, ever thought you would do this to me, just arrange it without a word. How dare you not ask? HOW DARE YOU. You have no idea, no idea at all how I feel."

"In time..."

"No!"

"Maybe if I came, we could talk."

"No. No."

"I was wrong to just write."

"Cancel it. Or get someone else."

"I can do that, if that's what you really want."

"Yes."

"Very well, but they want you, Jessica, the Philharmonia."

"Listen! I DON'T CARE! Ask Cliffe. Or Hoffman. I can think of a dozen people."

Rudi fights his guilt. Michael, Suzy, and now Margaret have told him that maybe it is too much, that he may have gone too far. He feels cruel, but he still can't see any other way. Given a choice Jessica would not do it. He must believe that. He's sure of it. This was bound to be the hardest time.

"It all moved so fast. I thought you might be ready, want to do it. Please don't be angry with me. I'm old and stupid. I got excited. I only thought of you. Crazily it was as if it was meant to be, you know? At first I just wanted your view on the music, that's all. That's all. Yes, I admit the thought was in my mind, but I'd wanted it to come from you, when you'd seen it. Then, about two weeks ago, I confided in Grace at The Barbican about the *Dances* and that I'd asked you to look at them. A day later she called me, telling me about the new season's programme and that there was a chance to weave them into the English concert next June. As you know the pieces are quite short, and she thought they would fit at the end of the first half of the programme. She said he'd spoken to several people. They were very excited. It was a definite if we got our skates on. She wanted an answer."

"You had no right."

"No I didn't. I'm sorry, Jessica. Of course I'll talk to her. I'd hoped, that's all."

Jess puts down the receiver. She looks out across the farm garden towards the broad. Two jet trails scar the blue sky. She feels numb.

Rudi's letter had sat on the kitchen table, unopened, for a day and a half. Jess wondered if it would be the question. Part of her wished it was. She was sure everything was leading towards him asking her to consider playing the *Dances* in concert, and when the letter was handed to her by Margaret she sensed it might be it. She was not sure how she would feel if she was right, and she kept looking at it, wondering. For sure her answer would be no. Whispering Reeds was a special place. It had been good to work again, to explore something new, away from pressure, away from people. She'd left the letter and kept reaching instead for her violin. They were wonderful pieces. They were fresh. Vital. She'd worked on them. Somehow, they fitted with where she was, who she was. Then, finally, the night before, she'd gone to bed, read the letter, and howled.

"Jess?" Margaret is at the door. "Please tell me to go away if you want to. Would it help to talk about it?"

Jess shakes her head.

"What will you do?"

"You know?"

"Rudi called yesterday, asking if you were OK. Rang twice, so I asked him why. Eventually, last night, he told me. I was about to come down to the cottage this morning to see if you were OK when you came. He was wrong. I think he was wrong. But don't leave, Jess. I'm worried you may go. There's no need."

"Not sure what to do any more."

"Come by whenever you want. You know you can do that, don't you? If you want to talk. Or not. Whatever. We're here."

Jess looks again at the telephone. She loves the pieces. She'd dared to imagine herself performing them. But she does not trust herself. It will be another disaster. She turns, hugs Margaret briefly, and leaves.

Margaret hears the back door close and steps closer to the living-room window.

She watches, arms folded, as Jess walks past the garden wall. She looks like she did the day she first arrived at the cottage. Margaret thinks of following her but doesn't. She will go later in the day. Jess needs a little time. Then she will go to her.

Margaret fetches David from the school bus, gives him and Phil their tea, works in her garden, her sanctuary, until the light starts to fade, then comes in and changes into cleaner clothes. She has felt uneasy all day. She tells them she is popping down to the cottage and David says he wants to come.

"Not this time, my lovely. Explain to Dad what homework You've done. I'll be as quick as I can."

The warmth of the day is fading, the wind has turned to the east and the air is fresher than it has been for days. Biba runs ahead, searching for pheasants among the nettles and grasses at the base of the blackthorn hedge as she always does. Margaret walks fast, thinking of what she might to say. She's certain, just as she'd sensed from the very beginning, from what Rudi had first said to her about Jess, that maybe she can help. Somehow. Jess needs space, but she needs someone to listen to her, someone detached from all she knows. Rudi has taken a huge risk. Maybe she should have done more to get to know Jess, to get close and to encourage her to be more open about her pain, and maybe it would have helped now, after the call, if Jess had more trust in her.

Margaret is about two thirds of the way along the track when she hears a boat's engine roar. It isn't the outboard. She quickens her step, half running. As she reaches the gate Margaret sees Otter at the end of the dyke, her wake spilling into the reeds on either side. Biba runs to the staithe and barks. Jess glances back, expressionless, then looks ahead again. Otter surges

183

out into the open water and turns sharply left, towards Potter.

Margaret stands beside the cottage and watches Jess's head moving above the reeds, the wind blowing the hair from her face, her forehead high and determined. She looks back towards the cottage for a moment and then is gone. Margaret stares blankly at the open water at the end of the dyke. The setting sun, reflected off a bank of high cloud, casts fire along Otter's wake. She's too late. She's left it too late. She tries the door to the cottage. It's locked. The lights are out. She calls Biba and turns for home.

"She's gone, Phil. I was wrong. Should have gone to her sooner. The call obviously upset her a hell of a lot. I thought she'd stay, though. She seemed to have settled, to be getting on OK."

Phil and Tom are in the milking parlour, washing down. They stop and wait. Margaret paces.

"Maybe she felt she needed to sort things out, clear the air or something. Maybe She's going to see Rudi. Don't know. It's such a bloody shame. She was settled. Seemed to be working out for her. I'll go and ring Rudi."

She turns to leave, then stops.

"D'you think I should, Phil?"

"No, Sweet Pea. Let it be, for now."

The sun sinks, leaving half-light. No other boats are moving. A line of motor cruisers and one yacht are moored along the bank. People are laughing. There is the smell of fried food. A fat man in a vest and jeans is on his knees and elbows on the roof of one of the cruisers clutching a small television aerial. Beneath him a woman and two boys, their faces illuminated by the TV screen, are shouting instructions. Holidaymakers on the other boats are hidden behind drawn curtains, save the last one. An elderly man on a small, tatty motorboat is fishing off the back of it. He is the only one who seems to notice the yacht moving through the dusk. He raises a beer can to Jess and calls.

"She's a bewty. Getting a bit late to be making waves, mind. Take you care, 'cos there's no more moorings until the end of Heigham Sound, 'less You're headin'' up Meadow Dyke or plan to use the ol' mud weight. Wouldn't leave it long afore you stop if I were you."

Jess hasn't thought. She's running. She'd spent the day locked away, crying, shouting, drinking. Then, on impulse, in a rage, she'd left. She's dizzy, half drunk. Otter goes on. Ahead to her left is the yellow post marking the start of Meadow Dyke. Straight ahead, about fifty yards beyond the post, three yachts are tethered together just to the side of the main channel. She can just make out their mud weight lines. People are sitting talking in the well of the middle boat. They hear Otter's engine and idly turn to watch. Jess is level with the yellow post now and she suddenly forces the tiller to the right, swinging Otter into Meadow Dyke.

18

How blessed I am, for something I once desired so much yet had grown to accept was not my destiny, has, finally, come to pass. I am with child. I am certain of it. After such a time, it being so many years now since our marriage, both Jacob and I had believed it was not possible and were reconciled. Yet now, despite my age, it seems we will be parents.

Jacob's joy has been unbridled, and the comfort and guidance of Ruby these first days has brought such reassurance and understanding. I will write to my Constance with the news, enclosing another letter for her dear father...

To open my door and see before me both Constance and Dr Brazington has stirred my heart so, and the two days in their company have been among the most vital of all.

I am able again and long returned to my work within the school, yet, until the week last past, my grieving spirit has barely raised its head since our child left us in March. That they should journey so far to visit us and have such concern as to our well-being has brought such comfort to our sorrow. My thoughts have been overwhelmed by loss and the beauty of our child, Thomas, who never drew a breath; of Jacob lovingly swaddling him in the shawl I had made for him before binding a rock to his back. I see Thomas's serene face constantly from when we lowered him into the calm water of the mere, the water into which he faded fired by the light of the lantern being held by Billy who had gently rowed us out from the reeds. This was the water gypsies" way when a child passed.

How many there are within that mere is impossible to imagine. I am now of the daily habit to walk to the water's edge and to talk to my son.

How strange it was to see Constance and Dr Brazington grown older, as it most surely was for them to see us, yet, if I reflect on it, they seemed so little changed by the years. While the Doctor has need of a stick and the sides of his head have turned for the most part to grey, his eyes and mind are as bright as polished glass and his eagerness to explore this wetland brought forth that keenness I know so well and which seems to know no bounds. He immediately, typically, wanted to check my health and proceeded to examine me, before declaring that what I needed most was rest, nature, and the goodness of the breeze and sun upon my face.

We passed the Saturday afternoon talking of all that has befallen us, and then, upon Jacob's return, we went back with them to their lodgings at the inn where we ate and talked a great deal more. Constance relayed that Dr Brazington had supposedly retired from his work but in truth had continued to care for many people. He, however, preferred to tell of his wildlife studies and his increasingly regular visits to Norwich for naturalist society meetings, as well as other more contentious gatherings where the evolutionary theories of Charles Darwin were discussed. Constance said she wasn't certain this was so good for his heart, but her father then began to debate quite forcibly why the evidence of evolution was abundantly clear to anyone with a wit to study it, confessing that he had little hope of reaching heaven if the comments of several clergymen were to be believed. It was clear he had some considerable knowledge of the wetland, far more than before my leaving Swanton Rectory, and he said he had visited some of the more accessible broads and rivers nearer the city. It was then agreed, to his most gleeful delight, that we should all venture forth onto Horsey the following morning, that he might see something of the wilderness and its many creatures, and Jacob left us for a short while to seek out Billy and Ruby, saying he would ask for the loan of their small boat, or some other of sufficient size with sail or oars. I asked of Constance's recent news, not having received a letter since before Christmas, and she told me of her happiness, and that both her husband and children were well. It was with sadness, though, that she also told how her brother-in-law, Captain Ernest Baker, had been killed in southern Africa fighting the Boers, having previously been much decorated for his actions in fighting during the Zulu war. The loss had affected the whole family deeply, especially Dr Baker, whose health was already quite frail.

Doctor Brazington asked if I had continued with my journal, and I told him that I had, it being something so important to me. He enquired also if Jacob could now read, which my husband, on his return, willingly illustrated by taking up a

188

newspaper left upon a seat and reading a few words from an essay about the life of Benjamin Disraeli, the once Prime Minister who recently passed away.

We began upon our short adventure the following morning quite early and took with us food and drink. Jacob had taken cushions so I could be most comfortable, and he had the sense also to bring a tarpaulin from the Duchess under which we might shelter should the wild sky become angry. He felt sure it would rain before the day was out and there was no denying it, but it did not stop us, and what sunshine there was between the clouds would, in the words of Dr Brazington, make the water flash as with phosphorescent fire. It was we who were supposed to be guiding the Doctor on this journey, but both Jacob, Constance, and I delighted at how, from the moment we were afloat, he talked incessantly and excitedly, both in whispers and roars, of what we could see. He began to write within his small notebook but then became frustrated that he might miss something whilst he was writing, so I happily volunteered to write for him, as I had done so many years before.

We passed young marshman Robert Tubbs rowing silently in his father's gun punt, looking for all like a giant insect, though Jacob remarked such stealth was probably as much to do with avoiding the bailiff as disturbing the ducks. There were a great many swallows and martins flying low across the water, but there seemed to be few insects on them to feed, for the mayfly has yet to appear. The Doctor surveyed the scene from the front of the boat, telling me all the birds he could hear, redshanks, plovers, and the bleating snipe, and then we had to take cover beneath the canvas as some great cloud discharged a tumultuous volley of heavy rain drops that set little fountains across the water. When this rain abated, we went along Meadow Dyke and onto Horsey, where we could see the sandhills in the distance and hear the beating of the waves carried on the keen wind, but it was less than comfortable, the Mere being so large and the wind so strong, so we returned to the relative shelter of the reeds in the dyke just beyond a little wood in which the herons make their nests and we stayed there for a while to listen to a sedge warbler that had ventured forth after the rains. The Doctor delighted in finding an orchid upon the grass bank and then, as we settled ourselves to eat and drink, there came from the mass of reed the distant, booming call of a bittern. It is a most haunting sound, one which Constance had not heard before, and the Doctor declared most contentedly that it was welcoming him...

To think that the coming year will mark ten years since our marriage makes me dwell upon the swiftness of this life. The time has passed at such speed, and now this journal, this heavy volume, is beyond three quarters full. I am minded that it has never been as the Doctor intended, having become from the outset a long soliloquy rather than notes on naturalism, and I have long felt it to be an account such as one might never offer to anyone to read, other than a loved one. Jacob has done so and is forever encouraging, for he knows the comfort and interest it brings during the times I am alone. If I am honest, as I must be, I must say also that it has become something that I do for my mother, for it is in some part an answer to my longing to speak to her.

This summer has been much different for me on account of the fire at the timber yards, and I am unashamedly grateful for it. That the Duchess was damaged in the fire and in need of considerable repair was a great worry to us for a short while, for we were fearful what this might mean regarding Jacob's employment, but when it was made known by Mr Cherry that the wherry would indeed be mended and that for a while Jacob would be employed once more upon the marshes, we were much content.

For some months now Jacob has been able to return home at the end of each day, and I have been able to walk out upon the marshes to join him in his work, or to sit close by and make the notes that Dr Brazington asked of me. For two years now I have been sending my observations to him and he seems much delighted, which pleases me.

Today I wrote how the sweet scent of new-mown hay was in the pollen-laden air, and as we ate our food it was as if we were in a wild-flower garden. The swifts were soaring into the blue sky, while hundreds of rooks and jackdaws were feeding on the marshes. Once in a while there came the harsh call of the pheasant and then, as the dusk mist began to rise from the dykes and we set off for home, we could hear the "crek-creck" of the corncrake. What I have not relayed to him, however, is the loveliest observation of all, for in the course of the day my Jacob took me far off across the marsh, through the feeding cattle, to a gateway beside a ditch that he'd worked to clear of weed the week before. Upon the wooden post he had carved our names, and with them a heart.

The winter has come once more and with it the severest freeze I have known. For days the thickness of the ice has prevented any boat, even the Duchess and the other wherries, from moving. Yesterday, to the music of the tinkling ice crystals on the reed stems, I stood and watched as Jacob joined others who had ventured upon the frozen surface of the Broad to race one another at high speed upon skates. I did not like to witness this, for I was fearful that the ice would crack or someone would suffer a terrible injury, for there were painful falls. Yet I am also glad that there is some distraction for them, for there can be no work in such weather that turns both water and ground to iron. We have some food, for Jacob has shot a pair of coots and a water hen, and there are other things within

191

the cupboard. But open weather, when the reed cutting may begin, is anxiously awaited.

A tumult of snow has, just yesterday and last night, turned all around us white, and where the ice has stopped all passages upon the water, so the wind-blown snow has now blocked all the paths and byways. I am thankful that Jacob is home, for he went out at dusk with his gun, there being a break in the storm. But he was caught within another fall, and on his return he declared it to be as discomforting as being overtaken by a dense fog, for he could see nothing and there were deep drifts along the frozen ditches and against the marsh fences and gates. It has suddenly become a struggle to keep warm and to feed ourselves, yet we have shelter and a little to eat. The starving birds and animals who leave their tracks in the snow do not.

How can I write this down? My dear husband, so deserving of life and the kindest, the dearest of all men, has gone from me and I am utterly lost. May is such a senseless month for death. About me are the natural things we always found so uplifting. Everywhere I look life is new and so vital in its glory. I suppose the matter of my staying here will come upon me soon, I am sure. What of it? For now I do not know what I am to do. And still there are no tears. Perhaps now. What shall I do? Again I find my eyes looking for him, my ears listening for him to come home.

Billy and Ruby, God bless these people, have been such a support to me during these desperate days. Their Bible sits beside me now. Billy rowed me to Martham today, to where my husband, who had been running a fever but was insistent on working so we had food upon the table, had fallen between the staithe and the wherry. I held mayflowers, ragged robin, and early poppies as if to a wedding. How Jacob loved them so. How he would urge me to guide him on our wanderings

192

on the Lord's day so that he may gather them. For Billy to grieve so moved me deeply.

Jacob was found today, far off near Potter and brought back to Hickling. Finally we may lay him to rest. And yet I dare not tell of my uncertainty. This is an end to it all, but part of me would have him stay within the water he worked and loved. How can I say this? The minister has shown such understanding. I pray the service, set for the morrow, will reconcile me.

I see it is a month and eighteen days since I last set down my thoughts. It is also nearly twelve years since I began this journal. I must confess I am suddenly grown tired of it and there is no sense in continuing, and this gift of Dr Brazington, who taught me so much and who first urged me to recount my life, is almost full. So be it. No more for me the scratch of this pen on your paper, dear book. This collection of thoughts and memories, such as they are, were firstly for you, Jacob, and I weep openly now at the way you first encouraged me then set yourself to learn to read. Without you I can find neither the will nor reason to continue, so I will close these pages. At the end of the coming week I must leave our house so another marshman and his family may make it their home. This is right and proper. I pray they will find the same happiness here between the reeds and blue heaven that we have shared. My journal I leave with you, Jacob my beloved, and with it my heart.

19

"Margaret, I..."

"Hello, Jess."

Jess is standing at the back door of the farmhouse, her hair blowing across her anxious face. Her jeans are brown at the knees and ankles, and her large baggy white T-shirt looks like she hasn't taken it off in days.

"It just ends, Margaret. It just ends."

"What does?"

"The journal. Anna's journal. Is there more? I want to know if there's more. Is there?"

"No, there isn't. As far as I'm aware there isn't. Come in. Come in."

Jess hesitates, then goes through into the kitchen. Margaret shuts the door and follows her.

"Sit yourself down now."

Margaret runs a tap and fills an electric kettle.

"Aga's out. Tea?"

Jess nods.

"Phil's off to Norwich to market and he'll bring David home later. He'll be gone best part of the day." Margaret glances at Jess as she reaches for two mugs, hoping she is listening. They can talk, if she wants to. "All here on my tod, save old Alan, our hand. He's clearing out at the top of the yard. You couldn't have timed it better. I've just given up on some foul paperwork. D'you know, it's one part of this farming lark I've not taken to my heart. Never will."

She sets the pot and two mugs on the table and pours some milk into a jug from a little churn. They sit facing each other. Jess looks at her. Her chin buckles and she starts to weep. Margaret leans across the corner of the table and rests her hands on hers.

"It's OK. Let it out now. It's all right. Let it go."

Jess howls, locks her arms across her stomach and folds in, rocking backwards and forwards. Margaret brings her chair closer to Jess and hugs her.

"Sorry. Sorry."

Jess blows her nose, sniffs, wipes her eyes with the ball of her hand.

"Don't be."

"Oh God. It's crazy. Crazy. I was so angry. Just wanted to hide, you know? I've damaged the boat as well. Because I kept going, don't know where, back and forth, until it was dark. Then found myself on Horsey and got scared. Saw a red sign and went into a channel. Hit the staithe very hard. Cracked the strip of wood that runs along the edge of the boat."

"That's repairable."

"He...he wants me to play *Three Dances* at a concert. You said you knew that, didn't you?"

"Yes."

"That's why he got me to come here."

Margaret waits, says nothing.

"I can't. I won't."

"Leave it for a while."

"I can't leave it, I can't." Jess starts to cry again. "And it means I can't stay either. He said he wants to give me the cottage. That's a bribe. A bribe. How the hell can I stay when I know that? Do you know how that feels?"

"Forgive me, but I think You're wrong. You mustn't feel you have to leave. Whispering Reeds is yours if you want it, whether you decide to play this concert or not."

"No."

"Yes. Because that's what Francis wanted too, you know? And he's not asking you to play anything. It was his, first and foremost it was his. He talked to me about it, that last time he was here, when he knew well enough he was dying. He knew Rudi wouldn't be able to manage it for long if at all, and I know they discussed it. He also told me there was someone they thought might just appreciate it; love it; gain from it. You."

Jess looks at her trying to understand. Margaret smiles.

"Francis talked about you, a little. Said I would like you."

Jess smiles back at her for a second through wet eyes. Margaret's expression is gentle, kind.

"Told me about those times when you first all met. He said it was an incredible time for him, that it was full of fun and music, that you all became very close. He never ever forgot that, you know."

Francis bowls into Jess's mind and she can see him, sense him, remembering so clearly the way he somehow weaved them all together, he, Jess, and Rudi, all those years ago. How he trusted her with his thoughts, showing so much understanding, and helping Rudi to make her feel safe there.

Margaret waits a moment.

"So you see, Jess, it was never a bribe. Rudi has this dream of helping you, of this music being played by you, that is all. But I definitely think he was wrong to take things this far without asking you. Remember, though, you don't have to do anything you don't want to. He'll have to understand."

"It's not that easy with him."

"Just tell him no."

"I did. But he won't let it go. I know him. He won't."

"I've known people like that. Problem is they push so hard they become the reason you don't do something."

They sit in silence. Then Margaret leans away.

"I confess we knew where you were."

"You did?"

"When you disappeared we wondered at first if you'd left the boat somewhere and made your way back to London, but we checked round the main staithes, rang Ted and some other people who know the boat well and there was no sign of her. Then Phil saw her mast above the reeds in Wendle's Cut when he was out on the north meadow."

Margaret doesn't say that she also let herself into the cottage and had stood for a moment looking round at Jess's things scattered about. She'd picked up the Fairy Liquid bottle from beside the sink to put it away but had stopped herself. Then she had found the violin beside the bookcase in the lounge and returned home, knowing that Jess would come back.

197

Jess looks down at the table as she speaks. "Just stayed there. Hiding, I suppose. Drank again. Slept. Took the journal; I needed to, because it's been wonderful, very real to me. Helped me stop thinking about everything, you know? I've loved it, from the moment I first started reading it on the train coming up here. There was something, just a few words, that made me think about my family, about growing up. And I feel I know Anna and have a real sense of her. But I can't believe it just stops, just like that. Stupid, but I feel it's like I've been left again. That's how I feel, Margaret. That's how it feels. I get to know someone, get close to someone, and they leave. Or die. What happened to her?"

"We don't know."

"God. I mean, it's as if I know her. I feel as if I know her. I've even come to sense her. She's there, isn't she?"

"I think so."

Jess whispers, "Bloody hell."

"Francis talked about trying to find out what happened to her, but I'm not sure he did anything. Couldn't. Once he set about typing it all out, it became something of an obsession, like he was prone to, but by that time he was pretty ill. So he didn't. No time in the end. Said he wished he'd thought about it when he was well enough but had sort of put it to the back of his mind as one of those things you are forever saying You'll do one day, in your dotage. But at least he got it copied out."

"Where's the original?"

"Rudi has it."

"In the flat?"

"Think so. You should have it really. It belongs with the cottage."

Jess stares into space. Margaret studies her.

"How do you feel now?"

"Shattered, anxious. A sort of hollowness. Hard to explain. It can all get too much, you know? What's different, worse in a way, is that I was starting to think I could actually stay here, be here, which is such a strange thing for me. I've tried to work out why that is. I've thought about it so much and I think it's because here I can breathe again. Can you understand that? I found after a while, when I got used to it, that I could sleep like I remember as a child."

"That'll be the fresh air."

"Yes, I suppose so. But I think it's the water too. I've had this really strong feeling that I had found my way back to the sound of water, something I realise now that I have missed. It's been a real comfort and has brought good thoughts. But now all this. Oh God. Truth is I don't think I belong anywhere."

"We all belong somewhere, Jess."

"Not me."

"You'll find it. Maybe it is here. Give it time."

"Have you ever been down to the sea at night, when the water's ink black? No white horses, just big waves on the beach and a swell and lapping like it's breathing? It's one of the most awesome things, isn't it? I used to do that when I was a kid. Didn't frighten me then, but later, after the accident, when I was far away, I started having horrible dreams about it, one of my nightmares, that I'm swimming, that somehow, I'm out there, trying to get back, thinking I'll drown. I could see the house on the shore but couldn't reach it."

"Here as well?"

"No, no I haven't. But the broad at night is much the same, isn't it? It sort of draws you to it. Bit scary. Maybe it's because it's such a long time since I've been this close to water."

"I think it's eerie in the dark. I think everybody does."

"I was frightened to begin with, and those first nights when I found it hard to sleep I stood on the lawn and thought about that dream, fearing it, rather than actually dreaming it."

"What about the other dream, the one about the crash?"

Jess shakes her head and half smiles in thought.

"No."

She looks down and runs her fingers along the grain of the pine table.

"Ever since my family died I seem to have been made to do things I didn't want to do. My father. At school. College. Wherever I've gone, whatever I've done, someone's either arranged it or, if I've tried to do something for myself, someone's taken over. My life's always been like that. It makes me feel physically sick. Whatever I've tried to do, somehow I end up feeling completely out of control. But I didn't expect it here. I wasn't sure about coming here at all and yet when I got here I really began to think it was different. And it is, I know that. I began to feel a sense of belonging here. Really did. There is something about it. Calms me. I do love it, if I'm honest. And I want to stay; I know that now. Just don't know if I can. I truly believed Rudi was trying to help, you know? When he said he was giving it to me, it was like a dream; a wonderful dream. But I was completely crushed by his letter, Margaret. In a blind panic, I suppose, a mix of panic and anger. I just wanted to run again, to hide."

"I'm glad you felt you could tell me."

"Well. You're not part of it, are you, Margaret? I think you understand."

"I do."

Margaret pats Jess on the hand, picks up the teapot and walks over to the sink, where she fills the kettle again.

"My mother died two years ago. Was in an old folk's home back in Kerry. Dad died in 1954 when he was only 48. Some things in this life aren't fair. She lives to be 83 and my dear Dad, bless him, goes just like that."

Margaret turns and leans against the sink, arms folded.

"Cancer. He was gone within weeks of being diagnosed. But d'you know what she did? She never told me. I was away at college in Dublin. He was dying and she never told me. Only saw him once again. I'd have nursed him. I'd have come back sooner. Her will be done, you know?"

"Why would she do that?"

"Oh I've been round that one a few times, Jess. So many times. I despised her for it. Still do. Always will. Mind you, I'd felt hate for a long time before that, since I was very young really. Because she didn't want us, either of us. Dad loved her, never gave up, worked himself to the bone trying to keep everything together. I loved him to bits and he loved me. Gentle soul, he was. Too gentle really. For she was forever off with other men, screaming at him for making her life a misery. Looking at me as if I did too. I never went home again after Dad died. Went straight from college to London, training at Charing Cross Hospital, where I met Phil. I was running too, in a way. Coming here was a bit of shock, but I'm glad of it, that I am." She turns and refills the teapot. "An aunt, father's sister, wrote and told me that's she'd died. I didn't even go to her funeral. But I had to go back later to sort through the papers and stuff which was dreadful. Needed to, though. I'd half hoped, but there was nothing of Dad's left. Nothing. It was as if he'd never existed. She'd chucked the lot. I went to the grave and came away in despair that she'd been buried with him. I stood there whispering "sorry" to him. He'd got away from her and now she was with him again, weighing down on him."

Margaret carries the pot to the table.

20

It is another dark dream, but not like those of old.

Jess is standing on a dusty track that falls away down a hill. Her violin and bow hang from her left hand. She can see a woman with a dark shawl draped over her head. Her clothes are dirty and ragged. She has collapsed against a tree, her cheek and palms pressed against the bark. She winces and cries out in pain. She twists round until her spine is against the tree, her head falls back and then jerks forward as her arms cup the heavy shape of her unborn child. Her face is as pale as death. Her eyes are shut tight, her mouth open with the labour of breathing. She pushes herself away from the tree and staggers up the hill towards Jess. She falls. Jess calls out, unable to move. The woman picks herself up and comes on. Jess calls to her again and reaches out. The woman says nothing. She walks past Jess as if she isn't there. Jess watches her go, feeling the coldness of water around her bare feet. She looks down. She is sinking slowly into black water, like the night sea at the Cape that haunts her. She is gripped by terror, yet when she looks up again she is in a sea of reeds, out in the wilderness. For a moment she is relieved, but then they begin to swirl around her, pushed by a rising storm. It gets darker and darker and the wind grows stronger. She feels it will push her over, but her feet and ankles are locked by the roots of the reeds, and she becomes one of them. Across the heaving, hissing bleached-gold stems she can see other people held in the same way, being beaten and bent by the storm; her mother, her grandparents, Francis, a woman whose face she cannot see. More and more people appear until there is an ocean of faces pinched tight, braced against the wind and rain. Music, the third of the *Dances*, fills Jess's head and echoes the storm. It pulls and strains her body. She shouts and cries but no one opens their eyes; no one can hear her. Her hands and neck are grafted to her violin and bow now, and she plays. She is desperate. She closes her eyes and sees musicians beside her, rolling like the reeds as the music tears through them. The pattern of the audience fades into the blackness. Jess strains to find the faces she loves.

The strings burn her fingers.

"MAMMA!"

The cry creases her stomach and drains her of air. She falls back on the bed, gasping. Her chest is bursting. She rubs her palms into her wet face that is itching with sweat. The cottage is creaking in the wind and she can hear the water slapping against the staithe. Jess curls into a ball and stares at the broken moonshine flickering on the wall. She relives snatches of her dream, and wonders what to do, whether to stay or to run.

It is a brighter day, like a watercolour, and the dawn air is cool and fresh. Jess shudders, but continues to lean on the corner of the cottage near the shed to look out over the reeds for a second or two more. Way off, low in the sky, there are iron grey clouds. She takes some deep breaths, then goes back into the kitchen. The kettle has boiled. She makes coffee and returns to the sofa where she had settled and pondered and snoozed since the dream woke her. The deep, soft sofa is cosy, comforting, as is the whole room which is cast in warm light by the lamp. She opens the curtains. Her fear has slipped away. Her eagerness to leave has faded to the state she knows well, the numbness of doing nothing. She looks across at the music stand and wonders what will happen, what Rudi will do. It is nearly three weeks since she called him. She doesn't know what he will decide now, if he will listen. She doesn't feel angry any more, or upset. There is nothing more she can do, only imagine. And a small part of her keeps seeing herself playing the *Dances.*

Jess sits up in the bath. She can hear Margaret calling. Her tone says something is wrong. Jess climbs out, wraps herself in a towel and goes through to the kitchen. Margaret is standing anxiously just inside the door, her raincoat shining with wetness. They both drip water onto the floor.

"Jess..."

Jess goes towards her.

"What? What is it?"

"Rudi, he's in hospital. They think he's had a stroke."

"No."

Jess folds a little, like She's been punched.

"Esther, his sister, just rang. I think it happened some days ago, though she wasn't very clear and was obviously very upset. Said he kept trying to say something, and she thinks it's your name."

Jess covers her mouth with her fingers, then turns away. She swallows hard, wondering what to do.

"I...I'll get dressed, get some things together."

"Look, I'd like to go too. Do you mind? I can drive. Be the quickest way, I think."

"OK. I'll be as fast as I can."

"I've got to sort some things too, so I'll go back to the farm and drive down here in about half an hour. There's a downpour coming and no need for you to venture out. You sure you want to go?"

"Yes. Yes. I'll be ready."

Just past Norwich the rain stops and sun glistens on the road. They don't talk, other than for Jess to offer to pour coffee from the flask that Margaret has packed in the wicker basket on the back seat. Only when they join the tide of traffic heading down the M11 towards London do they begin.

"I shouldn't have shouted at him."

"It's not your fault, Jess."

"Maybe it is."

"No. You mustn't think that. Rudi is elderly. He isn't a well man, you know that. Come on, now. You can't blame yourself. That's crazy. He did something wrong and you had to speak your mind. That's not your fault. Anyway, there could be a hundred and one other reasons for this."

"Why do I always feel so guilty?"

"You have done nothing wrong. Nothing. The reverse in fact. By coming to the cottage you have done something very, very important."

Jess turns and looks at Margaret. Margaret goes on.

"I told you, it was Francis who thought of you. He said it came to him one day that you should have it, and Rudi was so overjoyed that he managed to get you to come to and see it, live in it. It had been a great worry to him, Jess. He shared Francis's wish that you should have Whispering Reeds, thought it was a wonderful idea, but he couldn't see how. That place was the most important place in the world to them. After Francis died Rudi told me what he had to try and do. He was really, really worried. It was the last of Francis's requests of him and he did it. Or rather you did. As for the music thing, well, that's taking things too far. The main thing is that what they really wanted has happened. You made him so happy. Or rather both of them, if you believe in that stuff."

"Do you?"

"Ghosts? Yes, I suppose I do, in so much that I get a real sense of people sometimes, you know?"

"Yes."

"Could be the mind playing tricks, but I don't think so."

Francis and Anna live in both their minds for a quiet while, until they leave the motorway and the Volvo slows and joins the tail of traffic queuing at a roundabout.

"What's best, Jess? Parking's going to be a nightmare."

"Which hospital is it?"

"The Middlesex. Just north of Oxford Street."

"God, I don't know. Not driving I don't have a clue really. There must be some sort of parking at the hospital, surely?"

"I wouldn't count on it. Even if there is it's probably choc-a-block. Maybe I can leave it out here in the suburbs somewhere. I hate driving in London anyway. I shoved an A to Z in the glove compartment. There are a couple of sandwiches too. Must be getting on for three now. I'll have a bite. Just cheese I'm afraid."

Jess opens the foil and passes Margaret a sandwich, then studies the map.

"Well, if we park somewhere near Swiss Cottage we can get the Jubilee Line down to Bond Street then the Central to Oxford Circus."

"I vote we get a taxi. Not a big fan of the tube."

"OK".

Jess looks up. London is closing in on them.

Margaret pays the driver. They stand looking up at the building.

Margaret takes a huge breath. "Right. Are we set?"

Jess smiles weakly at her. "Don't like hospitals. Sorry."

"What are you apologising for? Because I'm a nurse? Away with ya. Different when You're not working, when you know someone in there. I'm not so keen on them either, not now." She leans towards Jess. "Not like it used to be either. If you ask me the health service is in a right pickle. Creaking at the seams My old ward sister, Sister Mann, a stickler if ever there was one, would have fifty fits."

She puts her arm through Jess's and nods her head.

"Come on."

They are told Rudi is on a men's ward on the third floor. They take the lift and Jess drifts behind Margaret, who goes through the doors onto the warm ward and asks at the nurse's station. A nurse points to the far end. They walk along the corridor past several open-ended rooms, each with six beds in them. One or two beds have curtains round them, while beside a few others there are one or two visitors sitting or standing. But most of the patients are alone, some sleeping open mouthed, others watching. She is conscious of wide eyes following her as she walks by. Some of the old men look dreadful, with tubes in their noses and arms, and pitiful expressions on their ashen faces. There is a calmness, a false quietness masking truth. The warmth and the smell make Jess blink and her shoulders tighten. She quickens her step and follows Margaret, who has turned into the last room.

Rudi is asleep, propped on pillows in the far bed nearest the window, a mask over his nose and mouth, a tube in his thin bare arm that's laid on top of the bedding, a huge spray of carnations beside him, his thin, flat hair brushed neatly across his forehead, his bony chest rising and falling. Jess's heart races. Margaret is on the far side of the bed talking softly to Esther, clutching her forearms and looking into her tearful eyes. There is a small pile of bibles on the windowsill beyond them. The top window is open and the hum of London drifts in. Esther turns her head and tries to smile. Jess goes round to her and gives her a hug. With trembling hands Esther takes a tissue from her handbag.

"Oh dear. I found him, you see, sitting on the floor in the kitchen. He was on the floor. Wasn't able to speak. I...I..."

Margaret takes her hands again. They'd met only once before, at the funeral, but had spoken on the telephone a couple of times since then. "Don't fret, now. He's sleeping. He's very comfortable. He's being well looked after."

"I hope you don't mind me ringing, only Rudi gave me your telephone number when he came up to Norfolk last year. Just in case, you know?"

"Yes, of course. Of course I remember. We spoke, didn't we? Now, Esther, has anyone else been with you?"

"No. There's only me. We don't have any other family."

"And what about you? You must be exhausted. Have you had anything to eat or drink lately? Esther? Have you? Look, Jess is here. She'll stay with him. Come with me. Come on, we'll go and find a nice cup of tea."

Esther sniffs and nods and picks up her handbag. Margaret looks at Jess and smiles knowingly, then walks slowly away with Esther.

Rudi looks very peaceful and, strangely, not so old. Jess sinks slowly onto the seat beside him, her back to the window. She looks at him for a long while, then her gaze drifts to the next bed along, where a sprightly man is sitting upright, looking down at a cup of tea in front of him. He glances at Jess and smiles warmly, then continues to gaze at the green cup and saucer.

Jess gets up and goes round to him.

"Can I help you with that?"

He raises his arm.

"Oh, no. Thank you. You're very kind. Very kind. But I can't touch it, you see. It belongs to London Transport. But if you would be so kind, I'd be grateful if you would get me a telephone. I wish to call the police."

Jess looks round. A nurse who has been with another patient across the room comes to the other side of the bed.

"Now, Mr Merriford, what's the problem? Better drink that tea soon or It'll be too cold."

"I'm not sure I should."

"I won't tell them."

The nurse winks at Jess and then helps Mr Merriford lift the cup to his lips. Jess backs away and sits beside Rudi again. The nurse comes round and stands beside Rudi and checks his pulse.

"If he stirs, rub his right hand and arm. Stimulation. He has some paralysis on his right side. You family?"

Jess shakes her head. "Just a friend. The woman who was here is his sister."

"Yes, she told me. In a bit if a state, poor love."

"How bad is he?"

"So hard to tell at this stage with a cerebro-vascular accident. He's had a CT scan and we're trying to get his blood pressure down. The mask is to make sure his brain is getting enough oxygen. If he gets through this and there's no further trauma then, apart from the drugs to try and reduce the risk of another stroke, he's going to need physiotherapy and speech therapy if he's going to regain some function. So, don't worry if he can't speak to you. Talk to him. Rub his hand. OK?"

"OK. But, I mean, what could cause this?"

"Again hard to tell. When you get to his age and you lose mobility, plus the fact he has high blood pressure, the possibility is always going to be there. We'll see."

She turns and goes back to the patient on the other side of the room.

Jess looks at Rudi. He is breathing deeply, his mouth slightly open. His pale skin looks so thin. The bones of his chest, bare at the nape of his pyjamas, hold her gaze. She locks her arms tightly across her stomach and leans forward in the chair, rocking slightly. The ache is there, and the guilt.

Margaret and Esther return. Jess lets Esther have the chair and Margaret beckons her out into the corridor.

"She's almost on her knees and really needs to get some rest. I've said I'll take her home, if that's OK. I'll be back as soon as I can. Do you mind staying?"

"No, of course."

"Go and get yourself something to drink first, though. Take your time. She said she wanted to stay a little longer just in case he wakes again. So don't rush. Give yourself a moment. When you come back I'll take her home."

"Is there a payphone here?"

"By the lifts."

"Michael?"

"Mum? You OK?"

"Not really. It's Rudi. He's had a stroke."

"Oh God."

"Look, I'm at the Middlesex Hospital. You know where that is? Just off Oxford Street between the BBC and Tottenham Court Road. Can you come? And, well, I'm not sure what I'm doing, but Esther can't deal with all this on her own, so I was thinking I may stay over tonight. I don't want to go to the flat, though. Can I stay with you?"

"Um..."

"What?"

"That may be a bit difficult, because Dad's here at the moment. Down for a couple of days."

"Oh."

"I can talk to him, though. I'm sure he'll understand."

"No. Don't. Please don't. I'll ring Suzy."

"Anyway, I can be there in about an hour. All right? Which ward?"

Margaret and Esther are still with Jess at the hospital when Michael comes in, bearing a bunch of yellow roses. A nurse is with him, and before anyone can speak she says that there are too many visitors now. Margaret explains that she and Esther are just leaving. Michael kisses Jess and Margaret, then hugs Esther and smiles at her.

"I might have known there'd already be a huge bunch of flowers here. I'd better donate these to someone else otherwise it's going to look like a florist's."

Esther looks at him intensely. "So kind of you to come, Michael."

"Mum rang me. We want to be here."

They all look at Rudi for a moment, wondering what to say. Esther leans over her brother and runs her fingers across his hair.

"They've given him some medication and washed him. Not woken up though."

Michael and Jess look at one another. Margaret moves to Esther and gently touches her elbow.

"Come on, Esther. You heard the nurse. Let's get you home. Take a taxi. Jess will explain to him when he wakes. You have a good night's rest and then you'll hopefully feel much better tomorrow."

Michael helps Esther with her coat and Jess takes Margaret to one side.

"Once You've dropped Esther why don't you head home? I'll stay

211

in London tonight, with a friend."

"You sure? We could meet at the car, or I could come back to the hospital."

"No need. Getting Esther home is a real help."

"I'll stay with her for a while, but I'm afraid I can't stay down. The girls are due home this weekend and..."

"That's fine. Don't worry. Only I ought to stay. Don't feel I want to go quite yet."

"I understand. How will you get back?"

"Train. No problem. Will just need picking up the other end."

"Fine. If you are sure."

Jess kisses her for the first time. They hold each other.

"Right, Esther, are we set?"

Jess and Michael watch them go, then sit either side of Rudi. Michael takes one of his hands, and so Jess does the same with the other. She tells Michael what the nurse said, then looks at Rudi.

"I can't stop thinking it's my fault."

"Don't be ridiculous, Mum. He's very old, he has high blood pressure, he sits for huge lengths of time. It happens to people his age. It's no one's fault."

"I shouted at him. Screamed at him."

Michael looks at his mother unsure if he should say it. He takes a deep breath.

"If you want to blame someone then blame all of us. We knew, Mum, we all knew that Rudi wanted you to play the *Dances*. You must have realised it too. Come on. It's just regrettable, wrong, the way he did it, without talking to you. I sort of knew he might do something like that, but

I didn't know what to say. I should have talked to you about it when I was in Norfolk, but didn't. And d'you know why? You seemed so happy there that I actually thought it was possible, that with a little more time you might agree. I was so happy to see the change in you, to think it might be possible, yet I didn't want to run the risk of upsetting you. I let Rudi down by not helping and I let you down by not being honest."

"I just reacted."

"I know, Mum, and no one could blame you."

"I...I felt as if the whole thing, the cottage and everything was to get me to do this."

"Not true."

"I realise that now."

She looks across the bed at her son.

"Oh God, Michael, what do I do now?"

"Nothing. Nothing. One day at a time. Don't make any decisions now. The cottage is yours because Francis and Rudi wanted you to have it. As for the *Dances* there is nothing wrong whatsoever, even given this, for you not doing it. In fact it's really, really important now that you don't do it unless you really want to. It's about doing it for yourself, Mum, not for Rudi, not for me or anyone else for that matter. You need to want to do it, and there should be no guilt about it. Honestly."

"Why would he do that?"

"Oh come on, Mum. You were his best student, his favourite. You are the best. He and Francis loved you. He wanted to help you. How many reasons do you want?"

Jess looks at Rudi again.

"D'you think he can hear us?"

Michael gets up. "I don't know. It's possible. I think I'm going to get a coffee. D'you want one?"

Jess smiles up at him and nods.

21

Jess unlocks the door and turns on the light. Her flat is cold, a chaos of things she tries not to see. She hesitates in the doorway, then gathers up a pile of post off the floor and dumps it on a table unopened, adding to the chaos. She goes quickly to a drawer in the cupboard by the window. She lifts out an old child's shoebox, removes the lid and takes out a worn book, her grandfather's book, which she studies for a few seconds, then lifts to her face and smells. She goes back to the table and searches for a pad and pens. She kneels and feels beneath the sofa, pulling a carrier bag out of the webbing beneath it and takes out what's left of her dope. She carries it into the bathroom, hesitates, wraps it in toilet paper and flushes it away. She sweeps all her toiletries off the shelf into the empty carrier bag, turns off the light and the water heater and goes through to the bedroom. She strains to reach and drag down a holdall from on top of the wardrobe, then drops the carrier bag and some clothes into it, along with her pillow. Back in the lounge she scoops up the book, pad, and pens and heads for the open door.

Suzy is playing the piano. It's almost dark, the Clapham Street is full of parked cars. The tree-lined Victorian terrace is patterned by lights in windows. Jess recognises the music; Schubert, an *Impromptu*. She stands on the step, her face close to the red door, waiting for the right moment to knock.

"Jess! How long have you been out there? Oh come here."

Suzy gives her a big hug. Jess drops her bag and holds on to her.

"You must have been listening. You were, weren't you? Give me that bag. So great to see you, although not under these bloody horrible circumstances, I know. The answer, me thinks, is food. Let's eat something. Yep?"

"But You're working."

"Panicking more like. I've got a recital in Guildford next Friday and, as usual, I'm not ready. Done enough for one day, though. Too tired to concentrate now."

Jess looks tentatively round the door into the long room that runs from the bay back to the grand piano and French doors. Suzy glances back over her shoulder as she walks down the hall towards the kitchen.

"Don't worry. I'm on my own. Have been since Easter."

Jess follows.

"Patrick?"

"Still friends. But it had sort of fizzled out. We needed some air, both of us. Now, sit yourself down and I'll see what I can find."

She brings plates, knives, a French stick, and several cheeses on a board to the table, and then a half empty bottle of white wine from the fridge door and pulls out the cork with her teeth. She grins and raises her eyebrows.

"Got my eye on a hunky bloke who works in the box office at St

John's, though. Early days. Half French apparently. He grew up in Paris and has this really sexy accent and big dark eyes. My imagination's been running riot. I plucked up courage to, well, you know, and we're having lunch tomorrow. Right..."

She pours the wine and hands Jess a glass.

"Here's to the good times, gone and still to come."

Jess looks down into the golden drink. She slowly puts the glass down. They talk. Jess tells her everything, and Suzy listens intently, leaning forward, elbows on the table, her face cupped in her hands. She sees that Jess doesn't touch her wine glass. She remembers that feeling of trespass when she went into the flat, her shock at the mess. Jess doesn't ask her.

Suzy didn't know Rudi well, and when he called out of the blue and said Jess was doing something for him she wasn't certain at first. But Rudi was adamant, and she had no way of getting in touch with Jess. Listening to Jess tell of his visit to the cottage she remembers that Rudi didn't actually say Jess wanted it. Jess talks on. Suzy knows nothing of the rest, and her face shows it.

"He's given you the cottage? Wow. Crikey, Jess. I mean, that's amazing. What are you go to do? Stay there, or..."

"I'm going back, tomorrow or the next day. Not sure. Depends. I'm not clear really, about anything, but I'm quite used to that feeling. There's nowhere else to go. Don't want to go back to the flat. I'll maybe spend some time at the hospital in the morning, although I'm not sure what I can do. It all feels really weird, but I want to try and talk to him, you know? Clear the air, say some things. Just hope he can hear me, doesn't die."

"Look, what Michael said to you today, about not having to do the concert, is right, of course. Don't make any decisions now. It's not the time."

"If...if I did decide to do it, I'd need to work with someone."

Suzy smiles. "Really? I'm in great demand, I'll have you know, and expensive. Seriously, though, you might have to come back to London. Don't think I could get up to Norfolk."

Jess sleeps late and is woken by Suzy playing. The house is warm. She lies listening for a while, then gets up and wraps herself in a white bathrobe. She goes to the loo, then drifts to the kitchen, makes herself a cup of coffee, moves silently through to the sofa and settles. It's so good to hear Suzy again, to see her. They eat toast and drink more coffee. Suzy continues to practise as Jess showers, dresses, and gathers her things. She comes down, ready to leave, and finds Suzy in front of the hall mirror looking at herself.

"He's quite a bit younger than me, you know, and if he decides he doesn't like me I'm going to blame you. After sitting up talking half the night I've got bags under my eyes. Listen, if you can wait for half an hour, I'm going to put some war paint on and change, then I'll come in with you on the tube."

"Half an hour?"

"Well, maybe a bit longer, but wait for me. Pleeeease. It's gone twelve already and I've got to get my skates on. You can reassure me I'm beautiful and that I'm not being an idiot."

"You are, and You're not."

"In which order!"

Suzy charges up the stairs, then suddenly stops.

"A...Are you thinking of staying tonight?"

"No."

"Right. Fine. I mean..."

"It's OK, I understand. Decided I'll head back today anyway."

"Good. Right, wait!"

Suzy continues to run. Jess stares bleakly at herself in the mirror, then looks away.

The phone rings and Suzy shouts down telling Jess to get it. It's Michael. He tells her that he's already at the hospital and that Esther is there, how Rudi has been awake for a quite a while but they've been asked to leave the ward while they bath him and then take him for some sort of scan. It's unclear how long that will be. He says he can't stay any longer because he promised Sally he'd take her to her parents in Hampshire, and he doesn't want to say no. Jess says that's fine, he must go. They agree she will call him from Margaret's when she's back in Norfolk.

Jess watches Suzy skip off the train and vanish into the crowd. At the hospital she takes the stairs not the lift, walking at a slow rhythm, pacing out words, thinking what to say if Rudi is conscious. She walks through the ward, turns into the end room and freezes. Esther and Tom stop talking and look at her. Esther comes towards her beaming.

"He's been awake quite some time, Jessica. Isn't that wonderful? Resting again, but what a change since yesterday. He smiled at me and squeezed my hand."

Jess is staring at Tom. She blinks, sees herself in the mirror. She swallows hard and walks towards him, her head and eyes down, scanning the floor until she can see Rudi. Tom comes to her side.

"Hi, Jess. Forgive me, only I was here with Michael, then stayed to keep Esther company for a while. Got talking."

She turns for a second and faces him, eyes closed, and snatches a huge breath.

"It's OK".

"I'll go."

"No."

She looks at him now, almost pleading. He touches her arm.

"I'll get you a chair."

219

Esther is sitting by the window, rubbing Rudi's right hand. Jess takes Rudi's left hand, rubbing her thumb across the back of it. Esther is leaning forward slightly, whispering a few words in Hebrew. Tom sits on the end of the bed and they stay like this for a while, all their eyes, if not their minds, on Rudi.

Jess tries to steady her breathing, to ease the tightness across her chest. She wonders if Tom meant to stay to see her, or if it was a mistake. She wonders what to say to him, what he must think of her, what will happen now.

Rudi's mouth and nose are not covered by the mask today. His cheeks look hollow and his lower face is strangely different, and as he swallows and moves his jaw as if he is eating. Jess realises his false teeth have been taken out. After a few minutes he yawns and opens his eyes a little. He rolls his head on the pillow and stares at Jessica, a slight smile slowly dawning in his eyes and on his thin lips. She feels the fingers of his left hand move. He holds her thumb and squeezes it.

Jess leans forward slightly.

"Hello, Rudi."

Esther stands and raises a glass of water to his mouth. Water dribbles down his chin and she wipes it away with a tissue. She remains standing, looking at her brother, who continues to look calmly at Jess. Tom gets up too.

"Maybe we should a leave them for a little while, Esther. Take the chance to stretch your legs. I'll come with you."

Esther kisses Rudi on the forehead. "I won't be long."

His eyes turn to his sister for a second, then he continues to gaze at Jess as they leave. Jess tries to smile, but the smile buckles, and her head drops.

"I'm sorry I shouted at you."

Rudi lifts his hand as if to tell her to stop.

"Only I was..."

He is rolling his head very slightly from side to side and patting her hand. He tries to say something. Jess fumbles for a tissue in her bag, wipes her eyes and nose, then clutches his hand. They stare at one another for several seconds.

"I don't know what to say to you, Rudi. I love the cottage, love it, and I've never thanked you, have I? I'm sorry for that too. Thank you. Think I'm going to stay there for the time being. Don't want to be anywhere else just now. Only..."

She must tell him. She feels she can now.

"Only this thing about the music. You have to understand, Rudi, I have to decide. Me. No one can do that for me. Not any more. Not any more."

Rudi smiles at her again.

"I love the Three Dances. They are wonderful. But I need to know you understand what I'm saying to you. Do you? I must decide, and I'm not ready to do anything right now. Do you? Do you understand?"

"Yes."

The word is a whisper, but clear. Rudi's smile grows until his face shines with it. He repeats it. Jess closes her eyes and lowers her head until it touches the bed. Rudi lifts his hand and gently rests it on her hair.

When Esther and Tom return Jess is talking softly to Rudi about Anna and the journal. She stops when she sees them, lets go of Rudi's hand and stands up. Rudi points at her and then at the way out.

"You want me to go?"

He nods, pointing again, only this time up at an angle. Tom is at Jess's shoulder.

"I think he means you should go home."

Outside on the pavement Jess no longer feels she wants to hide. Having Tom standing next to her doesn't panic her. Strangely, it's sort of a comfort, and there is a feeling she hasn't had for a very long time. She realises she doesn't want him to go. She is wondering what to say when he speaks first.

"Time for a coffee?"

"I'm not sure when the trains are."

"Actually, Jess, I was thinking. If you want, I could drive you back to Norfolk. I've got to go back to Suffolk anyway and it's not that much further."

"It is."

"Well, I want to, and then you won't have to cart your bag or to worry or wait about at stations."

"Er..."

She wants to say yes.

"Say yes."

"OK...Yes, OK. You sure?"

"Absolutely."

He is as tall as ever and much the same. A little round-shouldered, wide grin, hands buried in the pockets of his sagging beige jacket, the deep soft voice. His dark brown hair has receded, and his sideburns are quite grey. He looks tired.

"You can drop me in Norwich."

"No. Don't worry about it. I'd like to do it. Give me that bag. My car's outside Michael's, but maybe we can get that coffee first, though? Didn't sleep all that well the last couple of nights. My days of willingly sleeping on a sofa are long gone."

They find a café. He begins, gently asking what Jess thinks of Sally. They talk about their son, his music, the quartet. Jess asks about Tom's work, at the Britten Pears School where he's been for so long. As he answers she doesn't listen but looks at him and wonders about him and Michael in all those years in that house by the beach, that life in Aldeburgh, their son growing up, the rhythm of their lives separate from her, the things, the familiar things, and that feeling that must exist between them. It stirs the painful memory of her own childhood on the Cape; the love, the deepest feeling of love.

Tom talks and looks back at Jess. He senses that she isn't really listening, but it's OK. She looks different, a little tired and drawn maybe, but better, so much better than when he saw her at Francis's funeral. Some of the weight in her face has gone. Her skin has more colour and there is a depth and steadiness to her eyes he has never seen before. She is clearly, understandably, fragile, but there is a softness and openness, a readiness to smile, that makes him wonder what must have happened. Michael was right.

As Tom weaves north east through the traffic, back along the way Margaret had driven, Jess senses a deep calmness come over her. It feels so good to be leaving London this time, like another weight has gone. The sun is lower and there isn't a cloud in the sea of blue sky. They chat a little, carefully seeking memories of happier times. When thinking what to say, Jess keeps leaning and looking up at the faint white face of the moon floating above the harvested fields, waiting for the sun to set. He asks what the place is like, what sort of things she has seen, how old the cottage is. She tells him about the journal. He listens intently. He asks what happened to Anna, and Jess says no one knows. He insists there must be something, some information somewhere, and he urges Jess to check local records. She tells him she intends to do, but doesn't say that in her bag are pens and paper that she feels compelled to try and keep a diary of her search.

Tom watches her as she speaks, noting how her eyes brighten, how her hands move as she describes Anna's world. When she pauses, he asks gently, "Why does it matter so much to you? This woman you never knew?"

Jess looks out at the water for a long moment. "Many reasons," she says softly, almost wistfully, and offers nothing more.

As they near Norfolk the moon heartens. Stars begin to glint just before the last sunlight turns to gold on the western seam. Jess asks that they stop so she can go to the loo, and Tom says he needs to fill up with petrol anyway. They pull in at a station and Little Chef. Jess walks across to the toilet. At the sink she dares to face herself in the mirror, and pushes the hair from her face, continuing to brush it with her fingers. She goes back to the car and studies Tom as he queues to pay. He comes out of the sliding door and crosses the forecourt to the car.

"I'll just pop into the Little Chef for a sec. There's a payphone in there and I need to make a quick call. Only be a tick."

"Right."

She suddenly realises he might have someone and that he is explaining why he will be late. Why else would he need to call? Her back stiffens. When he gets into the car she suggests again that he drop her in Norwich, but he says it is far too late and he wouldn't dream of it. Nothing else is said. Then, beyond Norwich, on the edge of the maze of lanes in the last miles to the cottage, Jess suddenly realises that she isn't sure of the way. She bends forward and peers at the road signs picked out by the headlights, but nothing looks right and they are lost for a while. She tells Tom to stop so she can go into a pub and ask for directions, but it's still another half an hour before she sees a sign for Hickling. By the time they arrive at the cottage it's gone eleven.

Tom turns off the engine and smiles at her.

"Well, that was fun."

"Sorry. I never thought. Do you need a coffee or something? You've still got quite a drive."

"I don't want to impose."

"It's OK."

"Actually I need a pee now. Do you have a compost bin?"

Jess smiles and shakes her head.

They go into the dark cottage and Tom stands in the kitchen as Jess goes around turning on lamps. He follows her into the sitting room.

"I see what Michael meant. Jess, it's a pretty place. And a piano too."

"The bathroom's in there."

She turns and sees him looking at the music on the stand near the window.

"What's this?"

"Just something Rudi asked me to look at."

She waits, watching his musical eyes scanning the notes. She remembers that intensity in his eyes, the furrowed brow, from those distant days when they were students, when they first played together. He raises his head and looks at her inquisitively. Jess moves quickly towards the kitchen.

"I'll put the kettle on."

"Don't, please. Not on my account. I think I'll hit the road. It's getting late and it's better if I head home."

She blurts out, "You can stay if you want. I know what you said about sofas, but it's quite..."

"No. Thanks. It's been good to see you again, to have a chat. You know."

"Yeah."

"Just sorry about Rudi, though it looks like he might be improving a little. So, have to go, because, well...Right, I'd better go to the bathroom."

Jess waits in the kitchen, leaning against the sink. She wonders who his woman is, what she looks like, if she's a musician. Tom walks back through and comes straight up to Jess and kisses her on the cheek. Jess closes her eyes for a second.

"Thanks for bringing me."

"Pleasure."

"You must come again when it's light. Maybe with Michael?"

"That would be nice, really nice. I'll hold you to it. Take care. Bye, Jess."

"Bye."

She closes the door behind him and leans on it. She opens it again when the car starts and pulls away. She waves but he doesn't see her.

22

10 September

Another frustrating day. I took the dinghy to the far end of the broad, then walked to the village yet again. This time I was allowed, finally, to get into the church and see the records. Although there were no clues in the churchyard (I've walked round it often enough) I had hoped that maybe their graves, or just Jacob's, might have been there, unmarked, or that the stone had been removed or something, and that the records would tell me. But nothing. The vicar was adamant that no one could have been buried there without it being in the church books.

This isn't easy. I know she worked at the school, but without any obvious records of that either I'm not sure what to do now.

15 September

I've been re-reading the journal and have had an idea. I want to go to Gressenhall and see the place, and I also want to try and find Swanton Rectory, which can't be that far away. There's a chance Anna might have gone back to where she came from, that is, if the doctor was still alive, and hopefully the Rectory is still there. I doubt that anybody living there now will know what happened a hundred years ago, but it will be fascinating to see where she lived. I'll try and borrow a map from Margaret and Phil tomorrow and tell them. I think they said the old workhouse was now a museum or something, so that means it's open to the public, and I will see where she was born as well.

16 September

I'm very tired. Margaret has just taken me in the car to Horsey and we have walked for miles, first across the meadows to the bank of marram grass, then along the beach, back inland, then on a path beside the channel where I stayed that time on Otter, and finally through the village to the car which she'd parked beside the thatched church. It was very bracing, and I can feel my skin tingling from the salt air, and my legs itch from where they were spiked by the grass. From a distance the wind-blown marram hills, as Anna called them, looked in the sun like shiny blue-green fur, and the contrast of that colour against the sky was incredible. Down on the beach, where a galaxy of shells lay scattered across the almost white sand, we stood and watched two seals bobbing up close to the shore, coming quite near at one point to a family swimming. We talked constantly, and I'm glad that Margaret is keen to come with me to Gressenhall and Swanton. We have agreed we'll go next week, after the wherry trip this Sunday.

23

"Jibing! Look out you lot! Heads down!"

Jess, Michael, and Phil duck into the hold of the wherry Albion as the bottom of the huge black sail sweeps by inches above their heads. They are standing on the steep steps that drop down into the hold, where four of the narrow red hatches in the centre of the boat have been lifted and stacked, letting a band of sunlight into the space below. Jess and Michael are on the steps on the left, where they have been talking and leaning out, watching the yachts and motor cruisers go by. Phil is on the other side, taking pictures. Below in the windowless hold Margaret is with her eldest daughter Lizzie at the far end of a long wooden table that's already laid out for lunch. Margaret pouring a pre-cooked soup into a pot, ready to go on *Albion's* gas stove when they stop, Lizzie is cutting bread.

"People are hungry. Where are we, Phil?"

"Just passed St Benet's and have turned off t'wards Walsham Broad.

Wind behind us now so ten minutes at most I reckon. Need a hand?"

"Typical. Bloody typical. Men. Wait until it's done and then ask. Actually, yes, Phil Bunn, you can pour me some wine. How many of us are there again?"

"Hang on..."

Phil and Jess pop their heads up into the breeze and look round. Ted is standing tall, arms folded, high on the deck at the back of the boat. He is at home. Jess thinks to ask him if his family were water gypsies. By his knees in the deep, cramped cockpit Jess can see the faces of Margaret's son David and Nat Sparkes, the skipper. David's concentration and effort tell her he is grasping the hefty, subtly curved tiller. She had held it for a few moments, the weight and power of the wherry so palpable, Anna's account enriched all the more. And, there, in the cockpit with the thick rope coil of the main sheet that runs through Nat hands to the corner of the vast black sail, are the doors leading to the snug cuddy with its two bunks and stove. She imagines Anna everywhere. Jess turns. At the front of the wherry, sitting in pairs on the hatches either side of the towering wooden mast and looking ahead along the river are Helen and her mother, Pat, then Margaret's other daughter Jackie, and Michael's girlfriend Sally. When they'd first set off from Womack Water Jackie and Jess had sat there, lifting their legs out of the way as Ted and Phil had pushed the boat with quants, just as Jacob would do, out from the mooring and onto the main river.

Phil steps down to the floor of the hold and reaches for a bottle of wine on the table.

"Eleven, I reckon. Twelve, counting Nat."

"Right."

Albion slows a little as the riverbanks become wooded, but light gusts of wind keep filling the high sail and she glides quite quickly through two tight turns. The black canvas swings back and forth again. Sally, Jackie, Helen, and Pat lie flat on the hatches, laughing. People on holiday cruisers reach for their cameras and a couple of the boats bump into each other as they try to get out of the wherry's way. There was a bite in the air when they set off, but the midday sun is pleasingly warm. Jess can see that the river has straightened out once again, so she gingerly climbs out of the hold and goes towards the mast. She turns and smiles at Michael, who follows her, and they settle on the bow by the winch used for lowering and lifting the mast. Jess explains how it works, how vital it is for getting under bridges. Michael's head flops back and he stares up at the black sail and the end of the mast where it is painted red, white, and blue like *Albion's* decking. Jess follows his gaze. Right at the top, there is a long red wind vane with a white star on a blue square and a metal figure of a woman in a bell dress.

Jess says, "Ted told me that flag at the top, the vane, is called a Jenny."

"Is that why there's a woman up there?"

"Apparently."

Someone calls. They sit up. People walking along the bank wave to them and they wave back.

"How do they stop this thing?"

"They'll swing her nose into the wind and then drop the sail. Like any boat, I suppose. No problem if there's space. Margaret says we're going to stay out in the middle of the broad, South Walsham Broad. Look, there it is."

About two hundred yards ahead the river widens into a shiny expanse of water.

"What do we do then? Is there an anchor?"

"Mud weight." Jess points at the cone of metal with a coil of rope around it just in front of them. "All Broads boats have them."

"That? Bloody hell, I tried to lift that, Mum. It weighs a ton. And those poles..."

"Quants."

"Whatever. Those ruddy great things they were pushing us along with first off, they're ridiculously heavy and unwieldy. I couldn't do that, not in a month of Sundays."

"They used to do it all day long if necessary, on the old working wherries. There used to be hundreds of them, you know, carrying cargo up and down the rivers and from big ships in Yarmouth. Two people used to sail them, loading them by hand almost to the point of sinking, sailing in all weathers and then having to unload them again."

"How long ago was that?"

"Until this century and many before that. There's a book at the cottage, *Black Sailed Traders* by...by...Clark, that's it, Roy Clark. I started reading it this week, knowing we were coming. He was one of the founders of the trust that saved Albion. She's known as the last of the black sailed traders."

"Where did they sleep? In the hold?"

"No, there's a tiny cabin at the back, known at the cuddy. Go and have a look later. Have a go at sailing her."

"Nope. Don't want to ruin a glorious day. What worries me though is that with all these boats about and the yachts and stuff, there must be some horrible collisions. I mean, in places the river's barely wide enough for the wherry, let alone a great big holiday cruiser coming the other way."

"Bound to be, I suppose. But don't worry. We're bigger than everything else and our skipper knows what he's doing, I think. Character, isn't he? Just love the way Nat shouts at people to get out of the way. His grandfather was a wherryman, according to Ted. Anyway, everything should give way to sail."

"But when that twerp cut across in front of us earlier I thought his number was up."

"You mean like this bloke?"

"Oh shit."

A small pale blue and white motorboat, the sort people hire for the day, has veered out from the bank at full throttle and is pirouetting in the middle of the river, right in *Albion's* path. A wide-eyed young boy is at the controls and a man is standing at his shoulder, spinning the steering wheel and wildly over-compensating, throwing the boat into a figure of eight, while the woman sitting at the back is hanging on to the side, looking petrified.

Jess glances back at Nat who is helping David pull hard at the tiller, trying to change the wherry's course. Ted has his hands cupped to his mouth and is shouting, but the roar of the hire boat's engine drowns him out. At the last second, the day boat veers back towards the bank, missing *Albion's* bow by a whisker.

Nat slaps a hand to his forehead and shouts.

"HOLY FUCKIN' MOLY!"

Margaret's voice booms from the hold.

"LANGUAGE, NAT."

"Sorry, Margaret. Sorry, David. But, honestly, did you see it, boy? Tha's things like that why I gorn grey. Think on about what you said about wantin' to be a wherry skipper. Sailin' is one thing, but havin' to deal with them buggers is..."

"NAT!"

"Sorry, Margaret."

They are almost at the broad now and as Ted makes his way to the front, Nat calls for everyone to either get below or out of the way. Fifteen minutes later and the sail is down on the hatches and they are all seated round the table, steaming bowls of soup in front of them. Ted raises a glass.

"Here's to us all. Once again, a right nice day. Cheers."

"Cheers!"

Jess looks round at the beaming faces and smiles back. Word pictures, fascination, have become tangible. There is a happy hum of conversation and she watches Sally and Michael in the seam of sunlight beneath the open hatches, grinning across the table at one another. Beyond them Helen and her mum have returned to their deep conversation. Nat Sparkes, his cheeks crimson with the wind and sun, is laughing loudly, seated between Phil and Ted and recounting some of his close scrapes. David is listening eagerly. Margaret is at the end near to Jess, flanked by her daughters. She smiles at Jess.

"All right?"

Jess nods. "Thanks for this."

"We do it every year. Nat, Phil, and Ted have known each other since they were kids and it's a tradition, sort of. Nat always skippers, of course, and Ted is the mate. Glad you're enjoying it. Your Michael seems to be. She's a lovely girl."

Jess looks at Sally and her son and sees their softly spoken happiness, their knowing eyes as they look at one another. She feels a smile grow on her face.

After lunch Margaret commands the women to go on deck and to leave the clearing up for the "menfolk", so they climb onto the hatches to sit in the folds of the sail and talk as Albion swings slowly round on the mud weight. Jess settles close beside Margaret who is staring out across the rippling broad.

Margaret speaks without breaking her gaze. "Weird isn't, when you suddenly get a sense of someone. I do believe in ghosts, spirits, call it what you will, you know that, in so much that I can't disbelieve it, if you know what I mean. Too many times I've had a really strange feeling of something, someone. Could be the mind playing tricks, but I don't think so. I'm sure of it. Funny, but I've got this strangest feeling just now, like Francis is right here, you know? When we got up from the table I suddenly imagined him clear as day standing at the end, by the steps where he'd always sit entertaining us all, laughin', laughin' his head off he was, just like he used to. Maybe that was to remind me that I should be missin' 'im. I do."

Margaret pulls her legs up to her chest and rests her chin on her knees. Jess follows her gaze out across the dappled water. Margaret takes several long, deep breaths.

"We didn't come out on Albion last year, what with the funeral and Rudi being so frail nobody felt like it, so this is the first time without them. Strange thought. You can imagine it, though, can't you? Francis was like a big kid and would beam like the sun. God, he loved it. Such a lovely person he was too. Such fun. We had to fish him out more than once, you know, because he would insist on making quanting a competition, which, of course, was a complete nonsense. One year, on the river Ant I think it was, he got his quant stuck in the mud at the bottom of the river and when he got to the back of Albion he couldn't pull it out. "Stead of letting go he hung on, the fool. Ha! Then there were the times when he would insist on roaring about on the dinghy with the outboard. Times like this, after lunch, he'd be on it, nosing, exploring or the like. Couldn't sit still for one minute."

Margaret turns and smiles knowingly at Jess. "Handsome devil too, don't you reckon?"

Jess grins. The two women gently lean towards one another until their shoulders touch. Memories of Francis bond them. Jess sees him naked. She remembers his shape, the square-shouldered, tall form of him, the colour and beauty of him, that first occasion, so early on, when Rudi had let her into the flat without him knowing. He is standing in the doorway to the hall, facing her, asking her how life is, as he always would, yet bare, completely bare. She remembers him cupping her face in his hands after her first solo recital, saying nothing, just beaming, looking down at her, gently shaking his head, his large eyes bright like river water. He had kissed her on the forehead and hugged her with such tenderness. She had hung on to him. She remembers his feet, his huge brown feet, and how he hated shoes. How he would always go barefoot at home, and go to work and concerts and ride his cycle in all weathers in just his leather sandals. He was constant, always there, always life itself. She thinks back, and knows with a surging feeling of love, that without him it could never have been.

Margaret breaks the silence.

"Heard from Esther yesterday, by the way. Rudi's speech is coming back quite well really, but he can't walk, and not likely to again, she thinks, given how he was in the first place. She shouldn't be so sure. He's as stubborn as I am. Must be some Irish in there somewhere. Anyway, She's still talking about taking him to live with her, which in the circumstances seems to be the only option. God only knows what he'll think of that. But the alternative, some sort of nursing home, is unthinkable too, isn't it? Maybe he'll appreciate being with his sister, the company and all, and being looked after. Even before the stroke there was no tellin' how long he'd have coped on his own."

"No."

They both think about the music. Margaret wonders if Jess has decided yet what she will do. Jess tries to push it from her mind.

"Margaret? When can we go, d'you think? Gressenhall, I mean."

"Gressenhall? Oh, um, a Saturday would be ideal, to be honest with ya. No school run in the morning and David'll be at home to help Phil. Um. Next weekend?"

"Right. Saturday then."

"Best."

Jess looks out across the water, jewelled by light.

"Great."

24

Drips from the branches drum on the brolly. Jess slows and stops on the dead leaves near the end of an avenue of half-bare trees. She stares at the red brick wall of the workhouse and upper storeys of buildings beyond. She reaches a gaping gateway. Looking back at her is the face of an imposing red-brick house, a blue clock on its forehead, a white bell-tower on its crown. Something is missing. There is no grand entrance, just windows and two small doors in the corners. Two plain wings jut forward and from the one of the right the workhouse runs on and on to a three storey block before doglegging back towards the lane and another block of pitted bricks with the same regimented, closely spaced windows. To Jess's left there is a muddle of other smaller buildings, their slate roofs shiny-black with the wetness. Jess swallows. She blows out air. There is no sun but there are shadows. She can feel her heart. A few feet to the right of the gateway there is a dark green door beside the steep roof of a lodge abutting the wall. Her eyes linger. The knocker is an iron fist clutching a short bar.

From the moment the buildings had come into view through the sweep of the windscreen wipers she fell silent. She lent forward to take it in, her mouth open, too heavy to close.

Now, standing so near to the 200-year-perimeter wall she can feel its purpose, hear Anna's words. She looks over her shoulder at the way Anna's mother must have stumbled and crawled. She shivers, hunches and walks slowly through the gateway. Margaret is waiting in the shelter of a door off to the right. It's the entrance to a shop, and she calls to say She's going to try and buy a guidebook. Jess is standing in the middle of a pool of shiny shingle, her eyes fixed on the clock. It's almost half past eleven.

Jess can hear the footsteps and voices of more people coming in through the gate behind her. She looks again for Margaret. The shop is in a single storey building, next to the little house with the steep roof standing just inside the green door. Jess stares for several seconds at what She's certain must have been Walter Copperdin's lodge, then slowly turns full circle. To the left of the big house there is a free-standing chapel; another cottage that's been turned into a tea room; more low buildings abutting the boundary wall; the main entrance and tree-lined track falling away down the slight hill to the road; the porter's lodge; the shop; an area of grass and trees and then that long wall of windows running from the right side of the main block.

Margaret comes back holding a booklet and some paper.

"Plenty of info on the rural life museum, but not so much at all on the workhouse history. I've got this sheet, though, from a very helpful man in the shop. He's done a little map of the layout on the back. Said the shop's in the building where new arrivals were washed and de-loused, and, hang on a tick, yep, and that must be the porter's lodge next to it. See?"

Jess doesn't look or reply and continues to scan her surroundings. Margaret gazes round too.

"Strange, isn't it?"

Jess nods. Margaret senses her unease.

"Look, there's a cafe here. Do you want to have a cuppa or something, to warm yourself?"

"No. Let's have a wander. I don't think I want to stay too long after all. Sorry."

"No, that's fine. I think I agree with you. Come on, then. I vote we start in the main building. That's where the old dining hall was, although it's now filled with old wagons and farming stuff, apparently, which I'm curious to see anyway. And somewhere in there, off to the right, is the punishment cell."

"Punishment cell." Jess whispers it. "Alice."

"So he says, you know, where they kept a record of who was put there, or did anything wrong."

Jess blows out her cheeks. Margaret closes her umbrella, puts her arm through Jess's and they walk towards the clock.

"Ah, there you are. Thought I'd lost you. Have you seen this here thing they used to use for threshin' corn? It's quite..."

"Margaret, come and look at this."

Margaret follows Jess out from among the machinery crowding the large room, through to the back of the building and down a corridor to a door.

"Should we be down here? There are no signs or anything."

Jess opens the door and walks out into a narrow open space hemmed in by the tall buildings on one side and another high wall on the other side and at the far end. The rain is still falling and they put up their umbrellas again. There is a single feeble fruit tree starved of light, and the ground is covered by sparse, damp grass. Jess walks across to the wall, and, as she follows, Margaret can see the scratches on it. Crosses and names roughly carved.

"Jesus."

"What is it, d'you think?"

"I reckon it might well be where the men and women were separated when they were working. The man in the shop said there was something like this, though it's not on the map. I suppose this is where the men worked and over there, on the other side of the high wall, is the laundry where the women were. They weren't even allowed to talk. Fancy couples being split up like that. Oh God, it makes you think, doesn't it?"

Margaret runs her fingers over the names and lines and crosses etched into the red stone and whispers "It does that for sure."

Jess silently reads some of the names mixed with the myriad of crosses carved by people who could not read or write; R Worship: Caleb West; Tam Beedon; M Caulder; Jepp; Jeremiah Fowler; Will Coker; Benjamin Kemp; Napp; Hurst; Charles Roydon.

Margaret walks along the wall and looks at the tree.

"And how the hell does this thing manage to survive here? I reckon we're on the north side so the place must be permanently in shade. The tiny, dark punishment cell was bad enough, but this place is not nice, not nice at all, you know?"

Jess half nods. She turns and tries to look at the paper Margaret is holding.

"Where does it say the unmarried mothers, the jacket women, slept?"

"Um, buildings behind the chapel. Old schoolroom's round there as well, and the place where the vagrants were put."

They walk back through the main block and down beside the chapel to another small courtyard and a row of adjoining buildings. They stop, glance at one another, close and shake the water from their umbrellas again, then wander silently through the small rooms that have been filled with mock-ups of a village shop, a bakery and a craftsman's workshop. They stand aside as other visitors pass by discussing how rural people used to live.

There is nothing to tell people what the buildings used to be.

Jess walks out and leans her shoulders and head against the wall, letting the water fall on her face. She closes her eyes. Margaret comes to join her.

"Enough?"

"Yeah."

"Maybe not such a good idea to come."

"No. Maybe. Don't know. I might stay here for a fraction longer though, if that's all right. And on the way out I'd just like to see the orchard."

"The burial ground?"

"Yeah."

"Just near here, outside the wall, but you've got to go out the front and round to the right. I think I've had enough too. I'll see you back at the car. OK?"

Jess flickers a smile, then watches her walk away. She doesn't move for several seconds, closing her eyes again and feeling the cold, clean water washing her skin.

"Well?"

Jess gets into the car and shuts the door hard.

"Cold. You OK?"

"Irish, remember? Used to the damp. But I think I know what you mean. Find the orchard?"

Jess nods and blows into her hands and rubs them together.

"Just looks like a little orchard. Strange, you know, to think what's there. That we sort of know some of the people who are buried there."

241

"Reckon Anna's there?"

"No. I don't think so. Why would she come back here? It doesn't make any sense, unless she had no choice, but I don't think so."

"There may be records."

"I'm sure she isn't here. Well, I hope not. If she was I wouldn't want to know."

"I don't know about you, but I could do with a warm drink."

"Yes."

Jess looks back again at the workhouse, then turns to Margaret who has started the car.

"Margaret? You know what you said on *Albion,* about ghosts?"

"Mm."

"After mum was killed, when I was in hospital, I wished so hard that there was something. I don't know what exactly, but something. But I felt nothing, nothing at all."

Margaret turns off the engine and turns to face Jess.

Jess stares blankly out at the wet car park. She speaks slowly, quietly. "Even at the graves. I didn't feel anything there either. Shock, I suppose. I feel shocked now. Odd, isn't it?"

Margaret puts her hand on Jess's shoulder.

"Not really."

"When my father brought me to England, I really lost it, you know? Got crazy. I started seeing mum, or imagining her with me, sometimes my grandparents too. I really thought I could see them, in the corner of my eye, or feel them close by, but I'd turn and there'd be nobody. I thought about them all the time. Wanted them, but couldn't have them. I was completely lost. God, it hurt, Margaret. I can't tell you how it felt. Horrible.

It was like I was going mad, that my mind was playing tricks on me. They were there but I couldn't have them. Nightmare. And I've told you about the nightmares, about drowning, about the crash, me knowing it's going to happen and trying to stop it. I soon got to the point where I desperately didn't want to even think about my family, or feel them, if that makes any sense. But the more I tried not to, the stronger the feeling would be, and it always used to well up in me when I was really low, and I could only shake it if I was out of my head. I've been an alcoholic for longer than I can remember. It's true. I know it. That's why. But, d'you know something? I want to see them now. I shouldn't have tried to chase them away. Shouldn't have."

Jess's eyes fill with tears. As Margaret leans across to hug her she says, "I'm a mess."

"No."

"Oh I am." Jess rubs her eyes and pulls a tissue from her pocket. "I'm OK. I'll be OK. God, I'm crying a lot. Loads since I've been here. Can't seem to stop it."

"That's good."

"Before I came to Norfolk, I didn't know what I was doing. I was...was thinking more and more about killing myself. It's something that I'd thought about for a long time, but I'd got to the point of saying to myself more and more to just do it. Asking myself why I shouldn't. That's how low I was. Truth was I had nothing left, Margaret. Nothing. Drunk most of the time. Even the music meant nothing. I felt I couldn't do it any more. But at the cottage, I sort of started to come to terms with it. Who I am. I really have, I think. The place has calmed me, let me think more clearly. Without alcohol now, for some time, except when I read Rudi's letter. And I've thought about my family a lot, a lot, and have had good dreams, if you can call them that, without the crash, without the images in my head of them dying in the car. I never saw that, don't remember anything about the accident, but I've imagined it. But not recently. And I've started to have a real sense of other things. Reading the journal I've got these strong mental images of Anna, and all the people she writes about. Francis too. I see him everywhere."

"Like me on the boat."

"Yeah."

"But not here."

"No."

They both stare through the rain at the wet walls. Margaret softly breaks the silence.

"Nobody knows for sure, do they, what there is or isn't? They can't. But there's no denying what we feel sometimes. When you get an overpowering sense of someone. If people are in our minds, then they exist. That's a fact."

"I didn't like it in there at all. Before today I was looking forward to it, but I didn't like it. As soon as we got out of the car I was sort of dreading sensing something negative and was really wary of it. I knew what happened here because I read about it and could recognise it. But it didn't help. Just cold. Very cold. God, I hope she didn't end up back here."

"I know."

"What now?"

"That warm drink?"

Jess nods.

Margaret starts the car again and puts it in gear. "There'll be a cafe somewhere. Are you still up for looking for the Rectory at Swanton?"

"Yes. Need to."

"If the rain stops we could have a look in the churchyard too. But if that proves fruitless I don't know what we do then, Jess. That's it, I think."

Jess doesn't reply. She is still gazing at the workhouse as they pull away.

If Anna isn't there she just might be at Swanton.

The car moves slowly down through the village of Swanton, the sky still ashen, the rain falling steadily. At the bottom of the long street they turn left towards the church sitting proud on a rise. The lane climbs steeply to it then drops away down towards a wide river valley of flat lush grass with a band of water snaking through it. Cars are pulling away from the church. The rain is getting heavier. Margaret and Jess have agreed that if it is still wet when they reach Swanton they will go to the Rectory first.

Jess looks down again for a few seconds at the map on her lap.

"We're close. I think Two Bridges is just ahead, so it must be here somewhere. Oh..."

"Hang on."

Margaret pulls over sharply at the entrance to a drive on the left that disappears into some trees. They can't see a house, but the wrought iron gate is open and on the left of the two wooden posts is a little oval black sign with white lettering: *The Old Rectory*.

They turn and smile at one another. Margaret puts the old Volvo into gear again and the wheels spin on the gravel.

"Remember, if they look like they might bite, let me do the talkin'."

Just into the trees they can see through the pattern of bark the white walls and deep windows of the white-washed house, three floors high, with dormer windows in the roof, looking out over the lane and onto the Wensum valley. The copse of trees ends and the drive cuts between tidy lawns, widens and stops in front of a side door that's open. Two liver and white springer spaniels come bounding out followed by a woman in green Wellingtons in a long waxed raincoat with a large hood that shadows her face. She shuts and locks the door and comes towards the car smiling, the two dogs circling her, tails wagging. Margaret winds down her window and the woman, who must be in her seventies or more, peers in, smiling warmly.

245

"Don't mind my girls. Just off for a walk. Can I help you?"

Margaret apologises for rolling up unannounced, tells the woman briefly that they have discovered something of the history of the house, that they have just called on the off-chance, and suggests that maybe they should come back a little later.

"No, no, please don't go. I shan't be too long at all. Sounds fascinating. Goodness. Look, I'm outside now and they'll never forgive me if they don't have a short run. Can you wait?"

Jess suddenly leans across.

"Would it be OK if we walked with you?"

"Of course! Wet old day, but if you don't mind, then I'd be delighted. But, forgive me, only your face looks very familiar. Do I know you?"

"I'm Jess...er...Jessica Healey."

"Oh! good Lord. So you are."

"And I'm Margaret, Margaret Bunn. A friend."

"Well, this is unbelievable. Quite extraordinary. Wonderful. You will stay for tea, though, won't you? Richard won't believe this. He's down at the church just now, churchwarden, been a wedding today, poor souls, with all this rain, but he'll be back soon. I'm Rosemary, by the way. Rosemary Boswell. Oh dear, I'm completely thrown. Come on girls, we've got some special visitors, no jumping up now. Come on!"

Jess and Margaret get out of the car and make a fuss of the dogs. They walk down the drive with Mrs Boswell and into the trees. She calls the dogs to heel and they cross the lane into a meadow that drops down towards the river. Jess says nothing as Margaret tells of Anna and the journal, of Dr Brazington and Constance, and tries to recount some of Anna's stories of her time at the Rectory. Mrs Boswell listens intently, stopping in her tracks occasionally in open-mouthed wonder and to look back up at the house. She asks how the journal was found and if she and her husband can

246

borrow it, and Margaret tells too of Francis and Rudi, of Whispering Reeds and the account of life there, how Francis had painstakingly transcribed the journal before his death, and how they were now trying to solve the mystery of what had happened to Anna.

It is only after they have walked some distance along the riverbank that Mrs Boswell turns to Jess with a puzzled expression.

"Forgive me, but...how...?

"I am an old friend of Francis and Rudi. I'm staying at Whispering Reeds."

"Oh, I see."

Jess changes the subject back to Anna.

"Do you or your husband know, by any chance, if there are still church records from a hundred or more years ago? Is that possible? We know Anna was married here. Maybe She's buried here, too. We're trying to find out what we can."

"Of course. How very interesting. Richard knows a lot more than I do, being on the parochial church council, and, I must admit, considerably more religious. Look, let's get back. He'll probably be home by now and he'll be amazed when he hears what You've just told me, although I suspect he'll be even more flabbergasted seeing you. I should tell you he's a musician."

Margaret asks "What instrument?"

"Violin. He's going to go into orbit when he meets you. Music is how we met actually. He was a violinist in the orchestra of the Ballet Rambert before the war. Was just starting out when the ruddy war came and stopped everything. I was desperate to be a ballet dancer and had just joined the company. I ended up in the wrens. Richard joined the Royal Artillery and was away in north Africa and Italy for four years. We were married just before he left, and, thank God, he survived, but when he came back things were so tight he had to give up hopes of playing professionally again and went to join the family business."

"Here in Norfolk?"

"No, we are not from Norfolk. It was a printing press in Warwick, which is what his father wished Richard had done in the first place. He wanted to leave, get back to the music, but never did. Took over the business himself in time and built it right up. Very successful really, and our nephew took up the reins six years ago. Have been doing a lot of the colour catalogues for some while now. Quite a business, but Richard had long felt that any fun had gone out of it. That's when we came up here. Always said he wanted to live in a quiet village, so I agreed, and prices up here were low, relatively, and it's beautiful, of course. But if I'm honest I'd have preferred to stay in a city, or at least close to one. I was brought up in Putney, London. Richard's still devoted to his music, though, and plays, quite a lot more these days now he's retired. Complains bitterly that he can't do it any more, but he can. He has all your recordings, you know, every one of them. I can't wait to see his face."

The churchyard falls away down the side of the hill, a fold of damp, long grass, patterned by a muddle of green-grey headstones, some leaning, locked in by an old flint wall. The rain has finally abated. Richard Boswell, a tall, pale man with steel grey hair and a round, soft, tired face and dark brown eyes, walks ahead. He is using a stick but moving quickly, urgently, his head turning left and right as he passes through the stones.

"I'm sure it's in this area somewhere. Sure of it. Remember the name. Yes, here. Here it is."

They stop beside him and look down at the grave. Nobody says anything for a moment as they try to read the weathered, lichen-covered words.

"It was the name. I remembered the name. So unusual."

Margaret squats down to get closer and runs her fingers across the letters and numbers.

"He was 84. He lived to be 84, bless his soul. Not a bad age in those days, eh, Jess?"

Jess shakes her head. Her eyes go back and forth across the names: Thomas Brazington, and beneath it, beneath him, by her feet, Emily Brazington. She feels numb almost to the point of fainting. She blinks through a rush of thoughts. If Anna lived beyond 1904 she would have stood at this graveside at the funeral. Where she's standing now. This is the church where Anna was married, where Constance was married. Could Anna be buried here too?

Margaret buries her hands in her pockets. "Can we look for Anna's grave now?"

Mr Boswell swings his stick in the direction of the church. "I don't remember encountering the name Farrow. But it is not so unusual in Norfolk. She may be here. The grave may be unmarked."

They fan out, Mr and Mrs Boswell moving towards the east window, Jess and Margaret dropping down to the bottom of the graveyard. They all walk about slowly, stopping and starting, heads down, reading, gradually circling the church and meeting up again at the lych-gate.

"Nothing?" Mrs Boswell knows the answer but asks anyway.

They all shake their heads. Margaret asks Mr Boswell if there are records.

"Should be. I'll have a word with the Reverend Armson and the verger, Bryan. See what we can find out. We can look and see what there is under the weddings register as well. Now, why don't you come back to the house again and have some supper? You'd be very welcome, wouldn't they, Rosie?"

"Absolutely."

"And I could tell you all about the Lincoln bible."

"Lincoln bible?"

"Abraham Lincoln's ancestor lived here. The pub was once Richard Lincoln's house and he was churchwarden here. The church has the family bible."

"Really?" Margaret looks doubtful. "Only I thought his family were from, um..."

"The town of Hingham. Indeed they were. I believe one of the oldest places in New England is called Hingham, isn't it? But long before then one of the family came to live here at Swanton. The grandfather of the Lincoln who emigrated, I think I'm right in saying. You're welcome to see it."

Margaret turns to Jess who looks back anxiously, willing her to say no. Margaret understands.

"That's very kind of you, but no. Maybe some other time. Only I must get back to the farm. It would be lovely to stay and talk some more, but we've been away all day and I need to get supper ready for my Frank and our son. It's been wonderful to meet you, though, and thank you both so much for your hospitality and for letting us see round your beautiful home. Before we head off I'll just jot down my address and telephone number for you so, should you find anything, I'd be really grateful if you could get in touch."

"Fine, but You're sure you won't stay?"

"Yes. Thank you."

"Then come and see us again very soon. Maybe bring the journal with you? Would that be possible? Or we could come and collect it from you?"

"Either, I really don't mind."

"Well, we'll stay in touch now. Don't have to decide this minute."

Margaret and Mr and Mrs Boswell wander out of the gate onto the lane, but Jess stands still.

"If it's OK I'll catch you up. Just want to have a quick look in the church."

Mr Boswell turns.

"Oh, I'll come with you."

"Actually, if you don't mind, I think I'd like to be on my own. Is that all right?"

"Of course. Quite understand. It should be open."

25

11 October

Am feeling so sad and deflated because it doesn't look like I'm going to find Anna after all. Mr Boswell has written saying they have checked the church records and there is nothing to show she is buried at Swanton. I don't know what I expected, and now my excitement before the visit to the workhouse and the Rectory has gone completely. Do I mean excitement? It was more an expectancy, a hope, I suppose, given my stupid dreams, when I've taken flowers to her and talked to her. Maybe it was just the idea of seeing more of her life, the places she lived, that affected me, because, if I think about it, the chances of finding her grave were pretty slim anyway. It's been on my mind and I can't believe she'd have gone back to the workhouse. No. And if she did go back to the Rectory, and there is no guarantee that she did, and she survived the doctor, which is quite possible because she would have only been 57 or 58, then she could well have moved on. Truth is we've done all we can and there's nothing else to see or do, a strange feeling of loss again, disappointment and frustration. I want to know.

Am re-reading the journal, which helps. The Boswells are coming over at the end of next week to borrow it. Margaret is doing a lunch which I suppose I'll have to go to.

24 October

Mrs Boswell has called Margaret to say they won't be coming after all because her husband is in hospital after suffering a heart attack. Diabetic as well, apparently, but didn't know. He sounds quite ill. Didn't look well when we met him, and Mrs Boswell has told Margaret that she'd been worried about him for a long time, but that he is incredibly stubborn and would not go to the doctor. Margaret thinks it would be a good idea to take the journal for him to read. I agree. I will not go with her, though.

The feeling that's been hanging round me still won't go, but the music is helping. I can't say it's taken my mind off it because I've come to associate it with Anna, with the cottage, but it really does help. And I think I've come to a decision. I'm going to play it. For her.

7 December

Still no reply from Esther and Rudi to my letter and I am pondering if I should ring, only Mr Boswell's death has been a horrible shock. The funeral yesterday was very strange, being back there again at the church and the Rectory. I feel desperately sorry for Mrs Boswell. Got a real sense when we met her that she hadn't really settled, because of the way she talked about it being her husband's wish to move there. And without any children, or family close by, She's bound to be lonely. She said Mr Boswell had a second massive heart attack in hospital when they were still running tests, and that was it. She looked devastated, but very dignified, defiant even, and was already talking of spreading her wings, doing some of the things she had wanted to do for a long time, like visiting a friend in Italy, visiting Inca temples in South

America. *Strong person, I think. We've left the journal for her now. She says she wants to read it, that it will help to have something else to do in the coming days and weeks other than to sort through her husband's many possessions. Margaret has invited her over, which will be good. I like her.*

I got back to find a letter from Michael, saying he and Sally are up to spend a few days with Tom at Aldeburgh next week, and they thought it would be a nice idea for the two of them to come up to see me on the Saturday. I feel I want to see them.

26

Jess opens her mouth to speak, but in her surprise says nothing.

"Hi, Jess."

Tom leans towards her and kisses her on the cheek. There is a flicker of a smile on her face. She looks over his shoulder at his car and into the lane, confused.

"I...I was expecting Michael and Sally."

"Can't be that far behind me. They pulled over at some shops on the outskirts of Norwich and waved for me to carry on. I think they were just going to get some money out of a cashpoint. Actually, I half expected them to be here before me."

"I don't know what to say."

"You don't mind do you? I'll go if you..."

"No, no, don't. You took me unawares, that's all."

There is an awkward silence. They speak at the same time.

"Mi..."

"How's..."

They blush and apologise. Tom continues.

"Michael scribbled me a rough map in case we got separated. I've had to drive myself because they said they were planning to stay up tonight, n- not here, they said something about driving along the coast to stay in a hotel somewhere. I still got in a bit of a muddle, though. Lanes round here are a maze, aren't they? And I did it in the dark last time, remember?"

Jess smiles and nods.

Tom backtracks away from her, leans into his car and pulls out his jacket and a scarf.

"I hope you don't mind. I should have warned you, but I honestly didn't know I was coming until this morning. I only agreed to come at the last minute. But they were very pushy. Very. Anyway, I'm glad, really. Needed to get out of the house, and I've heard so much about this place, Jess, I confess I've been itching to see it in daylight. It looks amazing."

"Come, come round the front."

She takes his arm as if to lead him. They look at each other for a second. He walks with her. They move from the shingle to the silence of the grass, and the sound of the wetland grows as it fills the view. They slow and stop in the middle of the lawn between the cottage and the staithe.

"Wow!"

"Very blustery today, and it can get very bitter, but it blows the cobwebs away."

"You're not kidding. God it's beautiful. Incredibly beautiful. So open. Blimey, Jess. What a place to live."

"You should sense it when the sun's out. The colours, the water and reeds, the sound, the peace..."

"The pulse. The sanctuary and infinity of nature. A freedom. Like when you were growing up?"

"You always were so wise with words. Yes. That exactly. My childhood."

Tom realises they are venturing into deep water. He changes tack.

"And that's Rudi and Francis's boat?"

"Mmm. Otter."

"Michael said he sailed with you."

Jess smiles sheepishly and glances at him for a second. Tom has lifted his face to feel the freshness.

"I'd like to try that. But maybe when it's not so blowy."

Jess folds her arms and hunches her shoulders as a shiver runs down her back.

"The stove in the kitchen's alight and it's cosy in there. Just need to put a match to the fire in the lounge. Coffee?"

The trees beside the coast road bend away from the sea, moulded by the north wind. Jess looks out at the white horses racing to the beach and her eyes follow the faint curve of the watery horizon. It's warm in the back of Michael's small car and she can feel Tom's shoulder pressed against hers. Sally is driving like the wind, and Michael's hand is on her lap. The road is twisty and Jess begins to feel a little queasy.

"Is it much further?"

"Not far now, Mum."

Tom looks at Jess and pulls a face. He leans forward and peers over

Michael's shoulder.

"Where, pray, are you two lovebirds taking us? I'm rapidly losing my appetite."

Michael twists to face his parents, beaming. They are wedged on the back seat, slightly bewildered and comical as it bounces along. They know it, and Jess looks back at him wide-eyed. Michael feels elated. He points ahead.

"See that red and white lighthouse? That's the village, isn't it, Sal?"

"That's it. Margaret brought me and the guys here when we were up, that night Michael stayed over. Good seafood. I mean really good. Not far at all now. I'll put my foot down."

Tom and Jess look at one another in mock horror.

As they are getting out of the car Sally says she needs the loo desperately and runs on ahead into the pub. Tom stretches and says he wants to walk up to the church and take in a few lungfuls of fresh air. He tells Michael to order him a pint of bitter and some whitebait if they have it. He wanders off. Jess thinks to go with him, but Michael has already taken her arm and is talking to her.

"Hope you don't mind, Mum. But, well, I thought it would be nice to have Dad here too. He's having it a bit tough at the moment to be honest."

She looks across at Tom, walking hands in pockets up the gravel drive towards the church.

"Is he? Why?"

"Don't know, exactly, but he's not with anyone, hasn't been for a long time now, and I think he's wondering whether he should move on, get away from Aldeburgh, do something else with his life. That would be strange, in a way, because it's where he's always been, all I can remember him doing anyway, and he's always been into it so much. Maybe It'll pass, but it seems to be on his mind a lot of late."

"Did he tell you this?"

"Not in so many words, but yes. He probably just needs a good holiday, I don't know."

Jess continues to look at Tom as they walk towards the pub door. He is standing now on the brow of the churchyard gazing out towards the sea.

Jess stops, "Michael?"

He turns.

"You have always called me Mum. I have not been there for the greater part of your life. I don't deserve it. Why do you do it?"

"Because you are my Mum. And..."

"What?"

"It is how Dad has always referred to you. Always."

Michael goes into the pub. Jess stands and stares at the man on the clifftop.

There is a roaring fire inside the pub beneath a blackboard menu. Most of the tables are taken. Michael points to one in the corner where Sally has left her coat. Jess settles herself in the corner seat so she can see across the room and tells Michael she'll have a tonic water with lemon, but no ice. He tells her to look at the menu board and then joins the throng at the bar. Jess still feels slightly nauseous from the car ride. Sally comes round the corner, tall and beautiful, and puts her arm round Michael, talking close to his ear. He says something to her and she comes across to Jess and leans on a chair, smiling warmly.

"Michael says we ought to get our food order in now as well, to save waiting again. So what d'you think?"

Jess leans, trying to see the board. "Oh, um...Do they have a soup? That would be great, with some bread."

"Are you sure? They have a crab soup. How about something more substantial?"

"That's fine, honestly. I've had a bit of an upset tum for a few days. I think that's all I can manage. Some bread with it would be good."

"OK. And Tom said whitebait, didn't he?"

"Yes."

Sally goes back to Michael and waits with him. Jess hears the latch on the door and sees Tom come in, his hair blown into a wild twirl. He waves to her, and comes across, stopping for a moment to warm himself by the fire.

"Blimey, that cleared the sinuses. But you wouldn't want to be out there too long. A blow like that goes right through you."

"Margaret says they don't call it cold round here, just fresh."

"Mmm."

Tom comes round and sits beside her and they look at Michael and Sally.

"So, what's all this about then, d'you think?"

"About?"

"They stayed with me last night, came up yesterday afternoon, and haven't stopped grinning. Something's up. Reckon they're going to tell us something."

Jess studies Sally and wonders. She could be. Her voice falls away.

"She's pregnant?"

"Your face, Jess. It's a picture. Oh I don't know. I might be completely wrong. But they've looked like they've been itching to tell me something from the minute I saw them. Strange really, because I've been trying to find a way to tell them my news."

Jess's head snaps round. Tom looks down at his hands.

"I'm not getting any younger and I've decided I need to work out what I want to do, so I've taken some time off. Michael knew I was thinking about it and now, well, I've done it. Couldn't really think through clearly what I was going to do while I was still working, so I asked and they've agreed to let me take six months off. Sabbatical, sort of. Bit tricky financially, but I think It'll be OK. They think I'm trying to write something, which is a fib. Hilarious really, but what the heck. Just need some space, some time."

"Might you leave altogether?"

"It's possible, yeah. Been there a heck of a long time, Jess. Very comfortable in many ways, enjoyed it, and the house is full of memories, of course, which would make it hard in one way. I've really loved living there, and may stay, or go head off somewhere and keep it to come back to, don't know right now. But I think I want to do something else, travel a bit, find a new challenge, whatever."

They both glance round the room wondering what words will come next. None.

Jess thinks again about that house, Michael's childhood home, Tom holding that world together like an anchor. She tries to think of the words to say that it is so good to hear, to know that he'll take time for himself at last, do something for himself; to leave behind the time he's given, that selfless time that has always weighed on her guilt.

Tom tries to imagine himself telling the truth, admitting how emotional and weak he feels, that he's trying not to tremble with the feeling of being drawn to her again. How that time when they'd met at the hospital and he'd driven her to Norfolk had left him stunned, releasing a flood of old thoughts and emotions. How that morning, the second he saw her, he knew. And he wants to be honest about everything, to tell her that for a long time now he has felt lost, that the meaning for continuing at Aldeburgh has all gone.

They watch their son and his girlfriend walk towards them carrying drinks. Michael puts the tonic water in front of Jess and hands his dad a pint. Jess stares at Sally's glass. It could be tonic too, without gin. They sit, raise their glasses and wait for Jess and Tom to do likewise.

"Cheers!"

Michael's eyes flit to Sally. "It's great we're all together, isn't it? Can't quite believe it." He looks at Sally again and locks his hand into hers. "Yes. Right. Um..."

Tom leans back and towards Jess and whispers, "Here it comes."

"We've something we'd like to tell you both. We're...getting married."

Tom stands and goes to hug Michael. Jess also gets to her feet, emotion welling, and leans across the corner of the table to kiss Sally, cupping her flushed face in her hands, saying nothing. They all move. Jess does the same to Michael, water in her eyes now. Then she folds her arms round him and pulls him too her, holding her breath and holding him as tightly as she can.

Tom's face is alight with a huge smile. "Phew, I knew something was afoot."

"You thought I was pregnant, right?" Sally has raised her eyebrows and is grinning at Jess.

"Er..."

"Not yet. We plan to leave it a few years."

Tom puts his arms round Sally and Michael and kisses them on the head. "Oh, God. You two. Getting married. Bloody brilliant, don't you think, Jess?"

She wipes at her eyes. "Oh yes. Yes, yes. Sorry."

They sit again. Sally lifts her glass and mouths to Jess "gin", making her laugh away the tears. Tom leans forward, eager to know.

"So, come on then, when? And where, for that matter."

Sally turns to looks at Michael, waiting to hear how he will say it. He takes her hand again.

"Well, having decided we love each other madly, and still do after nearly a year, we want to tie the knot as soon as we possibly can. No engagement, just a fab wedding, probably in July if we can arrange it. Should be time enough to sort everything, and it would be the best time for us. The rest of the year is looking increasingly frantic. We don't want to wait any longer than we have too, do we, Sal?"

"Nope."

"But we want it to be special too, of course. I hope you don't mind, but Sal's parents know. We told them on Thursday, before we came up here. You'll really like them. Maybe we should organise something soon when we can all get together. Up here would be good, then they can see where it will be and everything."

"Here?"

Jess and Tom say it in the same breath. They glance at each other then look to Michael for the answer.

"Now, nothing is set yet, OK? Nothing at all, so this may not happen. We aim to go on tomorrow and try and set the wheels in motion. But..." Michael takes a deep breath. "We have this crazy, amazing notion to ask Lady Crofton if we can get married there, at Bembroke Hall, in the chapel. Remember we stayed there after the concert, mum, actually in the hall? I told you, Dad, didn't I? It was in one of those bedrooms like you file through in a National Trust house. It was wonderful, absolutely amazing. She didn't bat an eyelid that we weren't married; showed us round and made a fuss of us, and she's already booked us for another recital next summer. We like her a lot and she seems to like us. Anyway, the morning after the concert we were walking with her round the house and ended up back in the chapel, and when we were in there she half suggested it would be possible. There'd been no suggestion that we were going to get married, we hadn't even talked about it. But she dropped a large hint which, at the time, made us laugh. Well, that's it basically. We're going to see her tomorrow."

Sally shakes her head.

"No, it isn't."

"Isn't it?"

"Afterwards?"

"Oh yeah. And we thought we'd play. Have a sort of mini recital at the reception, but we haven't asked yet."

Tom flops back in his chair.

"You mean, Sally sitting there in her wedding dress and you in all your garb? Fantastic. Absolutely bloody fantastic."

"Not just us. Um, the idea was to sort of make up a piano quintet. Sebastian, who'll be my best man, has agreed to play, Sally will play the cello, me second violin, and we were wondering if..."

Tom laughs as he speaks.

"What? Piano and violin? Hang on a minute. Us? You mean us, don't you? Oh boy. Oh boy. What d'you think, Jess?"

"I...I..."

"Leave it for now, Mum, Dad. Just think about it. A piano quintet."

Sally reaches across to Jess.

"Please don't think you have to. Please don't. We'll do something, for sure, and can always ask friends to join us, so don't feel pressured. It's really important to us that you don't feel that. We just thought it was worth talking about."

"I can't promise."

"We know."

"Maybe. I don't know. I need a little time to get my head round it. Bit of a surprise. Actually, I've something you should know too. Maybe now's sort of a good time. I've...I've decided to play the *Three Dances*."

"Oh Mum, that's wonderful. Does Rudi know?"

"Not yet. Can you do me a favour, Michael? Go and see him when You're back. Tell him, and tell The Barbican. Set it, so it's impossible for me to change my mind."

Jess and Tom stand on the edge of the pool of light from the kitchen window and watch the red lights of the Polo bump down the track into the twilight.

"Well..." Tom pats his pockets looking for his keys. "I must be making tracks too."

She nearly reaches out. Her voice gives it away.

"Bye, Tom."

Tom goes to his car, opens the door, then turns to her.

"Oh, by the way. Been meaning to ask all day. Have you had any joy trying to find out what happened to the woman who wrote that journal?"

"No, afraid not."

"Nothing?"

"She just disappeared. I've looked everywhere I can, but no. Nothing."

"Oh, I'm sorry. Well, it's been quite a day, hasn't it?"

Jess nods nervously. She finds herself speaking as she feels, the words spilling uncensored.

"Tom? You know this recital idea? We'll have to rehearse, and, well, I was wondering..."

"Mmm?"

"Given what you told me, that you've got some time at the moment, I was wondering if you'd work with the *Dances* as well? I can try and get hold of the piano score for you to have a look at."

"I...I'd love to."

"Great. I'd really like to run through it some time soon."

"It's Christmas, Jess."

"Oh. Yes, sorry. Of course it is."

They both think what to say next. She wonders what his plans are, if he might want to come to the cottage for Christmas. He wonders if she means to ask him to be with her.

"My sister's invited me over to be with the family, still in Chiswick, and I've said I'll go, but to be honest I'm never that fond of big family gatherings."

"No?"

"You here?"

"Margaret has said I can be with them at the farm. Only to eat, though, if that. Not sure yet."

"Well..."

"Yeah."

"Good to see you again, Jess."

"You too, Tom."

"Lovely to be here, to be together with Michael...with you. And to see this."

He gets into the car and she steps closer, holding the door open. "Ring me, will you?"

27

12 January

*Yesterday the freezing mist that has clung to everything for days finally
lifted, and there have been sunny spells and showers since, though the
wind is still very cold. Out of the wind the sun's been quite strong,
strong enough to make me think about going out, and after lunch, just
after a downpour, I went for a brief walk. I didn't go far, because the
sun didn't last, but for a while, in the shelter of the hedge, in the last
of the sunny spells, I could smell the dead leaves and moss just as Anna
wrote in her journal. Today I don't think I'll get further than the
woodshed, because the wind stings like ice and the rain has turned to
hail. Sitting here, at the kitchen table, looking out at the broad, the sky
is a vast canvas, full of mountainous clouds with dark veils of falling
hail beneath them. Enough hail has fallen here already to turn the grass
white and I'm wondering if next it will snow.*

Meanwhile I've re-read Esther's enormous letter, the tiny words crammed onto both sides of six pieces of writing paper, and it has made me realise, given how ill Rudi is and the care he obviously needs, that it's good he's with her. Really good. Knowing him, the idea of him being in a care home is horrible, and when I try and think what Francis would have wanted for him in the circumstances. Even if they didn't talk about it, he must have known, I'm sure, and been relieved to think that Esther would look after him. She says he seems content and is now out of bed for part of the day. The way she talks about his bed in the front room and their routine it's as if it was always like that, and she seems to be relishing it. I just wonder what he feels about leaving his things, his work, his piano, and what he's managed, wanted, to keep with him. He'll need familiar things round him and I feel guilty I've not been able to help him with that, because it was something I could usefully have done. It just hasn't really dawned on me until now. There was no mention of the flat or if it's going to be sold, so maybe they haven't done anything about it yet. I should make the effort and go, but I can't with the weather like this. I'll ring.

The bad weather has also meant Tom has yet to come. I haven't seen him since Michael and Sally told us their news, and it's a strange feeling waiting for him. I'm not lonely, and have never felt like that here, but I must admit I'm anxious whether he'll come. I'm sure he will, and maybe I'll try and ring him too when I'm at the farm.

28

He is close again, almost touching. They have found their way to that delicate calm, no need to speak. The words are in their heads.

Jess sits in her dressing gown by the end of Tom's sleeping bag, nursing a mug on her lap and looking at the fingers of flame growing round the lump of oak she has dropped on the fire. Tom has put his empty mug on the floor, pulled his knees up to make room for her, and is half propped up by his pillow, hands behind his head, looking up at the flickering light on the timbered ceiling. He breathes out, long, contentedly, and closes his eyes. She tentatively turns her head and studies him, that jaw, the long eyelashes, the still strong curls of his now iron grey hair, the weathered tan of his forearms, his neck and pale shoulders and chest above the arc of the sleeping bag.

"You look very comfortable. So much for what you said about sofas."

"Well, I take it back. Anyway, I was talking about Michael's lumpy sofa. Have you never crashed on it?"

Jess shakes her head.

"Don't. Too small and too ruddy uncomfortable. I can't stretch out on it and always end up with a sore neck. Bit like riding in the back of his car. This, on the other hand, is a Rolls Royce of sofas, and lying here, by the fire, is bliss, frankly."

"More tea?"

"That would be bliss too."

Jess takes Tom's mug and moves to the window, pulling one of the curtains a little, the butter dawn falling on her face.

"Could be quite a clear day. Not as wild as yesterday with any luck." She turns quickly. "Why don't we take the boat out? We said we'd have a walk if it looked brighter, but hardly anyone's going to be out there midweek in winter. We could have the place to ourselves."

"It'll be freezing."

"We'll wrap up warm. Lots of layers. There's some all-weather stuff of Francis's that should fit you."

"What if I fall in? Be as stiff as a board in seconds."

"You won't."

"Sure?"

"Sure. Look, if it starts to get wild we'll turn back, OK? We don't have to sail, just motor if you like, but it would be great to get the sails up if we can. Oh, go on, Tom. I'll look after you. Promise."

"All right. But just snuggled here, by the fire, the thought of getting cold doesn't grab me."

"You sail in Suffolk. You said so."

"Fair weather only; nothing too strenuous, and always with someone who knows what they're doing. Got caught offshore in a squall once. Petrified, I was, I'm not embarrassed to admit."

"This isn't rough, just a little fresh, that's all. And I think I know what I'm doing."

"I know you do. That's not the point. Fresh as in freezing, you mean. That's what they call it up here, don't they? A howling arctic gale and it's "a bit fresh"."

Tom slips further down into his sleeping bag. "Maybe I'll feel more like it after that second cup of tea. If it's all right with you, I'll not set off for home until this evening. The roads will be quieter and It'll give us the whole day. D'you want to rehearse some more this afternoon?"

"Could do."

"Well, let's see how the day goes. How about we take the boat and have a bracing walk as well, down to the sea maybe? Then we could go to the pub at Horsey for a drink and a bite to eat."

Jess doesn't answer and goes through to the kitchen. Tom winces at his words and curses under his breath. Jess is on the wagon, fighting it. *Idiot. You bloody idiot.* He thinks to follow her into the kitchen but he's naked. No time to dress. He waits until she returns, wondering what to say.

"Sorry, Jess. I didn't mean to..."

"Don't, Tom. It's OK, really. Just that, well, I'm trying not to drink...you know."

"Yeah, I know."

Jess sits by his feet again. "But dodging it's not the answer either, I know that, so don't apologise. Please. Went to the pub with Michael and Sally and that was fine. The only way I'm going to carry on doing this is if I can go into a pub and not have a vodka or anything. I...I've really not had a drink for months now."

"That's good, Jess. Really good."

Jess locks her mug between her knees and pushes her fingers back through her hair, holding it tightly for a moment in a ponytail before letting it fall.

"Have managed to quit smoking too."

Tom looks at her profile, her forehead, nose, chin and ears, pink in the fire light. She looks thinner, so much better.

"Any other vices you want to talk about?"

Jess glances at him, sees his smile and grins. She gazes softly into the perfect circle of her tea. Tom wants to pull her to him, for them to be still, silent, to hold her and feel the calmness he's never seen before. He thinks of when he will, if they ever will.

"Jess?"

"Mm?"

"Remember when we were at college? You asking me if I'd play for you?"

She nods.

"Why did you?"

She sips her tea, thinks for a moment.

"I liked your face."

"My face?"

"Your eyes actually. You've kind eyes."

"Nothing to do with my playing then."

Jess shakes her head, tries to hold in her laugh. Tom nods.

"Wondered."

"And why did you say yes?"

"Well it wasn't your eyes. They were never still long enough to catch. Umm. Probably had something to do with the fact I was pretty boring really."

"What does that mean?"

"I was dull, sheepish, lily-livered, scared witless, if I'm honest."

"Still don't understand. And you weren't boring."

"I was, Jess. Definitely was. Come on, you remember, surely? Or maybe you didn't notice early on. You were in your own world, very much focused on the music. Anyway, I was completely daunted by the whole place, like a rabbit caught in the headlamps of a juggernaut, and I'd realised I was going to have to work bloody hard. Lacked confidence, I suppose. Didn't want to let my family down either, especially my mother, and so just worked my guts out all the time. Then you asked me, me out of all of them, to work with you. Schzamm!"

"Don't be ridiculous."

Tom pulls himself up and hugs his knees, looking at Jess earnestly.

"No, I mean it. It was. Believe me. You were brilliant, everyone knew that, but you were, well, sort of distant, unapproachable, quite volatile."

"Understatement."

"Frightening to someone like me, anyway. You asked me, quite forcibly I remember. I ummed and erred, and then you asked me again the next day, angrily, and I didn't have the nerve to say no. The next thing I know I'm with you, soon in every sense. I was never going to set the world alight, but those years with you, bloody hell. Bloody hell."

"Sorry."

"Sorry? Just imagine what a boring fart I'd been if I hadn't, if we...well, if it hadn't happened. It was a weird time in many ways, Jess, sure, and it hurt a lot, a lot, sometimes, especially at the end, even though I knew, right from the beginning I knew it would come. But I wouldn't change it, Jess.

God, no. I learned a hell of a lot, not least about myself. Best thing that could have happened to me."

"Really?"

"Yes."

"Don't believe you. I was a nightmare, freaking out all the time."

"Not all the time. Not with me anyway."

"I was. You're just being nice."

"No. I'm not. You were always, well, mostly, calmer with me. Even when you were having a tough time you held back with me most of the time, and when you did lose it you always came back, 'til the very last time. I understood, I could see just how hard it was for you. Anyway, I loved you."

They stare at each other. Jess feels the thumping of blood in her veins. Tom's certain eyes ease into a smile.

"Couldn't last, though, could it? We were on two radically different paths, weren't we? You the virtuoso, me the plodder. Glad they've crossed again, though, Jess."

"Yes."

Jess wants to say more, but She's barely breathing now. Tom leans further forward and touches her shoulder.

"And we did get something incredible out of it, didn't we?"

She nods, looks away, everything turning to water. Tom's hand gently tightens on her skin.

"Accept it, Jess. We do. Don't keep beating yourself up over it. We tried for a while, didn't we? But it didn't work. Couldn't. Accept it. I believe there was nothing else you could do. And Michael does too, and he loves you; he loves you so much."

"Oh Tom..."

She looks at him, her eyes flowing. He opens his arms

"Come. Come here."

A pair of Mallard ducks rise from an inlet where others are feeding. More follow, calling, and they cross in front of Otter, turning in flight to lead the way along the line of the river. The keen wind pushes the boat down towards Meadow Dyke, faster than the beautiful rhythm of the waves that are running beside them and sparkling with sunlight. Coots hurry busily along the edge of the dry reeds that pulse in the air, and there is a rare clarity, a depth of colour and crystal cleanness to everything around them. Jess is at the helm, her chin high, cheeks crimson in the cold. Tom is sitting sideways, dressed in Francis's red and yellow all-weather gear, arms folded to lock in the warmth until his darting eyes see something else and he points a gloved finger again. Gulls floating in the shelter of an island of alder trees in the reed mass watch them glide by. They haven't seen and cannot see another boat, another soul. Jess turns Otter into the narrower Meadow Dyke and hauls in the mainsail. No longer running with the wind they feel its bite again. The canvas stretches and the boat leans and pulls forward, the music of the waves tinkling on her bow. Tom switches sides, turning his back to the cold and pulling the tall collar of the sailing jacket as high as it will go. The reeds are close now, close enough to hear, to see the detail, the dense forest of bleached gold rising from the ink-deep river, the stems and seed heads flowing back and forth, fizzing.

They venture out onto the rougher water of Horsey and Tom grasps the sides as Otter tilts and water sprays up from her bow. Tom shakes his face, grinning from beneath Francis" black woollen hat. Jess runs the main sheet through her hand to spill wind from the sail and settle the boat, glancing over her shoulder for a moment to see the smoother water of their wake rolling behind them. She feels so alive. She nudges Tom with her boot and he turns and looks at her, excitement and light in his face. She points ahead to the distant sandy wall on the horizon: *the long ridge of sandy marram-hills, standing between the country and the sea and drawing a strong sweep of gold between the blue of the sky and the green of the marshlands.*

They are just about to play when Jess and Tom hear Margaret calling from the back door. Jess puts down Rudi's violin and they go through to the kitchen.

"Margaret?"

"Oh, I'm so glad You're home, Jess. And You're still here, Tom. Lovely."

"Going home tonight, a bit later. Is everything all right?"

"Fine, absolutely fine. Only I came down here just before lunch to see if you were about, because Rosemary, Rosemary Boswell from Swanton, rang asking if it was all right to come over this afternoon. She's still up at the farm and would love to see you again. We walked down here mid-afternoon but no sign of you and I saw Otter was still out. She had a wander round outside. I hope you don't mind. I figured you'd be back before nightfall, so She's waited. Anyway, she's got some news. Quite a lot actually. I'll let her tell you. Can you come?"

Jess looks at Tom.

"Go ahead. I'll sort my gear out, load up the car. Don't worry, I won't disappear. I'll wait. You go. And don't hurry. We can work later, or next week maybe. Go."

Jess puts on her coat and she and Margaret walk purposefully into the night. The beam of Margaret's torch flits about the track.

"What news exactly?"

"About Anna. She'll tell you."

277

"So, after Richard died, I pretty soon made up my mind to sell and move back nearer my friends, to where there's a bit more going on to be honest, familiar ground, nearer my nephew Simon and his lovely family. They're all I've got now really. My sister, his mother, has been long gone, died of cancer in her forties, so Simon was with us for quite a few years before he went to college. Parents were divorced. His father remarried and had another family so it was never an issue that he came to us. Simple truth is I've missed him and Jane and the children a lot. They're nearly in their teens now. I'll find somewhere with a big enough garden for the girls, my dogs, and hopefully it won't take too long to sort everything out. The Rectory goes on the market next week which seems strange in a way, because after all this time when I've had no real feelings about the place at all, there's now this Anna thing, the journal and so on, and I look at it differently. Strange, isn't it?"

"Margaret said you'd found something out about Anna?"

"Yes, I have. It's been a bit of a happy distraction while I've been sorting through Richard's things and all the horrible stuff I've had to deal with. Well, basically, when I finished the journal, which I thought was absolutely incredible by the way, I kept thinking there had to be some way of finding out what happened to her. So I took myself off to the records office in Norwich, dug round as much as I could, but got nowhere. Then I went to the church and was checking the graves again when the vicar saw me and asked what I was doing. Can't say we've ever hit it off, not surprising really given my steadfast refusal to go with Richard to church, but he was pleasant enough and very interested. He told me to check the registry office in Dereham because he was pretty sure that's where some of the old church registers were stored for safekeeping. So off I trawled and began wading through the tomes."

Jess leans forward in her chair, listening hard.

"It took quite a few hours, but I found two things. The entries of Anna's and Constance's weddings."

"Can I see them?"

"I knew you would want to, and the registrar has kindly let me leave sheets in the books so it should be easy to find them."

Jess looks at Margaret and then back at Rosemary.

"But...what else does that tell us? We know from the journal that they were both married there."

"Well, it didn't strike me at first, but I kept churning it over in my mind and then I realised the information about Constance's wedding might give us a clue."

"What?"

"Well, do you remember that her husband's name was Edward Baker, and that Anna mentioned in the journal that they had three children, George and twins, girls, called..."

"Emily and Alice?"

"That's it. Emily and Alice."

"Anna wrote about visiting them."

"Yes she did, somewhere in Breckland, but without saying where."

"I don't get it."

"The wedding entry gave Edward Baker's address. Pine Heath Farm, Denwell. That's where Constance lived, where Anna visited with Dr Brazington."

"My God. She could have gone to live there, to be with Constance. She said in the journal how she wrote to her, but there was never any mention of the address. Her going there would make sense, wouldn't it? Where is it? D'you think the farm's still there, still called that?"

"It is still there, but not in the family any more."

"You found it?"

"Yes. Spent a day down there. It's about fifteen miles south of

Dereham. Lovely farm, a couple of miles out of the village, and nice people too, but they didn't know anything about the Bakers. Seems it'd been with another family before the current people, and they've only been there about 20 years. But I'd got the bit firmly between the teeth by this point and went back to the church and was on the point of going to the registry office again to go through yet more church records, the Denwell one this time, when the idea struck me to ring the post office in Denwell."

"Why?"

"To see if there were any Bakers still in the village or the area."

"And?"

"Not in that village, no. But, amazingly, a woman who helped in the shop, the post office is in the village shop, who'd lived there all her life, apparently, said she knew a Grace Baker who'd had a cottage there a few years back. Said she was pretty sure she'd gone into sheltered housing in Weston Wheatstone, the next village. Well, I went to see her last week. She's George's youngest daughter. Constance's granddaughter."

"Oh my..."

"She's 89 but honestly is as bright as a button. I couldn't spend long with her because no sooner had I arrived than an ambulance turned up to take her to hospital. For an operation on her waterworks, was all she said. After she'd gone the care warden, nice but fairly abrupt woman, said she'd ring me when she was allowed home but obviously couldn't say how long that would be. I'll write to her, to remind her. She did tell me, though, they're anxious it isn't cancer."

The last word stalls Jess. She repeats the question in her head several times before asking.

"Do you think there's any chance she knows anything about Anna?"

"Oh for sure she does. I did get a chance to tell her briefly about the journal and about you, and she seemed to take it all in. Was quite taken aback I think. Excited. Made the ambulance crew wait. Said she knew

Anna well and that she had some things you should see. She'd very much like it if you'd go and see her when she's back home again."

Jess finds it hard to take in. There is someone alive who knew Anna. In a daze she says,

"Do you think she will?"

"See you? Of cour..."

"No, I mean go home again. If it's cancer then..."

"We'll just have to wait. If not at the bungalow, then maybe you can talk to her in hospital. I'll write to the warden tonight, then I'll ring her later this week and see how Grace is."

Jess stops by the back door and listens. The music shakes her from her thoughts about Anna. Tom is playing the piano, a piece she cannot name. She eases the latch and walks through, leaning in the doorway, arms folded, watching him playing. There is no score. Still she doesn't recognise it.

He finishes. She waits for the notes to fade to silence, then tells him it is beautiful. He jerks round.

"Blimey, you made me jump."

"What is it?"

"A nocturne."

"I can hear that. Just don't know it. Who wrote it?"

"Me."

Jess pulls away from the doorframe. She looks at Tom trying to take in this other part of him, and wonders what else she doesn't know.

"Wrote it years and years ago. When Michael was very young. First piece, really. Lots of black notes. Not too clever really."

"It's lovely. I never knew you composed."

"I try."

"How much?"

"Quite a few pieces over the years. For myself. Maybe one day...So, how did you get on?"

"Me? Oh, I'm a bit numb to be honest."

Tom gets up and walks to her and gently holds her arms.

"Why? You OK?"

"Yeah, I'm fine. It's good news. A surprise, that's all. Just can't quite believe it."

"What?"

"The granddaughter of Anna's friend Constance is still alive. 89. Rosemary Boswell found her. She knew Anna. She knew her, Tom, and so probably knows what happened to her. After all the searching maybe now I'm going to find out. It has been a bit of an obsession, but I thought it was over, so I tried to let it go. Now, well, that's the shock."

"When will you go?"

"I'd go immediately, but I can't. This woman, Grace, is in hospital. She may be very ill, don't know. This is the last chance, Tom. I know it is."

29

The Brecks Home, a line of terraced bungalows guarded by pruned roses and a low wall, waits on the brow of the hill on the edge of Weston Wheatstone. The tiled roof, heavy in the half darkness like tilled wet earth and cropped with aerials, cuts into the hues of dusk. Nearly every window shows light, either through great squares of netting or chinks in curtains, and here and there flickering television images beam out at winged armchairs, some empty.

Jess wonders which of the women she can see is Grace.

It's only a day since Rosemary's call to say the warden had been in touch; a long month and two days since Jess first knew that there was someone still alive who knew Anna.

She walks slowly along the path outside the wall, looking in, conscious of the weight of the carrier bag in her right hand. At the gap in the wall, where a broad path leads to the main entrance, she hesitates and turns to look back at Tom sitting in the car. He nods once, slowly, urging her on.

Jess opens the door and walks in as quietly as she can. It clicks shut. The warmth hits her and she tugs at her scarf as her eyes dart round her, from the empty reception desk to an equally deserted open area full of yet more winged chairs and through to the bright light and white tiles of a small kitchen. There a short, stocky woman, the sleeves of her cardigan pushed up to her elbows, is busily drying her hands on a tea towel. The woman sees Jess and walks briskly towards her.

"Can I help you?"

"I'm here to see Miss Baker, Grace Baker?"

"Oh, I see. Yes, of course. I rang Mrs Boswell yesterday to say Grace was home again and she told me someone'd be along, although she didn't say it would be today, to be honest. It is quite late in the day."

"I'm sorry."

Jess sees no sense in trying to explain that she planned to come the next day but that afternoon felt she couldn't wait any longer.

The warden frowns, thinking. "Umm, right, bear with me a moment." She walks back towards the kitchen and calls to someone. Another woman looks round the corner and the warden tells her to finish up and go home and that she'll see her in the morning. She then comes back to Jess.

"Grace has been home a little while now, but we thought it best to see how she was, to keep a close eye. I'm Jean Berry, the warden. And, er...?"

"Jessica Healey."

"Ah, yes, now I remember. Mrs Boswell mentioned your name in her letter. I suppose it's not too bad a time to come really. We've just cleared away after the evening meal, so I can take you through to her. Likes her privacy, does our Grace, and loves to read and listen to the radio. Got back into the routine quite well, all things considered. She's probably sitting there at the table. Been ploughing through all manner of papers and things since she got back from hospital. Been quite full of it really, this thing You've come about. Something about a relative, isn't it?"

"Er, sort of, yes. Her health?"

The warden, who has started to lead the way along the corridor, stops. "You do know she has cancer?"

"No I didn't. I only knew she wasn't well."

The warden walks on, talking over her shoulder. "They did tests, kept her in and even did an exploratory operation in the end. Nothing they can do, it seems, which is not surprising given her age. No telling how long she has, but for the moment She's doing all right. We're keeping a very close eye, as I said, making sure She's as comfortable as we can, and we'll try and keep her here as long as possible. That's how it is. As for Grace, though, you'd never know, to be honest. She knows what's going on. A little thinner perhaps, so we're trying to keep her well fed. Taking it one day at a time. She's a darling, a real darling, bless her. Wonderful really. Just one who knows her mind that's all. Right, here we are."

The warden knocks and opens the door at the same time. "Only me, Gracie, lovely. Brought someone to see you. About the relative."

Jess follows her down a short corridor past a bathroom into a square bed-sitting room where a tiny old woman is gritting her teeth, pushing herself up out of a chair on the other side of a table set against the left wall. She's in a faded floral night gown, a crimson shawl round her shoulders. Tortoiseshell glasses with thick lens perch on her nose. Her grey hair looks like it's just been curled and is slightly blue against her flushed face. She balances, tries to hold herself tall, squints, beams and reaches out to Jess.

"How good of you to come and see me."

Jess takes her hands and looks at her, saying nothing, not sure what to say, her head slightly to one side, a smile weighed with emotion on her face.

The warden moves to the door.

"Can I get you a cup of tea, Miss Healey?"

"Oh, um, no, thank you."

"Grace love? D'you want another one?"

Grace doesn't take her eyes off Jess.

"No thank you, Jean. Now you, my dear, come and sit here by me. I can't see too well these days, but if you sit here, by the light, I can see you well enough. That's it."

As Grace turns and slowly lowers herself back down into her chair Jess looks round the bright room. The curtains are drawn. There's a single bed with its pink padded head against the far wall. A low table to the left of it, by the window, bears a lamp, a plastic jug and beaker of water, an inhaler, a glasses case and a round, hand-wind clock with two bells on top. On the other side, squeezed in between the bed and double sliding doors of a built-in wardrobe, there's a small oak sideboard with a pretty lace doily, several framed photographs and some newspapers and library books on the end of it. Beside Jess the leaf of the oval table is half covered in little piles of paper, stacked on a battered box.

Grace takes her hand again and pats it.

"Well, my dear child. So you are living in Anna's old cottage, is that right?"

"Yes."

"How wonderful. I want to hear all about it. Now, remind me, what is your name?"

"Jessica. My name's Jessica Healey."

"That's lovely. And so are you, my dear. The lady who came to see me has very kindly written to me, her letter's here somewhere in the muddle, and she told me all about you. You're a musician, aren't you? American, though, if I may say so, you don't sound like one."

"I've lived here since I was very young."

"And a violinist I understand. I think I have heard of you, you know. I can't quite remember things as well as I used to, but I like to listen to music. You'll have to forgive me if I'm a little vague. So, I expect we both have lots of questions. I have one very important one, one I have been dying to ask from the moment I first knew of all of this. Have you brought the journal with you?"

"Yes, I have."

Jess reaches down and pulls out the original journal and a copy of Francis's manuscript and puts them on the table. She offers the old book for Grace to see.

"Goodness me, that's heavy. Would you be a dear and open it and lift it so I can see some words?"

Jess does as she asks, and as Grace peers down at the pages the old woman's eyes narrow, her bottom jaw jutting forward in concentration. Her head moves back and forth. Jess starts to feel the weight of the journal. She looks down at the copy she's had made of Francis's manuscript.

"I've also brought you a typed copy, which may be easier to read."

Grace continues to peer at the journal. "Oh good."

She turns some pages, reads a little, then gently turns some more. She lifts aside a small slip of paper. Jess takes it. It's Francis's writing, a small poem: *The Finding*. Jess reads it again and again, thinking of him, hearing him speak the words. Grace's finally lifts her face away from the journal.

"This is definitely Anna's handwriting, you know. Definitely. I've been looking at some letters of hers I've kept. It's quite distinct. Quite small." She notices the pile of bound paper Jess has put on the table.

"Is that the copy? Goodness."

Jess puts the poem back into the journal and closes it. "It's quite a lot, I know, so I've split it up into sections which might be easier for you."

"Oh, thank you, dear."

"It's for you to keep. I thought you'd like to have it."

"Really. Are you sure? Oh how very kind of you, Jessica. But tell me..." Grace turns and looks intently at Jess. "When does the journal finish? When she leaves the cottage?"

"Yes. About 1884, I think."

"How old would she have been, then? Let me think now..."

"I'm pretty sure she'd have been about thirty-six or thirty-seven."

"I wonder why she left it behind."

"I've wondered the same thing, but I think it sort of becomes clear when you read it. Her husband had died and it seems she wasn't sure where she was going or what she would do. She said the journal had been for him. Maybe she didn't see it as being very important either, although it is, obviously, and maybe she didn't want other people to see it. I don't know. Another mystery. It's quite possible, too, she left with very little, because she would almost certainly have had to begin her journey on foot, and it would have been something else to carry. Depends where she was going, how far. That's what I would love to find out."

"I'm pretty certain she must have gone straight to my great-grandfather's again at Swanton, because I don't remember her mentioning anything else, and I do know she was with him quite a few years until he died. She talked of it, you know, this cottage of hers. In a great wild place, she'd say, and she'd tell us children countless stories of what she'd seen and done there. It was like some big adventure. We lapped it up, and she loved to talk of it, was a wonderful storyteller. Some of the characters, the water folk she called them, tales of catching eels and cutting reeds, sailing on big boats with vast sails. We all longed to go there, but it was never possible.

Too far, I suppose, then the war years. I remember, though, how, much later, not long before she died, she said she'd never really wanted to go back. I think she wanted to remember it as it was."

"Where did she die?"

"At home, the farm, Pine Heath. Look. I thought you might be interested to see this."

The old woman stretches to the table, pulls an old photograph out from beneath some letters tied with red ribbon and hands it to Jess.

"My brother Sidney's wedding, taken in the garden. 1917. Killed in the war the same year, poor soul, which broke my father's heart. Just months after this picture was taken. Dreadful war, so dreadful. So many good people, young people. And as for poor Virginia, my sister-in-law, barely married three months and widowed."

Jess looks intently at the eighteen faces. The bridegroom is in uniform. So too is another young man sitting cross-legged at the front of the rug laid out on the grass.

Grace leans and taps the photograph with her finger. "That's me, down at the front with the ribbon in my hair. Just turned seventeen then. That's father next to Sidney, and that's grandfather next to him."

"Edward Baker?"

"That's right. Edward. Some moustache, isn't it? Grandfather was very handsome, even then. He adored his horses, was still riding horses when he was in his eighties. He had a lovely mare called Candle, safe as houses. Her coat was the colour of candle wax, and they would plod for miles round the farm or off to the village."

Jess notices that the soldier sitting next to Grace is holding her hand. "Who's the other soldier?"

There is a change in Grace's voice. She slows, her eyes glaze.

"That's Hughey, Hugh Miller. I called him Hughey. My Hughey.

Scottish family, had a big Ayrshire herd on the farm next to ours. We grew up together. A very good man."

Jess waits, wondering. Grace stares at the photograph, deep in thought, but says no more. Jess looks again at the photographs on the sideboard. He's there too. She understands. She studies the other faces in the wedding photograph, then glances up at Grace to ask a question.

"A...and the woman sitting in the chair behind you, in front of your grandfather, that must be Constance?"

"No, it isn't. Grandma died when I was very young. I don't remember her I'm afraid. No, that lady in the picture, Jessica, is Anna."

Jess's heart jumps. She leans closer to the photograph and looks at the thin, serene face looking back at her. Anna is wearing a simple, dark hat with a flat brim and a broad ribbon of a different, slightly lighter shade round it. There is a large oval brooch at the neck of her white lace blouse. She's got a dark shawl round her narrow shoulders, and her slender hands are locked on the lap of an ankle-length black skirt.

"She lived very close by, you see, and was to me like my adopted grandmother. She had one of the farm cottages, one of the pair just beyond the stables quite close to the main house. She was almost my constant companion when I was young, and I lived with her later on. Mother was not able to do much at all, I'm not sure why, she was just unwell for reasons that were never really explained to me, so Anna sort of helped to run the house, and minded us children for a lot of the time. She was wonderful."

"This was after Constance had died?"

"Yes, I'm pretty sure that's how it was. I may be wrong, but I think that's what happened. I always understood that Anna looked after great-grandfather, a Dr Thomas Brazington, in his dotage, lovely name don't you think? Just perfect for a doctor, right up until he passed away, so that would have been about 1903 if my memory serves me correctly. I've found the family tree I did quite a few years ago now to check on the dates. I've written some notes. Let me see."

Grace peers at some of the papers on the table, bringing each close to her face until she finds the one she wants.

"Here we are. Yes, my great-grandfather was born in 1816 and died in 1903, aged eighty-seven. My great-grandmother, that's Emily, was born in 1825 and died in 1862 at Swanton. They were married in 1847..."

"The year Anna was born."

"Yes, I do believe you are right. I remember her telling me. Now then...Grandmother Constance was born in 1850 and died in 1902, the year before her father. So that means Anna probably came to live at Pine Heath in 1903, after Thomas Brazington died."

"Do you know if Anna wrote anything else? Was there another journal?"

"Another journal? No, not as far as I'm aware. I think I would have known."

"I wonder why."

"When she let slip that she'd kept a journal, this one, she said it was no good at all, seemed a little embarrassed that she'd told me, but did say writing it had become a comfort to her at that solitary time, being on her own as much as she was. It must have been quite a change, given where she had come from. No. Thinking back, I'm absolutely sure there wasn't another journal. I remember her writing letters, though, a great many, to friends mostly, and to me. She would write to me regularly whenever I was away, telling me news from the farm and other things."

"Do you still have those?"

"Yes, my dear. They're just there, the bundle with the red ribbon."

Jess picks the bundle up from the table. "May I read them?"

"Of course, dear. Bring them back to me when You've finished. I trust you. I've been re-reading them. She'd write the most wonderful letters, you know, full of colour and life, and I knew, just knew, that her journal would be precious."

"It is."

"Still can't believe that it's here. Actually here."

"Why did she write to you? I mean, I thought you were together on the farm."

"I left the farm for a while, after the war, and went to Norwich. Felt I needed a change, and father found me some lodgings with a family he knew. But I was sort of running away, and that didn't solve anything. Anyway, I'm not a person for cities. Country girl. Went home again. Then I caught the travel bug, seeing as much of the world as one could in those days. Went as far as Rome, actually. Was a little reckless, really, a woman travelling alone like that, but I just got on with it. Met some very interesting people. Very. Anna was always a great encouragement, and while I was away I was very glad to receive her lovely letters."

"But she was clearly a wonderful writer. You'd think she'd want to write more."

"Well, I know from what she told me about her time at Swanton she very much enjoyed helping great-grandfather with his work. He was a naturalist. A very knowledgeable one by all accounts."

"Yes, so I understand."

"Does she write about that? Oh I can't wait to read it. My eyes are a bit frail these days, but I'll manage. Just hope I have time to read it all. I'm not too well, you see, but I'll read it. I will. I still cannot believe it, after all these years..."

Jess picks up the journal again and opens the front cover. "The journal was a wedding gift from Dr Brazington. He gave it to her and encouraged her to fill it, to write. Look, there's a note from him here which you might be interested to see."

Grace bows to the journal again, reading slowly, then lifts her head and looks at Jess, a great smile across her face.

"How delightful."

She takes off her glasses and wipes her eyes with a little handkerchief she pulls from her sleeve. "Oh, that you should bring this to me. Forgive me, silly woman that I am. Only I loved her very much. Very much, you see. Anna was a very special person. And I'm so thrilled, so glad that you have brought me this. I still can't believe it. But Jessica, d'you think I might presume to ask to have the old journal for a little while too? I'd just love to have it here, to be able to look at it, hold it."

"Of course."

"Maybe just while you have the letters, until you come and see me again."

"Perhaps, I was wondering, would you like to come to the cottage? We could fetch you and bring you back."

"Really? Would you?"

"Willingly. If they will let you."

"Not their decision, dear. Yes, I'd like that very much. Thank you."

Jess takes Grace's hand and imagines her standing on the grass beside the irises and moon daisies, looking out across the reeds to the dancing water of the broad.

Grace pats Jess's hand. "There was one story, far-fetched some might say, but I'll tell it all the same. I like to think it could be true. Everyone would remark how similar Anna and my grandmother were, and how they were both like Emily."

"I know. That's clear from the journal, when Anna was writing about her early years at Swanton. Someone who saw her with Constance, by the river at Swanton when they were young, took them for sisters."

"Well, apparently, on one occasion my father pressed Anna about her mother, asking where she'd come from and things like that. This was when Anna was still caring for my great-grandfather and he was there and became quite angry and told my father to stop. Anna, though, willingly told my father what little she knew, which as little. Basically, her mother had been a maid at a big country house and that, during some shooting weekend, when there was quite a gathering of titled people from all over the area, she was, well, attacked by one of these guests, and became pregnant. That, and being born in the workhouse, was all she could tell him. Then, some years after that, great-grandfather, who was very, very frail by this time, told my father that he'd long believed, with no proof at all but just a sense, and perhaps because of the resemblance, I don't know, that Anna and his wife Emily might have been half sisters. He said he felt it the first time he watched Anna, as a child. It seems that Emily, who was a regular visitor to the workhouse, had, the year before her death, asked him over and over again to bring this one orphan to the Rectory, but he never agreed. Once she'd died, he was grief stricken, and then suddenly felt compelled to go and see this child. Why Emily wanted to bring Anna we'll never know, of course, but Thomas wondered if somehow she knew something, or sensed something, an affinity maybe with Anna. He then went to this country estate where Anna's mother had worked and found someone who remembered her and also a bit about what went on. It seems there was a certain Lord there that weekend, a member of the shooting party, who had a reputation for such abuse, and the gossip was that he was her father."

"I still don't see a connection, other than Emily and Anna looked alike."

"He was Lord Crofton, from the estate where Emily was raised. And Emily was an orphan too, left on the dowager's doorstep."

Jess lifts her hand to her mouth. Grace smiles at her.

"Well, it's a good story, isn't it?"

"But Anna was twenty-two years younger than Emily."

"Yes, but not impossible if you think about it. The resemblance was remarkable, by all accounts. We'll never know, dear, will we? Time may have embellished it, as it always tends to, but it's not out of the question, and I prefer to think it might just be true."

"Did Anna know?"

"Yes, she knew. Chose never to say anything about it, save to me, just the once."

Jess leans back in her chair. She picks up the photograph again and looks at Anna, with Grace as a young girl sitting by her feet. Grace looks at her.

"Why don't you take the photograph with you as well? Maybe you can get a copy done of it. And be sure to read all the letters. There's even one with news of a friend who went to live in America. Very interesting indeed. Oh yes, and there's also something else I'd like to give you. A present. Would you be a dear and go to the cupboard for me?"

Jess puts the photograph down.

"On the top shelf You'll see a blue, green and crimson quilt. Can you reach it?"

"Yes."

It's heavy. Jess takes it to the table and sits with it on her lap.

"Take it with you. I'd like you to have it. I've no need of it any more. It's so warm in here all the time."

"Are you sure? It's very lovely."

"Handmade. It'll help to keep you warm in that cottage."

"Did you make it?"

"No. Anna did, as a wedding gift for me. She'd have been making it about the time the photograph was taken."

Jess hugs it to her. "I'll treasure it."

"When Hughey was killed I went to live with Anna for a while in her cottage. She saved my life, I think. I don't know what I'd have done without her."

"How old was she when she died?"

"It was in 1933. The September."

"That means she'd have been...about eighty-five or six I think."

"Yes, I think You're right. It had been a dry summer and she was still quite active, well to the last really. She couldn't walk very far at all by then, but we'd go as far as the stream or into the woods, for picnics, or for me to read to her. Then one day she just died. Sitting on a chair in the garden. I thought she was asleep, but she'd gone."

"I'd very much like to visit her grave, to take some flowers. Is she buried at Denwell?"

"No, dear, not there."

"But..." Jess hesitates "you know where she is?"

"Oh yes."

30

14th April, 1989

Jess curls into a ball in the corner of the bed, bunches the quilt in a fist under her chin and listens to the soft echo of her mother's whisper. Count with me the petals of the moon daisy. Sleep, my sweet Jess. Sleeeep.

She lays still, the familiar soothing words slower to work than they have done in recent months, because her ears and mind are open to the April storm outside and to thoughts of leaving. The rhythm of waves slapping the staithe just a few yards from the cottage grows louder in the night. She pinches her eyes tight. *You must sleep. Tonight of all nights you need to sleep.* The wind pushes harder at the window. Rain rattles on the glass. The storm she watched building from the south-west late that afternoon is raging in the great darkness outside, round the little cottage and across the wetland. *Think about the day. Forget the gale and think about the calm of that day, that beautiful day.* She pulls the quilt over her ears. *Remember how certain and relaxed you've been. How much stronger you've become.*

That crystal morning the blackthorn hedge in the meadow beyond the track had been a mass of tiny white flowers, bright and alive in the sun. She thinks how it must be almost bare of petals now, its glory shaken to nothing by the squall. She remembers the bird song, and how she followed it, wandering through the open gate into the empty pasture, standing in the lee of the white cloud of blackthorn, ankle-deep in grass, looking up into the blue for the first skylark. She senses again how, there, in the lush pasture, in a dream-like moment, the breeze filled the air round her with the tiny white blackthorn petals. It reminds her of the cherry blossom of her youth. A huddle of trees in woods she would explore would, for one or two days in the year, shed their colour upon her head like confetti. She thinks how, as the day was fading, she was drawn out of the cottage again, this time by the honey light, walking slowly round to the bench that looks out across the reed mass to the open water, propping her head against the cottage wall as she has done in so many timeless moments before, and watching as small clouds scudded north east and grew in number. The sails of the few yachts on the water became tilted and taut, moving fast. The reeds were starting to dance. She remembers gazing impassively as the western sky darkened.

With the feeling of the keen air on her skin her mind begins to fall towards sleep, knowing that a year ago she wouldn't have seen the signs or noticed the storm until the rain was falling. She opens her eyes a little one last time and looks at the candle flame and photograph of Anna and thinks of the grave. Her last thoughts are familiar ones; the sense that Anna and Francis are close, that they are with her. The last things she sees before her lids close are the shadows on the wicker-backed chair beside the window.

Jess is standing on the grass, looking at the blades of the irises still yet to flower. Michael joins her, mugs in his hands. The storm has gone and the wind has turned to the north. She looks into his eyes as he hands her coffee.

"You needn't have come all the way up here, you know. You've only just got back from Amsterdam."

"Wanted to."

"I could have got the train. Margaret said she'd run me into Norwich."

"I know. But I wanted to. OK?"

"OK."

"Listen, Mum, the air tickets. Saw them on the table. I had no idea we were going to Cleveland first. Didn't you tell me your grandfather, the writer, was from there?"

She smiles up into his eyes, wondering how to begin to tell him the story; their story.

"Yes. Yes he was, but there is more, much more I know now. Our roots, our seeds, our history. I'll explain everything. There's such a lot I have to tell you, Michael." She touches his face. "So much. And to think you are coming with me."

Michael nods and smiles lovingly back at her. Jess studies his face.

"When you were a baby I used to say a bedtime rhyme to you. You're not likely to remember that, are you?"

Michael shakes his head.

"About the moon daisy, counting the petals of the moon daisy." Jess turns and looks out across the wilderness, feeling the freshness on her face, the air in her lungs. "I still cannot believe it, what has happened here. What I've learned here, been shown. I get this incredible sense that I was guided here, that it was meant to be." She looks down again at the tall sharp leaves rising from the water's edge. A few more weeks, a month maybe, and the first of the yellow irises will appear. She slowly squats, reaches her hand above the water and strokes a leaf. "Pity."

"What is?"

"These are irises."

"I know."

Jess stands again. "Yellow flags they call them. You see them all over the wetland. Anna loved them. Not out yet so I can't take some to put on her grave."

Michael looks to her open mouthed.

"You mean you've found it?"

Jess nods. "Finally. I'd like to call by there on our way, if that's OK. Take some fresh flowers. Maybe some more of the primroses from the bank in the lane that I took a few days ago, and then go back with some irises when I am home again."

"Where is it? You've looked everywhere."

"Except under my nose."

"What d'you mean?"

"She's buried with Jacob, her husband, a wherryman who was killed in an accident on the river. Looked in the churchyard here, but didn't think. He, of course, wasn't from Hickling. He was from Horsey, the village across the water, across Horsey Mere. You know, I've walked past that church several times and didn't think. I was moored not far from it that time I was on the boat, after Rudi's letter, remember? Well, she was there all the time. There's even a headstone. She died in 1933. She was 86."

"How on earth did you find out?"

They stop beside the farm. Michael stays in the car. Jess starts to walk round to the back door and Margaret appears, wiping her hands on a tea towel. They hug and, their arms still locked, smile at one another.

Tears brim in Jess's eyes. "Thank you."

"You're thanking me? Away with ya. We'll see you in London in a couple of weeks. At the Barbican. I can't wait."

"Come and see me afterwards."

"Try and stop me."

"Not sure how I'll be, but I know I'll want to see you."

"I'll be there. We all will. You'll be fine, Jess, my lovely, absolutely fine."

Jess tries to nod. Her chin buckles. They hold each other tightly.

"Then when you and Michael are back from America we'll go sailing, just you and me. Yes?"

"Yes."

"Go on now. Go do it."

Jess looks up into the trees and listens to the faint music of the wind ringing the young leaves. She looks out across the waves of reeds to the sparkling, choppy water, knowing their sounds. There is a pureness to the air that sharpens everything. By her feet the posy of primroses leaning against the headstone brings the grey to life. She steps back until the sun-dappled grave is at the forefront of everything, the timeless wetland of water and gold, the vast watercolour sky. She sighs, a peacefulness running through her veins, and stands breathing it in.

She looks over her shoulder at Michael who is motionless in a pool of light, leaning on his elbows on the wall by the gate. His eyes are closed, and he is smiling up at the sun. She decides then to delay their journey a little longer, to take him down onto the beach, to walk the sand, to begin to tell him there, there on the sand with the music of the sea. To show him the letter, the wonderful letter. She turns again towards Anna.

"Time to go. But when I'm back I'll bring you irises from your garden. Promise." She blows a kiss. "God bless you, Anna. God bless."

Back at the cottage that evening, before they leave for the airport, Jess sits at the kitchen table and writes a brief letter.

Dear Records Office,

Thank you for your help in locating the grave of my great-grandmother, Alice Breeze, née Hall, in the Franklin County archives. I intend to visit Columbus as soon as I am able, to see where she lived and to pay my respects.

With gratitude,

Jessica Alice Healey

She looks at the name she had written, the name her mother had given her, understanding now why. The seeds Peace had whispered about, the poppy and moon daisy seeds Alice had carried across the ocean, they had scattered forward through generations, through her grandfather the writer, through her mother, to her. She and Anna had both been connected to Alice, that spirited, defiant girl from the workhouse who would bellow her anguish and smile at anyone who sought to control her. Jess feels something settle deep within her, a flowering at last.

THE FINDING
By Francis Hatherly

Answers And Truths

Self And Time

Reason And Cockle Shells

Right Words And Rhyme

Wait

Wait On The Sands

With Peace Of Mind

For The Finding

Pine Heath 7 October, 1921

My dearest Grace,

I know it is only a matter of a few days since I last wrote to you, but do not worry yourself to receive another letter from me so soon. All is well at the farm and with us all here.

Your father's mare Star has given birth, a beautiful grey foal that he is inclined to call Breeze on account of how briskly he already moves. But that happy event alone is not the reason for my haste in writing again so quickly. I'm compelled to share some truly wonderful news with you.

Just yesterday I myself received a letter, delivered by the gentleman who now lives at the Rectory at Swanton, he so very kindly taking it upon himself to discover my whereabouts and to bring it here. This letter had been delivered to the Rectory, addressed to me, and the gentleman thankfully judged it to be of some importance, bearing, as it does, two stamps of America.

This letter is from someone I have most certainly told you about, namely my childhood friend Alice who was also born within the workhouse. Do you remember me telling you of her leaving to seek a new life in Canada? Well, to my astonishment, after all these years, she has written to me! It was, as you can imagine, the greatest of surprises. And what a letter this is, telling of such ordeal and adventure that I feel certain her life would make some great literary work, were people to

303

believe it. I will relay some of it now, because it is such a story.

Firstly, Alice has not been, as I imagined her, living in Canada. She had told me before leaving England that it was her husband Walter's intention to seek work in the ports there just as he had done in Norfolk, but I find that she has been long settled some great distance from the sea and in another country. She has told me that events led her to make her new life in the American state of Ohio, which all sounds quite wild and beautiful. The reason, however, is heavy with tragedy which, though she makes simple reference to it, must have been a most dreadful experience.

She recounts how she and Walter and their two young sons left England aboard an iron ship that sailed from Liverpool. It seems there was a great crush upon it, with people from many parts of the country sharing the journey with others who had already travelled some distance from countries across the continent of Europe. People with little means were below the decks, and Alice and her family were placed in something she refers to as the steering, which must have been close to the mechanism by which they directed the vessel, an experience which was by her vivid account not at all comfortable. People with greater means could afford cabins, but they were but a few. The ship then stopped in Ireland to take aboard yet more emigrants, to the point of it being almost unbearable, but for the prospect of the new life awaiting them all across the ocean. After some days at sea, some people began to fall ill with a fever, and then began the deaths. In a short time there was the darkest possible news, namely that the ship was gripped with the disease cholera. In the course of the journey more than five hundred souls were taken, including Walter, their bodies all being dropped into the sea.

On reaching land there was no relief, for they were not allowed to leave the ship for some considerable time until the authorities were satisfied that the disease had abated and could not be carried ashore. How truly awful that must have been, and Alice now faced the prospect of trying to begin a new life as a widow with two sons. It seems, however, during that long wait upon the ship she made some vital friendships, including a man, a tailor by trade from London, who himself had lost his wife and young daughter to the illness. She tells me how their grief proved a bond, and before they were finally taken ashore, it was agreed they would accompany one another, following his intention to leave his former ambitions behind him and to take a train west and south into America to the places just beginning there, where he considered there were the best of opportunities.

They travelled to a city called Cleveland on the shore of a vast lake, there hiring a wagon and making their way south to where they were to settle in a place called Columbus in the county of Franklin, which, by her description of it, was growing apace and already had a population of many thousands, a great many of whom, like them, had travelled from Europe. Alice soon after married this tailor, Ernest, and bore him a son, whom she proudly declares has grown to become a man of writing, working upon a newspaper. Her two other sons have also made their way, one learning the skill of tailoring and the other understanding the workings of engines and beginning a business that repairs motor cars. It seems it was her youngest son's suggestion that she should write this letter, for she had spoken to him often about Norfolk, although it seems she has not told her family a great deal of her beginnings and childhood. I suspect it might have been difficult to revisit her past in this way, but I am so grateful that she has done so and I have already penned my reply.

So it is that I now know she and her husband are now living not far from this city of Columbus, in a small town where they have a little house and quite a large amount of space where they spend such time as they can growing things and savouring the great outdoors, and where the children of her two older sons spend some happy hours with them.

And there is one further thing she mentions that I must tell you and which stirs in me such emotion and the richest memories of my own childhood.

Alice has always, she says, kept the old land, her birthplace, with her, for on her journey from Norfolk across the ocean and across that continent to her new home and life, she carried a little package, full of moon daisy and poppy seeds. Think of it, the seeds of our childhood now scattered so far far away. I will end now, because I am set upon beginning my reply to Alice. How wonderful that her children and her children's children, and the generations that follow, will echo Peace's rhyme, and like me and you, will fall asleep counting the petals of the blessed, beautiful moon daisy.

My heart is so full of joy. Stay safe, my darling Grace.

Anna

Field Poppy (*papaver rhoeas*) – a settler on fallow land all over the temperate world, growing in fields since the Stone Age with just one plant able to produce as many as 50,000 seeds.

Yellow Flag (*iris pseudacorus*) – a native perennial of marshes, wet woods and wet ground by rivers and ditches. *Iris* is the Greek word for rainbow. To the Greeks it symbolized life and resurrection, and is also associated with *Osiris*, the first Pharaoh to "become immortal".

With special thanks to the Norfolk Wherry Trust, The Hunter Fleet Trust, Norfolk Wildlife Trust, Broads Society, Broads Authority, RSPB, National Trust, Norfolk County Council, Eastern Daily Press, Children's Society, Andrew Millinger and the Herbert Howells Society, the people of The Broads past and present, and especially Maggie Whitman, Ella Kirby, Joe Kirby.

Extract from the score of Herbert Howells' Three Pieces for Violin and Orchestra reproduced by permission of Novello & Company Limited

Author's Fotnote

The great English wetland known to millions simply as The Broads is a treasure trove of beauty and nature – a different world that must remain, as Norfolk naturalist Ted Ellis so aptly put it, '*a breathing space for the cure of souls*'.

This work of fiction is based on many truths and one indelible fact, the wetland's wonder, both present and past. To find out more, about the wildlife, the history, and the Broads today here are some places to begin your journey.

Broads Authority
www.broads-authority.gov.uk
18 Colegate,
Norwich NR3 1BQ

Tel 01 603 610734

Norfolk Wildlife Trust
www.norfolkwildlifetrust.org.uk
Bewick House
22 Thorpe Road
Norwich NR1 1RY

Tel 01 603 625540

RSPB
www.rspb.org.uk
Regional office - Stalham House
65 Thorpe Road
Norwich NR1 1UD

Tel: 01 603 661662

National Trust (Horsey Estate)

www.nationaltrust.org.uk – do a search for Horsey Wind Pump
Tel 01 284 747500 (Regional office)

Ted Ellis Trust
Wheatfen Nature Reserve
www.wheatfen.org
The Covey, off The Green, Surlingham,

Norwich NR14 7AL
Warden: David Nobbs –

Tel 01 508 538036

Broads Society
www.broads-society.org
Administrator Miss Carol Palfrey,
Solar Via,
Happisburgh, Norwich, NR12 0QU   Tel: 01 692 651321

Norfolk Wherry Trust
www.wherryalbion.org.uk
Wherry Base, Womack Water
Ludham, Norwich

Hunter Fleet and Norfolk Heritage Trust
www.huntersyard.co.uk
Hunter's Yard,
Horsefen Road, Ludham,
Norfolk NR29 5QG,
Tel 01 692 678263

Museum of the Broads
www.northnorfolk.org/museumofthebroads
The Staithe
Stalham
Norfolk NR12 9 DA

T e l 01 692 581681

British trust for Conservation Volunteers
www.**btcv**.org
Sedum House
 Mallard Way
Potteric Carr
Doncaster DN4 8DB

Tel 01 302 388 888

You may also be interested to visit the relevant website or contact

Herbert Howells Society
Andrew Millinger
32 Barleycroft Road,
Welwyn Garden City, Herts, AL8 6JU.
Tel: 01707 335315
Membership: Ros Saunders at
saunders@amews.freeserve.co.uk

Children's Society
www.childrenssociety.org.uk
Edward Rudolf House Margery Street
London WC1X 0JL

Tel 0845 300 1128

www.ingramcontent.com/pod-product-compliance
Lightning Source LLC
Chambersburg PA
CBHW051517260626
47170CB00003B/659